XOXO

BY

KATHRYN R. BIEL

XOXO

DEDICATION

To Julie:
I don't know how to properly respond when someone I've fangirled for so long starts fangirling me. From the first time I read your blog, I knew we were destined to be friends. I'm just glad you now realize it.

This book would not be what it is without your support and encouragement. I should make some incredibly witty comment here, but, well, my brain is fried. I'm sure you understand.

CHAPTER 1: OPHELIA

These are the five things you should know about me.

One. My name is Ophelia Finnegan, and I was named after a character in Hamlet. I'm not a fan of Shakespeare, probably because his Ophelia falls in love, makes terrible decisions, goes crazy, and ultimately kills herself. Not exactly uplifting or inspiring. Thanks, Mom and Dad.

Two. I'm an accountant, but I don't really want to be. The thing is, I've always been good at math and anything with numbers. I like my job well enough and I'm lucky to have it, but just because you're good at something, doesn't mean it's your passion. On the other hand, numbers just make sense to me, and I find the hours spent lost in equations and spreadsheets oddly soothing.

My deepest desire is to write the next great romance novel. Unfortunately, all my life people have told me I can't be right-brained and be creative at the same time. They say accounting is practical and smart, while romance novels are frivolous, and writing is a waste of time.

In some kind of bizarre rebellion, that only makes me want to write more. It seems fitting, considering my whole life I've never done what people expect of me, right from the moment of my unplanned conception, as my mother so often reminds me. Writing is therefore on-brand for me. Three years ago, I even went so far as to publish a short story about growing up as a misfit.

My best friend, Marley, loved the story. It was critically panned on Wattpad and in one scathing ClikClak video, and I haven't been able to write more than a sentence since. So, I remain an accountant.

Thanks to COVID-19, I'm a stay-at-home accountant. My job is now permanently remote, so I've been working from my tiny one-bedroom apartment in Boston, which I rarely leave.

As a result of my limited human interaction, I've become a *little* addicted to social media. I've lost more hours on ClikClak than I want to admit. There's something voyeuristic and satisfying about scrolling through strangers' videos, and I can't seem to look away.

In lieu of a real social life, I've spent the equivalent of weeks learning trendy dances that I dream of posting (but don't). My draft folder is full of them, and that's where they'll stay. I'm not sure the world is ready for my dance moves. What I actually post are things that involve my cat, Sundance, who should probably have his own account.

Yikes. I just realized that my five-point list has strayed a bit. I promise I'll stay on topic from here on out.

The third thing you should know about me is that I have an overwhelming fear of birds. Like seriously, if I see a sparrow I immediately assume it's plotting my death. I have no real explanation for this fear, but it's there. My adrenaline and cortisol rise the mlnute I hear the flapping of wings.

Best I can figure, it may be related to that one time a seagull stole my hot dog before pooping on me. I've considered getting therapy for my bird phobia, but there's a lot more to unpack in my brain than just birds. It seems like a low priority.

Luckily, the pigeons in this city and I have come to an understanding. If they stay away from me, I won't kick them in the head when I walk by. Let's be clear, I've never actually kicked a pigeon, but if I had to, I would, in the interest of self-defense. So far, it's worked for all parties involved, and I don't have to pay for a therapist.

Number four: I'm a hopeless romantic. We're talking candy hearts, bouquets of wildflowers, and all grand gestures that include, but aren't limited to, Heath Ledger singing during Kat's soccer practice, that little kid in *Love Actually* running through the airport to catch the girl he loves before she moves to America, Reese Witherspoon and Josh Lucas on the beach in the rain in *Sweet Home Alabama*, and drum roll please … John Cusack and his boom box in *Say Anything*. Yes, I know it's an old movie, but it's a classic for a reason. These are the love stories that fuel my dreams and feed my desire to find a love of my own.

I used to view writing as a way to merge the analytical and romantic sides of my brain, but since I can't do that anymore, I've been focusing on immersing myself in a fictional world full of over-the-top yearning and forbidden romances. I get googly heart-eyes just thinking about it.

Sidenote: the heart-eye emoji is my favorite. I use it all the time, along with "XOXO" when I'm on social media. I picked it up from reading so many British romantic comedies. I'm obsessed with all things British. I'm looking at you, Colin Firth and Hugh Grant. Just not as you are now—how you were in the '90s.

So "XOXO" it is.

As long as I don't use it on a work email. Again.

This leads me to fact number five.

I can be pretty dumb, usually in the name of love. I have made a complete ass of myself in my quest to find that which poets write about. I've decided to call it research. I mean, how can I write the greatest romance novel ever written if I've never been in love myself?

Not that I don't act that way at other times. As a kid, my parents would often tell me to stop being "so Ophelia." That was code for acting without thinking, having too much energy, and not following typical social conventions, like playing quietly and neatly. My grandmother used to tell me children should be seen and not heard. I always had trouble—a lot of trouble—with that one.

The first instance I can distinctly recall of my major social faux pas in the name of love was when I was in the fourth grade. I was writing my own life story as an American Girl, and I was sure I was destined to marry Bobby Daniels. So one day, I kissed him during recess. As a fifth grader, he was definitely not into my younger, nerdy, awkward self, so (with good reason) he pushed me into a mud puddle. I jumped up and kneed him in the 'nads. Fail number one.

My hussy-like behavior ended up with me in detention writing an apology letter. My face still burns with shame when I think about that. Not my finest moment.

I wish I could say it was a low point for me, but alas, it was only the beginning of dumbass decisions made because of a cute boy. I haven't forced myself on someone or committed violence since then, so that's good. Yet, I completely lack the knack for picking the right guy.

I'm thirty, and I still haven't quite grasped the concept of choosing men who are even remotely interested in me.

CHAPTER 2: OPHELIA

If there was an award for going after guys that are totally out of my league, I'd be the MVP.

Don't get me wrong, I'm a solid six. If I bothered with hair and makeup, I could probably make it to 7.5 or even an 8. But that's a lot of time, energy, and motivation that are hard for me to muster up on a regular basis.

And since my mom likes to remind me that I'm "not getting any younger," I've decided to take a different, well-thought-out approach. A plan, if you will. This time, I'm being smart about it. No more flying by the seat of my pants. No more impulsive decisions. No more online dating—oh man, the stories I have from that. I know for a fact that Trent Carson is a real person, not someone hiding behind a profile waiting to catfish my trusting, hopeful soul.

He's everything I could want in a man. Not too tall. I'm only 5'2" so I don't like to feel overpowered and overshadowed by a hulking presence. Trent's 5'8", so we look cute together, not like a miniature poodle and Great Dane.

I'm sure he has other redeeming features, but they're escaping my brain currently.

Trent and I have known each other for years. We first met when we were in college, me at Boston University and him at Northeastern. Nothing but friendship happened back then, but we always stayed in casual touch.

Although there was that one drunken make-out session, where he got to second base, but that's not important. The bottom line is that when we graduated college eight years ago, we didn't see each other in person anymore but moved our relationship over to Instagram.

When COVID hit, Trent ended up back in Boston. He's an athletic trainer, working for the US Soccer League. His team was sidelined (well, they all were). That meant that we started hanging out, and one thing led to another.

It brought new meaning to staying in touch. We've been sort of together for over a year now.

We'd totally be together if the world were still shut down.

But now that it's opened back up and sports have resumed, Trent's back on the road. Also, he's now based out of Maryland and working for the Baltimore Terrors soccer team.

It plain sucks.

He's out having a real life again and I'm still here, in my apartment.

After that disastrous publication on Wattpad, I lost my writing flow, and even though story ideas plague me, when I sit down to write, nothing comes out. It's got to be because our relationship is stagnant.

Or non-existent.

I've decided that if I want to make this relationship work, I have to turn it into the stuff of romance novels. I need to step out of my comfort zone—which is my apartment—and do something drastic.

Trent only comes to Boston twice each season, which is dismal as soccer has a freakishly long season. We're never going to reach the Bridgerton level of passion at this rate.

I miss him dreadfully. I mean, I miss having him here and having someone to hang out with.

Cue a grand romantic gesture.

It's been four months since I've seen him. July seems like it was years ago. So, I'm going to visit him.

Get this: he has no idea I'm coming.

To be totally honest, I didn't know I was going either until I cruised the internet three days ago and found a Columbus Weekend special flight for $39 to Baltimore. How could I pass that up?

It's like the Universe is trying to reunite us. The only sign to make it clearer would be John Cusack and his boom box.

This is going to be great.

At least that's what I try to convey to my best friend Marley.

"Ophelia, are you sure?"

I want to tell her that I need support and not doubts about Trent. She says her concern is because he was a dog in college, but those days are long past. I mean, it's not reasonable to expect that he's the same person he was a decade ago. We all grow and change. It's not like I'm still trying to force boys to kiss me like I did with Bobby Daniels. I'd hate to think he still thinks I'm like that.

It's called maturity, and Trent is plenty mature.

I, on the other hand, may not be, as I stick my tongue out at my phone. Unfortunately, we're on FaceTime, so Marley sees this.

"Real nice. What was that for?"

"For doubting Trent. For doubting me. I mean, this is the kind of thing I live for. Grand romantic gestures. Flying halfway across the country to surprise him. Do you know how hard it is for me to do something like this?" I shove my makeup bag in on top of my clothes. It's a tight squeeze in my rolling carry-on. I'm not sure what he's going to want to do while I'm there, so I had to bring outfits for every possibility.

"Baltimore is hardly across the country ... "

I ignore her as I shove in the new lingerie I bought from Yandy months ago. The move to online shopping has been a real boost. Never ever in a million years would I have had the nerve to go into a store and purchase a sexy little French maid costume, complete with props, but there they are, in the bottom of my bag. I try to get something new every time I see him, but this is the first time we'll be delving into role-playing if all goes according to plan. I'm ready to act out things I've only read about in some of my spicier romance novels. I'm willing to bet Trent is going to love it, so long as I don't fall and break a leg on the stilettos I can barely walk in.

Clearly getting frustrated that I haven't responded, Marley repeats, "Baltimore is not halfway across the country from Boston. They're both on the east coast. It's not even a two-hour flight. But I suppose I'm impressed that you're setting foot outdoors. You probably won't even melt in the sun or start to shine like your skin is made up of diamonds."

"I told you never to bring up *Twilight* again. I'm still upset that Bella chose Edward over Jacob."

Her response is a frown, her ebony curls bobbing as she shakes her head slowly.

"What? Jacob was clearly the more stable choice. Edward was too controlling." Marley and I will never see eye to eye on this one. She's a fan of the domineering alpha male, while I much prefer a cinnamon roll beta hero, like Hugh Grant in, well, anything.

"I'm proud of you for putting yourself out there again, but are you sure it's the right thing to do?" Marley asks again. "I … I have a bad feeling about this."

I laugh. Marley's *feelings* about things are akin to my fear of birds. Totally unfounded and irrational. "It's going to be fine, Marl. In fact, it's going to be better than fine. I'm going to document the whole thing on ClikClak, so you can watch it happen practically in real time. This trip is going to be a turning point. I know it without a doubt."

I don't mention that I'm hoping to use this trip for inspiration for my novel. I'm always on the lookout for real-life plot bunnies. Folding in realism is the best way to make my novel seem legit, provided I ever get my mojo back and can start writing again.

I'm pretty sure I see her roll her eyes. "You'd better get going if you're going to make it to Logan in time. Are you taking the T?"

I shake my head. I love FaceTime. I don't have to actually say anything, and she still knows what I'm saying. Honestly, it's one of the reasons I'm addicted to ClikClak. I can use sound bites and emojis and GIF graphics to help me find the words I need to communicate my thoughts and feelings. When it comes to actually talking, I have a habit of being … well, awkward is the adjective that comes to mind.

"I'm taking an Uber. Getting all hot and sweaty on the T is not a great look for me. It's not romantic to smell like a locker room."

"He works for a soccer team. I'm sure it's a familiar smell for him."

I wrinkle my nose. Eww. "If that's what turns him on, the whole trip is doomed."

I pretend not to see Marley's smirk as I disconnect. She really doesn't like Trent, but she's not dating him, I am.

I hurriedly pull out my phone and open the ClikClak app. Taking a deep breath, I record the most personal video I've ever done. And since I've already done my hair and makeup, I don't even need a filter. My bangs, freshly trimmed thanks to a ClikClak tutorial, are on point. It would be criminal not to document a good hair day like this. Sundance, the big oaf, takes his customary perch on my shoulder, his yellow tail wrapping around my neck.

Okay, so I'm doing something crazy. Once sports started up again, my boyfriend moved to Baltimore because he works for a major team there. I only get to see him once or twice during the season, so I'm flying down to surprise him! He already told me they don't have a game until Sunday night, so he's having some friends over to his place. Can you imagine the look on his face when I walk in? OMG, he's going to be so happy! I'm going to do a series on the weekend, so make sure you tune in to see his reaction! Kisses and hugs, 'bye!

Removing Sunny from my body, I assure him that he has plenty of food and water, and that it's his job to watch the house. He responds by licking his butt. Classic.

I haul my suitcase and backpack down the long driveway and out to the street to await my Uber. I take the opportunity to add a kissy sticker and my "XOXO" trademark onto the video before posting. In addition to the trending hashtags, I add my own, including #xoxo, #liainlove, and #romanticsuprise. And then I post.

I have a small following of about a thousand people. Trent isn't one of them. At least not on ClikClak. I don't think he's even on here. But still, other people follow me. It's nothing to write home about, and my most popular video involved an unfortunate incident between my cat's weak bladder and my computer. Like I said, I generally don't have the guts to post anything really daring. The documentation of my trip is pushing me out of my comfort zone.

The bright side is that since Trent doesn't follow me here, as long as I don't post a clue on Instagram, he'll have no idea I'm coming!

Once my car arrives, I record another video.

I'm in the Uber, on the way to Logan. My flight leaves in just over two hours, so four hours from now, I'll be walking through my boyfriend's door, surprising the hell out of him. I totally love romantic surprises, and I know he will too! Are you getting excited? I am! Kisses and hugs, 'bye!

By the time I land at BWI, I have three more videos filmed and scheduled for release. The next one will be me, walking through Trent's front door.

This is going to be epic.

CHAPTER 3: XAVIER

It's one night. You can take a break from being boring and stuck up for one night."

It's not polite to growl at one's trainer, especially when he's working on a particularly delicate hamstring area, so I resist the urge to tell Trent to bugger off. He's an annoying bloke, but he's an adequate AT, so I bite my tongue. I need this hamstring mess cleared up, so I'm not known as a liability, especially when the Terrors have had such a dismal season.

Schwindel, the last AT was much more palatable. I wish he'd never gone to work for Boston. He was a solid mate, but when the front office sacked the coaching staff during the shutdown, most of our athletic trainers went with them. If they start cleaning house with the players, I'll be thrown out in the bin with the rest of the rubbish.

Either way, now I'm stuck with Trent, so I'd best make nice.

"It's just a casual gathering, not some big fray, right?" I don't need any more rumors about my partying lifestyle. Image is everything, and if I hope to keep playing in the US Soccer League, I have to keep my nose squeaky clean.

I'm at a distinct disadvantage. There are strict guidelines about the number of international players that can be on the roster. Personally, I think some of these Yanks are still worked up about the Revolutionary War, but I'll never say that out loud.

There's a long line of players looking to get into this league. All I'm looking to do is keep my spot. I've already lost a spot once. I can't afford to do it again.

"Totally casual. Nothing wild or crazy. You know me better than that, Bird Man." Trent is such a wanker. I hate that he calls me that. It's reserved for mates, and I'm not sure we're there yet. Or ever will be.

"Alright. I'll be there." I sound about as enthusiastic as if I were agreeing to be boiled in tar.

I've always felt that Trent is a bit dodgy. My opinion is partially based on the fact that he walks around here like he's God's gift, with a bigger head than any of the footballers who actually play. It's also based on the fact that he's trying to get me to go to a party when he knows it's not my scene.

Nonetheless, I'll be headed to his place tonight, instead of staying in, as I do almost every other night when we don't have a game. We've only one regular-season game left, two days from now, and naturally, we're not making the playoffs this year. Essentially, in three days, my season—and maybe my career—will be over.

So yeah, I don't feel much like partying.

On the other hand, I don't want people to remember me as a naff or a stick-in-the-mud. This season has not been stellar, which is why I'm laying odds on it being my last.

Most of the other players on the roster don't have a big huge black cloud hanging over them like I do. And being that everyone likes Trent—almost everyone (as in, not me)—I figure it can't hurt to show up.

I spend the rest of the afternoon dreading this social outing, but as I've already committed, I know I need to get over myself and show up.

As I reach Trent's place in the upscale Butcher's Hill neighborhood, I can't help but wonder how he can afford to live here. Last I knew, athletic trainers didn't make that much money, but here he is, living in a nicer place than most of the players.

I hear the music pumping down the street before I even reach his townhouse. Totally casual, my arse. I bet this nobhead went all out. I'll stay for one bevvy and that's it. Enough to be cordial. I don't have the stomach for what I'm sure is awaiting me.

Once I reach the door, it's as bad as I feared. There are people everywhere, filling Trent's multi-level home. It's about a thousand degrees inside, so I instantly shed my coat, dropping it on the pile of outerwear forming in a corner of the living room. I hear someone shout something about a roof deck and immediately guess it's more comfortable there than pressed up against all the hot bodies inside.

As I search it out, I decide that Trent must spend all his money on rent because there are barely any furnishings. An old couch, covered in a sheet. A few folding chairs. A high-top table and pub stools. That's about it.

Well, except for the massive flatscreen, which is probably to make up for shortcomings elsewhere. Ahem, the bedroom.

I wouldn't be surprised if he had a waterbed with satin sheets too. I shiver and want to pour bleach into my brain to erase that image.

I spy Trent along with several of my Terror teammates. There must be two females for every male here, leaving little doubt about the intention for the night.

Trent's on the couch, squeezed in between three women wearing low-cut shirts and short shorts. It looks as if they just got off their shift at Hooters. Trent has his arm around one and his hand on another's thigh.

Yeah, this twat definitely has a waterbed and satin sheets. Probably a mirror too.

My skin feels tight, and it's hard to swallow. This is exactly the type of scene I avoid. There's a good reason I'm no longer into the party scene, and I'm finding this show excruciating.

After grabbing a lager out of a cooler, I take the stairs to the roof. It's cooler and calmer up here. I could almost pretend I'm not at a party. Actually, with the right furnishings, this could be a quite fab flat. Of course, it's wasted on Trent.

"Hey, mate. Didn't expect to see you here." Alastair claps me on the back. We've known each other since we were practically in nappies. We first played together in the schoolyard in Gloucester.

"Didn't want to be here. But I didn't think I should say no, either. You know, being a team player and all."

Alastair shakes his head. "We're a rubbish team."

I nod. It's the truth. "I wish they hadn't sacked Bjorn. He and Kenley were a right stellar pair."

"They're killing it up in Boston. The Buzzards are in a good position to advance in the playoffs. And to think, before COVID, they were dead last in the league."

While the powers-that-be here in Baltimore used the pandemic to disassemble a moderately strong team, the Boston Buzzards swooped in and gathered the remnants, which has put them near the top of the league.

"I wish they'd taken me with them," I sigh, not even realizing I was thinking about it. But as soon as the words are out of my mouth, I know I mean them. I've been with Baltimore for four years, but I don't feel I owe them anything any longer.

On the other hand, I don't want to look a gift horse in the mouth. As a professional athlete, I'd be foolish not to realize that I'm only ever one move, one play, one injury away from hanging my cleats up forever, and a five-year contract is a solid deal.

As I drain my bottle, I debate getting another, but I know that's a slippery slope toward bad decisions and regret.

Not to mention there's nothing worse than a massive hangover at practice.

"Right, mate. I think I'm going to pack it in. This just isn't my scene."

Alastair claps me on the back. "Sure you don't want to stay? It could finally be time for the Bird Man to pick up a chick of his own, and there's a right attractive lot downstairs."

"No girl is worth sticking around here." Definitely not the type of women I saw on the way in. Highly made up, some high. No, sir, not my scene. We head down the stairs, through the bedroom, to the main level. I can't help but glance. Not a waterbed.

I'm slightly disappointed.

I wave at a few of my teammates as I head down the last set of stairs to the door. Trent better not get too sauced. He's going to have to treat everyone for heat exhaustion. It's like a steam bath in here.

Speaking of our slimy host, I can't figure out what those women see in him. As far as I'm concerned, the areshole is as appealing as a turd in a punch bowl.

As I finally make it out to the sidewalk, the cool night air washes over me, enough to lower my body temperature to just below boiling.

After walking away from the party, getting far enough away that the music is down to a dull roar, I stop and inhale deeply. I release my breath and repeat this a few times before I feel more like myself. I hadn't even realized being there would make me feel so uncomfortable.

It's been five years, but still.

The exposed skin on the back of my neck prickles with goose pimples, making me realize I left my coat in there. *Bollocks*. Good thing I'm only about a half-block away. Turning in my tracks back toward Trent's townhouse, I end up falling behind a young woman who is carrying a backpack that looks like it's about to burst at the seams. It takes up all of her back and then some. I'm not sure if the pack is oversized or if she's simply petite. She's also rolling a small suitcase behind her. Her other hand holds her phone which she appears to be talking at.

Small pet peeve of mine: there's no need to be video chatting with someone when you're out in public. Call me old-fashioned, but put the phone to your ear and have a regular conversation like they did in the good old days. You know, like the 1980s.

That's when I realize she's not having a conversation, she's making a ClikClak. My legs are quite a bit longer than hers, so I inadvertently move right next to her. I don't mean to listen, but well, if she didn't want people to hear, she wouldn't be filming out in public.

"Okay, so I'm almost there." She pants, a little winded from her brisk pace and the load that must weigh almost as much as she does. "I can't wait to see him. Mostly, I can't wait to see the look on his face when I surprise him." She beams widely into her phone. "Stay tuned for the next video. Kisses and hugs!"

She stops abruptly, tapping away, probably hashtagging and posting her video. I slow down so we wind up in front of the building at the same time.

"Are you going to 104 too?" the woman asks while smiling wildly. I wonder if she's on something. After I nod to confirm my destination, she hands me her phone and asks, "Would you mind doing me the biggest favor?"

I want to sigh but resist the urge. Of course, she wants to have her picture taken with me. Even though I don't get noticed here in America like I did back in England, I'm still spotted by the occasional groupie. I wouldn't have pegged this girl for a fan, though.

I could see her in a library or at a comic con, but not at a football game.

Except she's heading to Trent's party, so clearly I'm wrong.

I briefly feel sorry for her as she's going to stick out like a sore thumb, in her jeans and hoodie, her dark brown hair piled up in a messy bun, bangs fringing her face. It's too dark to tell if she's wearing any makeup, but she definitely doesn't seem like the heavily contoured and Groucho Marx eyebrow set inside.

She would be the last person I'd expect here, but football fans come in all shapes and sizes. However, they usually dress to impress. But actually, her casual dress and demeanor are refreshing.

Cute, even.

I decide to oblige her with a selfie. It's not terrible for my image to get tagged in things here or there. It makes my fan base appear stronger. I'm simply happy we're outside the party rather than in the throng of people. I don't need *that* in my image again.

"Right. Sure. No problem." I reach for her phone, knowing that my arms are much longer than hers, and I'll be able to get a better angle.

She makes one of those *squeeing* sounds that only females appear able to produce. "Thank you so much!"

Here comes the fangirling.

"Okay, so I want you to start recording right before I walk into the room."

"Pardon?"

"I'm here, surprising my boyfriend. I need you to record me walking in so I can get his reaction. He's in there."

Well, that's a sweet gesture, for sure. I can't imagine anyone I've dated traveling to surprise me. It would be nice if someone cared that much.

I take her phone and follow her in. I wonder who the lucky bloke is?

CHAPTER 4: OPHELIA

It's the moment.

I should have stopped to fix my hair, but when I saw that guy about to walk in, I knew I had to seize the opportunity. I wasn't sure how I was going to record the whole thing, but fate put him in my path.

It's like it was meant to be. I just hope my bangs have lasted.

Except, this is not at all what I pictured. Firstly, I've got to go up steps to get into the house, hauling my overstuffed bag behind me. Not exactly the easiest thing to maneuver. Next, it's wall-to-wall people. And holy hell, it's hot in here.

Dammit, if my bangs were still looking good, that's no longer the case. I can feel my hair both frizzing and going flat simultaneously, tendrils springing out in the most unattractive way while also sticking to my face as if covered in glue. Sweat is pouring down my back where my backpack now seems to weigh a thousand pounds. I feel my chest grow damp as well as my armpits.

I'm going to smell like a dirty sock by the time I find Trent in this crowd.

Also, this is *not* what I thought he meant when he said he was going to have a few guys from the team over. Last I checked, the Baltimore Terrors do not have this much cleavage.

I pull my shoulders in slightly, straining against the straps of my bag, trying to camouflage my C-cup chest that now feels woefully inadequate. Not to mention, I'm dressed like a suburban mom in my ankle jeans, a comfy striped T, and a hoodie. I'm normally content with my short, curvy size six frame, but in this room … let's just say this is not the ego boost I was hoping for.

I should have thought this through better, but it's par for the course for me. I either overthink and can't do anything, or I jump in without thinking at all. This seems like it's falling into the latter category with each passing second. Still, I turn to the guy holding my phone and smile. "Well, I guess it's time to find him. Make sure you get his reaction, okay?"

And then I see Trent. He's on his couch. It's the same one he's had since college, and I know it's seen better days. Good thing he's got a sheet over it.

But man, he looks good.

"Trent!" I call out, trying to make my voice heard above the din. The party goes quiet for a moment, except for the kicking bass in the background. I don't think I'd even heard the music when I walked in. Then voices rise, excited about Trent's surprise.

It's so nice that he has people who support him and are happy for him.

"Trent! Surprise! I'm here." I throw my arms open wide, leaving my suitcase as I step toward him. The overstuffed backpack makes it awkward to move, and I'm legit scared I'm going to tip over backward.

Slowly, he stands up. His eyes grow wide and his mouth forms an O.

I did it. I pulled off the surprise of the century.

This is so going in my book.

I squeal, attempting to raise my shoulders in excitement. "I know! I couldn't wait until the end of the season to see you." I'm still standing there, arms wide open. His face grows flushed, and he runs his hand through his blonde hair, which is what he normally does when he's nervous. Aww, that's so sweet! He's so surprised that he doesn't know what to make of it all. After a moment, he steps toward me, and I throw my arms around him. Tears threaten to fill my eyes, I'm so happy.

I didn't even realize how much I missed him.

Still nestled against Trent's chest, I turn my head toward the guy with my phone. His face is stony. Definitely not into the moving sentiment of my gesture. He probably doesn't have a romantic bone in his body. You can see it in his blank expression.

Whatever.

I don't need him to be romantic. I just need him to have accurately recorded my romance awesomeness.

"Thanks," I mouth, taking my phone back.

I cannot *wait* to post this video. People are going to love it.

Trent still hasn't said anything. The noise level has resumed, and if possible, is even louder than before. I've stunned him speechless. This is an even better reaction than I'd hoped for. And I've got it documented forever.

One day, we're going to look back at this pivotal moment in our relationship and smile.

"Aren't you excited that I'm here, babe?" I look up at him, hopeful. He blinks rapidly, his pupils wide in disbelief, like I'm too good to be true. "Where can I drop my stuff?"

"Uh, bedroom's upstairs." Trent jerks his head toward the stairs. "I just hope no one steals your stuff. Imma get another drink. Why don't I get you one while you put your stuff away?"

Trent heads toward the kitchen. Okay then.

He's too stunned to process this. That's all. I admit it is out of character for me. Usually, I think about grand gestures, but I wait for them to happen to me. This is the first time I've tried to make it happen myself.

And I totally pulled it off.

I haul my stuff up the stairs, looking at the flight as if it might be Mount Everest. With all these pro-athletes here, or who I at least assume to be athletes due to the high percentage of joggers and T-shirts, you'd think someone would offer to help me carry my bags up.

I guess chivalry is dead.

Or at least sleeping.

Or possibly drunk.

Once in the room, I pretty much collapse on the bed. This is not what I had in mind in terms of falling into Trent's bed the moment I walked through the door. Of course, now I'm so gross and smelly that I don't want him near any of my lady bits and all my anticipatory horniness has worn off like a cheap perfume.

There's no way I can be all sexy without a shower, and there's no way in hell I'm showering in a house full of people.

I guess the maid costume will have to wait for tomorrow night.

Not to mention that people keep passing through the bedroom like it's the terminal at Logan on their way to the roof deck. And Trent still hasn't come to find me yet. I bet he's working on getting rid of everyone so we can spend some time alone.

That sounds like a good plan.

While I wait for the place to clear out, I'm going to upload my video to ClikClak. Of course, I've got to set it to Ellie Goulding. It's like the song was meant for us.

It's so good. I don't need to edit it at all. The guy from the street captured it perfectly. I walk in, navigating the crowd, and then there Trent is, too stunned to speak as the music climaxes. Like it's too good to be true, and he can't believe his eyes. This is what true love and happiness look like, I add in my hashtags, #liainlove, #romanticsurprise, and of course #xoxo, and then I post it.

Now, all I have to do is wait for people to see it. That, and for Trent to come upstairs to me.

CHAPTER 5: OPHELIA

It takes me a minute to realize where I am. Still on Trent's bed.

Alone.

I glance over toward the bathroom, where light seeps out of the partially open door. Yup, Trent's still passed out on the floor.

After I realized he wasn't coming to greet me properly, I went back downstairs to find him pounding Jägermeister shots, just like he did in college.

And a few minutes later, he started puking, just like he did in college.

I wanted to text Marley, but I know her response would be about him refusing to grow up. I make sure Trent's breathing, which he is, and then pull out my phone.

Whoa.

This ... this can't be right. Over 150 ClikClak notifications.

Who the hell is notifying me?

I've never had this many notifications. My heart rate speeds up. It's finally happening.

I click on my landing page. What? My video of walking in has over four thousand views. In ... I check the time ... four hours. My most viewed video only has three thousand views, and it took a week, not to mention a super funny shot of Sunny falling off my desk, to get there.

People love stupid cat videos.

4,500 views.

Holy crap. I'm going viral.

Yes.

People love a good romance. I knew they would. The world wants romance and big sweeping gestures.

I glance toward the bathroom door again. Ha. Romance.

If they only knew the truth.

I open a new draft.

Okay, so you've all apparently seen the surprise. I mean, right now, at three a.m., it's had almost five thousand views. I didn't even think five thousand people saw my videos ever, so thanks for watching. Buuuut, yeah. The night didn't go as I'd planned.

I turn the video to peek through the bathroom door, catching a glimpse of a bare leg and the sound of cacophonous snoring. I should probably turn him on his side. Again.

So yeah, apparently he was so overcome with my surprise—and Jägermeister—that this is how my night went. In his defense, he was probably pretty drunk by the time I got here, so this was a short trip ... to the bathroom floor.

I turn the camera back to me and shrug.

Oh, well, wish me better luck today. I'll keep you posted. Kisses and hugs!

Part of me wants to cry. Part of me wants to kick Trent. Part of me wants to explain this all away as poor timing. Part of me wants to admit that I'm settling.

I glance at my ClikClak account. The views keep climbing. My brain cannot wrap itself around these numbers. I'm used to posting great videos and getting like twenty-two views. Not ... 5,352.

Holy shit.

My hands shake and I don't know whether to jump up and down and shriek, or vomit. Of course, Trent has the second one covered.

There's a good chance I jump on the bed for a minute.

See? I knew it. I knew the world would love me being in love. They'd flock to and share this moment of happiness in a world that's been nothing but bad news and worse news lately.

My #romanticsuprise is making the world smile.

I want to call Marley, but it's the middle of the night, and no one is bleeding. I text her instead to check out my account, followed by a string of exclamation marks. My inbox is continually pinging. I'm not ready for the inbox yet. Especially since the reality has not met the expectation of the video. Instead, I check the comments.

Girl.

What a dog.

She's an idiot if she thinks he's happy to see her.

Look at that body language.

This isn't happiness to see her.

#romanticsurprisefail

I see the hashtag *#romanticsurprise* over and over. Of course, I'd put it on the series of videos myself, along with my trademark #xoxo and #liainlove.

My stomach sinks into my toes. I might really vomit. Or pass out. The pit in the depths of my gut started when Trent chose to get plastered and puke instead of spending the time with me. It's only continued to extend down further and darker until I can't imagine there being a bottom to it.

I sag back into the bed, fatigue—and despair—washing over me. I'm going viral. And not in a good way.

I start sweating, the cold, clammy kind. My heart pounds and my hands shake. Bile rises in my throat. What a colossal disaster.

They hate me. All of ClikClak thinks I'm an idiot and my boyfriend sucks. Okay, well I agree with them on the second part, at least at the moment, but seriously, what's with all the negativity? Doesn't anyone believe in love anymore? How can they be so cruel when I was trying to do something so sweet?

I bury my face into the pillow. Maybe I can accidentally smother myself so I never have to face the light of day again.

For the first time, I'm glad my username is @lovelylia. I don't know what made me use Lia instead of Ophelia, but now I'm thanking my lucky stars I was too embarrassed to put my real name on there. Can you imagine if people actually knew who I was and what a fool I'd been to think this was a good idea?

Of course, now my face is going viral, so people might recognize me from that, but at least they don't know my real name. They shouldn't connect this to my account on Instagram or anything like that.

The door creaks open and Trent stumbles out, his blonde hair matted in some areas and standing straight up in others. He's scrawny, yet doughy, all at the same time. I can see this because he's only wearing his underwear.

I can't believe I was ever attracted to him.

Eww.

If it wasn't the middle of the night, I'd be hightailing it home. As it is, I'll be on the phone with the airline first thing in the morning to change my flight.

"Hey, babe. Sorry about that. I was feeling an epic rager, and I didn't know how to process new information."

Epic rager.

We're thirty. At what point do epic ragers become sad?

He staggers to the bed, almost lurching as he grabs my leg. I *think* he's trying to come on to me but doesn't quite have the motor function to pull it all together. "Why don't we wait until you're a bit more sober?"

And smell less like bad choices and desperation.

He crawls onto the bed. "Yeah, I'm not sure I can get any wood now anyway." And with that, Trent begins snoring.

I know, despite my tiredness, sleep is not going to come anytime soon for me. So, I do what any rational person would do. I continue reading the comments and messages on ClikClak.

Three hours later, as dawn is threatening the horizon and after I've watched my own video several—dozen—times, I've come to realize three things:

One. Trent does not want me here.

Two. Romance is dead.

Three. Going viral isn't all it's cracked up to be.

Over eight thousand people agree. Or eight thousand people are laughing at my expense. That's more like it.

I can't take it anymore. I pull the blanket off the bed, leaving a mostly naked Trent uncovered, and head up to the roof deck to watch the sunrise. This'd be perfect if I had a steaming hot cup of coffee in my hands on this crisp October morning.

Actually, it'd be perfect if I had a boyfriend who loved me and was happy to see me and wasn't still passed out. As if to kick a woman when she's down, a large mourning dove lands on the railing right next to me. The stupider cousin to the pigeon, this bird doesn't seem to understand the arrangement I have with its feathered relatives up in Boston.

My heart quickens and my hands start to tremble ever so slightly. My mouth goes dry. I flick my hand at it. It doesn't move. I wave the corner of the blanket. Still, it sits there, black eyes staring at me.

"What are you looking at? Shoo. Go away." I swish the blanket like a can-can skirt. The bird takes a step closer to me. Then another. It puffs out its feathers, trying to intimidate me.

It's working.

Oh no. This is it. It's going to jump on me and peck my eyes out. Or poop in my hair. Either way, it would be the end of the world. I hop to my feet, waving my arms in the blanket like my own set of massive wings.

The blasted thing doesn't move, except to bob its head.

Then, it rears up, spreading its wings. This is it. It's about to attack. If I don't defend myself, it's going to kill me.

"Go away. Get. Get. GET." I'm yelling now. I'm sure, if asked at a later time to analyze this situation, I might say that my reaction was intensified by my lack of sleep and extreme stress. However, at this moment, I don't have the clarity to think that. Instead, I start shrieking like a banshee, screaming that this bird is trying to kill me.

For the record, when you shout from a rooftop, "Help, he's trying to kill me. Help. Help me please," it's bound to get a police response.

Four cop cars pull up, seemingly out of nowhere.

And it's not like anyone believes that I felt threatened by a mourning dove. Oh no, they look at Trent, who has stumbled out to the deck, still in only his skivvies. It takes the police almost two hours of talking to us, both together and separately, to leave us be, finally convinced that there was no domestic incident.

Trent glares at me.

"What?" I finally ask. I'm clutching my toiletry bag in my hands. I'm going to take a shower and then head to BWI and *beg* someone to put me on a different flight.

"You're crazy. Like absolutely nuts."

"I don't like birds. He was taunting me. He was about to attack me." I would go to my grave believing that. I saw the malice in its cold, black eyes. I firmly believe that if I don't run a good offensive, birds will be the death of me someday.

Trent shakes his head. "You know, I don't think this is working."

Screw the shower. I can stink on the plane. I need to get out of here as soon as possible, otherwise, the police may be called back when I rip his pubic hairs out one by one. "Really? What gave you that idea? I'm so surprised. This is my surprised face," I deadpan before shoving everything back in my suitcase.

"What did you expect? That we'd last forever? You don't even live here."

"Um, you were the one who moved *here*. And without even asking me!" I mean, we weren't that serious, but you'd have thought he'd at least have discussed it with me. Or, if he wanted to be with me, asked me to come with him. I mean, I work from home. That can be done anywhere. And it's not like there aren't accountants everywhere. Everyone needs their money counted.

Of course, I'm not going to let him off the hook by being all reasonable or anything. "It's been good, Trent. Or actually, it hasn't. Not really. Lose my number."

He scoffs. "I don't think you have to worry about that. I wouldn't touch you again if you paid me to."

I roll my eyes at the loser I've wasted the last eighteen months on and begin hauling my stuff down the stairs. Just like my romantic surprise that wasn't, it's hard to stomp off in a dramatic exit when I'm practically toppling over with my backpack and a suitcase that keeps flipping on its side.

There is a *slight* chance that I spend too much time lost in the fantasy world of books and movies, and that it's setting me up for a world of disappointment.

And by slight, I mean one hundred percent definite.

CHAPTER 6: XAVIER

Our last game is a home game. It doesn't matter though. We've got the second-worst record in our division. All I need to do is make it through the game without an injury that could jeopardize my place on the team. Or my availability to be traded in March.

I'm in the holding pattern from hell.

The game starts in a half hour. I look around the locker room and take a deep breath, holding it before exhaling slowly. Everyone's going about their pre-game rituals, but I can't seem to get into mine. Ninety minutes more and then I'm onto the next step. It's how I've always looked at things. I identify my end goal and then immediately break it up into small, manageable steps to avoid an absolute panic.

It works.

Most of the time.

I don't like not having plans.

And whether I care to admit it or not, I don't really have plans right now. I don't want to stay with the Baltimore Terrors, but I'm not eligible for trade until March. That's a long time to be working and training with an organization you don't believe in.

My heart thumps a bit harder and my breath becomes more shallow.

Ninety minutes. All I have to do is focus on the next ninety minutes.

I put my earbuds in and pull out my phone. I need to distract myself for a bit before I totally lose it. I open ClikClak. I'm about three swipes in when it pops up. I recognize her disheveled dark hair and oversized fuchsia backpack, not to mention the suitcase rolling along behind her.

Bollocks.

I cringe inside, knowing what I'm about to see. Also, my filming skills leave a lot to be desired. When my career as a footballer dies, I think my chances of being the next Christopher Nolan are slim. Even though I was focused on her, as she approached the couch, I cut to Trent.

The expression on his face is undeniable. It's not shock or disbelief that this woman did this for him. It's not love. No, he's annoyed.

And his hand is completely on Hooter Number One's upper thigh.

Wanker.

But the comments. They're brutal and unrelenting. It's almost as bad as the British paparazzi. The lion's share is talking about Trent's body language. Not that they identify him. But there is a fair number calling her a fool and idiot.

Over a hundred thousand views. In about a day and a half.

Poor girl.

I wonder how the rest of her stay went.

At that moment, Trent swaggers into the dressing room. "All right, ladies, I've got plans for tonight so if you can keep your injuries to a minimum, I'd appreciate it."

Like any of us want to get injured. To be in pain. To miss playing time. To possibly have our career ended because of a wrong slide tackle or missed header.

Also, he's calling us ladies like it's some kind of insult. Has he seen the US women play football recently? They've made it into—and won—the Global Games much more recently than the men have. But it doesn't shock me that he thinks this way.

He's a complete and total tosser.

"Yeah? You got plans with *romantic surprise* girl?" someone calls from the other side of the lockers. Laughter erupts, and I find myself sniggering a bit as well.

Trent freezes and then at least has the decency to look down at his feet. "Um, no, she left."

"Did she rip you a new one?" That's Maken asking. "She caught you red-handed. The world is on her side."

"What are you talking about?" Trent looks confused. If I hadn't thought so before, I've now come to the conclusion that he has a very punchable face. I sort of wish we could get him out on the field, even during a practice or something, so I could give him a proper elbow jab. I'd take the yellow card.

"Check ClikClak. Search *hashtag romantic surprise*," Maken advises.

We all watch as Trent checks his phone. His face grows pale and then seventeen shades of red all in an instant. "I'm gonna kill her. That bitch. I can't believe she did this to me!" he finally sputters, a vein popping out in his forehead.

It's not a great look for him.

Of course, neither is how he's portrayed in the video. The comments are ruthless and scathing. In other words, what he deserves.

"Isn't she your girlfriend?" Alastair asks.

"Was. I thought by moving away, she'd get the hint. Should've just ghosted her dumb ass," Trent mutters, still scrolling through the comments. "Stupid booty call gone wrong."

In my humble opinion, girls don't make the effort like that when they're simply a booty call.

She didn't know she was a booty call. She thought she was a proper girlfriend. Maybe she didn't know he was a wanker.

"Are you going to respond to Lia?" someone asks.

"Lia? Who the hell is Lia?" Trent asks, still flicking at his screen. "Oh, yeah, that. It's stupid. Her name is Ophelia. She thought she was being all sly and everything, making a profile that would keep her from getting trolled. Ridiculous. Her name is Ophelia Finnegan. You all should find her and harass the shit out of her for doing this to me. Bros before hos, am I right? *Ophelia Finnegan*," he repeats slowly like we're jotting this down.

I think he's expecting a high five or arse slap from the team collectively, like he's one of us. He's not a player, he's a trainer. He's not part of the team, he's part of the support staff. Of course, he doesn't pick up on those subtleties.

I'm guessing nothing short of a massive lorry running him over would be subtle enough for Trent.

But enough about him. The Terrors have a game to play.

And lose. We lost. Again.

We knew the season was ending tonight, but none of us wanted to go out like this.

"This blows." Maken slams his locker shut. As the captain, he feels a large chunk of responsibility for the team. Personally, I feel like that rests on the shoulders of the front office who fired most of our coaching staff and traded or released our highest-paid players. They cheaped out and got what they paid for.

Maken, Alastair, and I all want out. Maken's the only one who can be traded in the off-season. Al and I have to wait for the March international trading window to open. And the five months until then seem interminably long.

The US Soccer League—USSL—is serious about developing American talent to increase their competitive standing on the world stage. In other words, they really want Americans playing who can represent the National Team at the Global Games. Ones who won't get their arses handed to them in the first round, assuming they qualify at all.

The USSL's solution is to limit the number of non-American citizen players to twenty percent of the roster and to restrict the trading of international players to two narrow windows during the long nine-month season.

Because a team might get stuck with a player or a salary that they can't trade, they're more likely to seek to fill the spots with American talent. At least that's the idea. It's not like we don't all have leagues in our home countries. Alastair is here because his contract paid him tons more money.

I'm here because I have no choice.

Alastair sits on the bench next to me, stuffing the contents of his locker into his large duffle bag. "I'm considering going back to the BFL."

Heading back to Europe would be a good way to extract ourselves from the Terrors organization. Alastair has that option.

I do not.

"I wish I could, mate. But you should look into it. Anything to save you from another season here."

"Ah, but what'll you do? Other than sit in your flat and sulk all the time. I'm worried about you, mate."

"I'm thinking of volunteering with a rescue organization for the next two months. That should keep me busy. You don't have to worry."

"Bird Man, you're too much. Really." Alastair stands, clapping me on the shoulder. "I feel terrible that you're stuck here."

"At least until March. I'll work to see if I can get traded then."

Alastair leans in and whispers, "You know no one likes to deal with Camacho. He's screwed over so many people that they don't trust him. I don't either."

That makes two of us. Our owner is as crooked as the day is long. I don't trust Camacho not to screw me over royally. And it wouldn't surprise me if other owners didn't want to trade with him because they felt the same way.

Once my locker is cleaned out, I look around. I can't believe I have no other options than to stay with the Terrors. As I head toward the door, I realize I'm not the only one having a terrible night.

"Take it down." Trent's screaming into his phone. "Ophelia, I mean it. I'm going to sue you for defamation of character. You made me look like an asshole."

I keep walking, knowing that Trent needs no help in looking like an arsehole. I'm not sure what Ophelia can do with this momentum, but I hope she profits tremendously. Or at least enough to recoup the cost of her plane ticket.

47

CHAPTER 7: OPHELIA

I keep waiting for that sick feeling to go away every time I look at my phone. Nope, still there.

The necessary evil is that I need my phone. At least I do if I want to talk to my best friend. Marley works in a busy doctor's office, so I can only text with her during the day. And since it's Monday, that means I have to pick up my phone to get some much-needed emotional support right now.

Marley: 400K+

Yeah, I didn't need that text message.

I don't need to know that over four hundred thousand people have witnessed one of the most embarrassing situations in my life. And that's an impressive statement because remember, I'm the girl who had the police called because she felt her life was threatened by a dove.

And we won't even talk about the sock incident.

What's so embarrassing about this is that I didn't know. I had absolutely no idea. I didn't *see* until thousands of strangers—literally—pointed it out to me. I mean, things were over with Trent anyway, obviously, but the video ...

A wave of nausea rolls over me.

How could I have been such a fool?

Yet another check in the column of "stupid things Ophelia Finnegan has done in her quest for love."

I had to shut down my direct messages. I turned off my notifications. I thank my lucky stars that my ClikClak account is not under my name so that no one can find and troll me on my other social media accounts. Sure they could look for my face, but that's like trying to find a needle in a haystack of short, average-looking brunettes. At least they can't link my ClikClak to my real name.

Lovelylia.

More like "Laugh at Lia."

Here's the thing—I don't know what to do now. Hell, that's the story of my life. My follows have gone through the roof as my video—and all the ones in the series—have blown up in views. I could, and should, use this as a springboard for more.

It's just … I don't know what more. I have no idea what else to do with my life. Try as I might, I don't really have a long-term plan or goal. My dad will tell me that I need a plan. It's only … for what? I've no clue.

I don't have tons of causes I feel passionately about. My life is pretty much all work since my social life is non-existent. I'm really good at my job, which is how I ended up doing it. I do admit that getting myself lost in numbers is soothing, and it passes the time, but I wouldn't identify it as a passion. Growing up in the shadows of my uber-successful brothers, being good at math was the only useful commodity I had. I didn't even do that well in school overall. Frequent comments on my report cards included, "disorganized," "talks too much," "talks out in class," and my personal favorite, "unmotivated." We all know that was their nice way of calling me lazy.

I wasn't lazy. It was just … hard to get my shit together. No one understood that though. I was smart enough to do homework. Just not smart enough to turn it in. My impulsivity and awkwardness negated any sort of popularity I might have had. Owen was the captain of the football team. Aiden played baseball. I was a mathlete.

That was not a compliment.

I might be good at crunching numbers, but it doesn't spark that *thing* inside me. It relaxes me. It makes the days go by fast, but it brings me no passion. The only thing I feel that way about is … passion. Romance. Love.

The things I'm pretty much totally incapable of figuring out. I mean, I'm thirty. It's not like I'm a kid anymore. Yes, Mom, I know I'm not getting any younger. But … I still just don't get it. Why doesn't anyone want to love and romance me the way books and movies imply it should happen?

I know I'm loved. My parents, my brothers, and even Marley. Sunny the cat loves me. Well, when I have a can of cat food in my hand, he does.

It's not nothing.

But it's not enough.

Me: You're not helping. I should shut my account down.

Three dots wave.

Marley: Don't. This could be good.

Good for what? Pointing out that I'm an idiot when it comes to men?

Let's face it, I'm not cut out to be an influencer, and no one in their right mind is going to take makeup tips from me. I mean, if I ever sat down and actually wrote the romance novel I've been dreaming of writing, then ClikClak would be a benefit to me. Like if even half of the people who are following me went out and bought a book, I'd be golden. ClikClak has literally made authors' careers. If I had a book, then I might be set.

All I have to do is write it now.

I ignore the fact that the last time I tried to write, it was garbage. I haven't been able to pen more than a random tidbit here and there. Not an outline, and certainly not enough for a story.

I take another drink of my vodka cocktail. Okay, it's pretty much straight vodka with a splash of orange juice so I don't feel like a total lush. Mimosas are totally acceptable, so this should be too. I'm fresh out of champagne to make a mimosa, and I need the hard stuff anyway. I'm off work today since I was supposed to be away. Sunny looks at me through squinty eyes, obviously judging my day drinking.

Whatever. He had his nuts removed before he can remember. He doesn't know what heartbreak feels like.

I open ClikClak.

Yeah, so obviously I'm an idiot when it comes to men, as several hundred thousand of you have pointed out. No, I didn't see his hand on her thigh. No, I didn't realize that he was not thrilled to see me—I honestly thought he was just surprised. But yes, I can see it now. Also, I should have clued in when he got totally shitfaced and spent the night on the bathroom floor rather than with me. I guess I thought because I knew him before and because we'd hung out all during COVID that it meant something. Maybe it did and the distance thing was too hard. Maybe I'm just an idiot. Maybe I'm drunk and rambling. I think number three might be the winner, but number two is a strong contender. Anyway, my big romantic gesture was ruined. I'm a viral laughing stock, and I still have no idea how to date someone who's not a total loser. Even though I love romance, I'm not any good at it. I'm an accountant, so maybe that's just not compatible with true love. So yeah, that's where I'm at. If you have any tips or tricks for me, I'm game. ClikClak, work your magic and bring me Mr. Right. Kisses and hugs.

I add my signature "XOXO" to the screen and the appropriate hashtags.

I try to scroll through, but my own video keeps popping up. Sometimes it's a splice, where someone else records themselves watching along. Those are the worst because their judgy judgment is on display.

Then my phone dings. It's a text from Trent. Trent!

What else could he possibly want? I mean, he already screamed at me.

And no matter what he says, I'm not taking him back. I may be lonely, but I'm not desperate.

Okay, I'm a little desperate, but not that desperate.

Trent: You need to take down the video.

I roll my eyes hard enough to strain one of them. I wonder if there's a medical diagnosis for eye strain due to an idiotic male. I scribble on a post-it to look that up. If there isn't, there should be.

Me: No.

Even though, like ten minutes ago, I was totally gonna pull it down. Now, I'm not gonna pull it down, if only to spite him.

Trent: You have to. It's defamation of character.

Me: You would have to have some character for me to defame it.

Boom. Stick that in your pipe and smoke it, Trent.

But I'm not done. Not yet. One more.

Me: Plus, it's not like I identify you anywhere in the video. If you claim it, it's on you. You're defaming your own character, you stupid asshole.

And then I block his number.

I finish my drink and immediately pour another. And then I open ClikClak again.

So, like, he just messaged me and told me to take down the video because I'm defaming him. Or his character. Or whatever. I was like you'd have to have some character for me to defame it.

I mimic a mic drop.

Can you believe he has the nerve to do that? Like I'd take it down because he asks. No, I want everyone to know what a loser he is. Of course, I was chasing after him, so what does that make me? It's like my milkshake brings all the boys to the yard, but only if they're narcissistic, immature, and unstable. I gotta try making a different flavor. I'm sick of this one. Kisses and hugs!

I then do what any sane, rational human being would do. I stalk Trent on social media. I mean, we were already friends everywhere before, but now I want to see what he's posting. I should have known something was up when he didn't follow me on ClikClak. Hell, I didn't even know he was on here until one of his many rants post-viral video. I wouldn't have to be a gambler to guess he's ranting and raving about the injustice of me exposing 'Im on ClikClak. And I know I have a small window before he blocks me everywhere.

This, of course, conveniently overlooks the fact that he was supposed to be in a relationship with me, but *obviously* had plans with the girl on his couch.

I wonder who she is?

I start scanning through his followers on ClikClak, but can't tell, especially when a lot of them have something like "ID23879077" as their username. Hell, I go by Lia on there, so it's hard to tell who's who. Instagram, though ... Instagram is a different story.

His followers are numerous, with a high percentage of busty women on his list. It looks like if they're not a set of boobs, his followers are soccer players. At least that part makes sense.

I don't follow soccer, so the members of the Baltimore Terrors are unfamiliar to me, mostly only recognizable by their team gear. There's one guy who is wearing a Terrors jersey, in addition to a thick leather glove with an owl sitting on it.

I shudder and swipe past as fast as I can.

I mean, birds are bad enough, but owls … they mean death. Or at least bad luck. Everyone knows that bad luck befalls you if you hear an owl hoot three times. Not to mention owls are the only creatures that can live with ghosts.

Maybe this guy is why the Baltimore Terrors were so bad this year. Do they know he cursed them?

I keep scrolling, looking more closely at the women. And there are so many women. If I were the flexible sort, which I'm not, I would be kicking myself right in the ass for not realizing this before.

I send a quick text to Marley.

Me: You are fired from being my best friend.

We fire each other at least once a month, if not more.

Marley: Good. I was gonna quit anyway. What'd I do now?

This is why she's my best friend. She gets me.

Me: Um, you didn't social media stalk Trent and you didn't tell me to either. A good best friend is supposed to act like a PI. Look at all the boobs he's friends with.

I throw in an entire line of red flag emojis.

Me: I'll give you one last chance, but you need to totally vet the next guy I sleep with.

After I send the text, it occurs to me that maybe I should have her vet the guy *before* I sleep with him. Between the two of us, we haven't exactly been doing a bang-up job. This calls for reinforcements.

It takes me almost two hours, but I look at my finished product and smile. Perfectly timed to music, short enough to be spliced with someone else's video. Animated graphics and of course my trademark "XOXO" at the end. I toss back another shot of vodka and hit "post."

Why yes, I did just post a ClikClak video asking my 75,000 followers to find me the man of my dreams.

CHAPTER 8: XAVIER

My body loves this day. My brain hates it. After a long season, we're done. There's no practice on the schedule. No game to play. Nothing to do with my time.

Downtime is my brain's archnemesis.

I'm bruised and sore, the season taking its toll on my body. That hamstring injury still nags, right up in the middle of my buttock, and I know it's only going to finally heal with some rest and relaxation.

I do neither well.

Normally, I'd fly back to England to visit my folks for a few weeks. But with COVID and travel restrictions, I'd be nervous that I'd spend my entire visit in quarantine. Or worse, that I'd take something home to my mum, who already struggles with chronic asthma. I keep asking my parents to move here, but since I'm gone so much, it hardly seems worth it.

Not to mention, they don't want to leave their flock behind.

So here I am, no schedule, no routine, no nothing for at least a week while I let my injury heal. I'll probably head up to Boston to catch the Buzzards in the playoffs. If I can't be on the field, I can at least support Coach Janssen. Bjorn took a risk on me when I was blackballed in Europe. If he asked me for a kidney, I wouldn't think twice before heading to the hospital.

To say I was livid when the Terrors gave him the ax would be an understatement. I wanted to walk myself, but with my international status, finagling a trade requires more work. There aren't a lot of teams who will invest in a player with a history like mine.

I pull out my phone and make travel arrangements to fly to Boston. I should probably let my agent know where I'm off to since he's the only one who has an interest in me off the field, but this trip is totally for pleasure.

After my reservations are made, I open ClikClak. I'd be fibbing if I said I didn't take some kind of pleasure in the embarrassment it caused to Trent. I've half a mind to tag him in the video, just so everyone knows who the wanker is.

It pops up several times in my feed of suggested videos. I like each one if only to help with the traction of the video. Though I do feel bad for the girl. Lovely Lia. But wait, that's not what Trent called her. He said her name … Ophelia Finnegan.

I wonder why that's not in her ClikClak profile.

I open Instagram. I take a quick selfie, lying on the couch and caption it, "What exactly does one do on a Monday?" After posting, I scroll through my followers until I find Trent's name. His latest post makes me stop.

It's a graphic of the quote, "Karma is a bitch, and so are you. No one will ever touch you again."

It's crude enough to make me pause. But my blood begins to boil when I see he's tagged @OpheliaXOXO in it.

That poor girl.

I think back to how excited she was to be seeing her boyfriend. To be surprising him with such a gesture.

I click on her name and her profile comes up. It's mostly pictures of her cat, a big, fat yellow tabby. She's not very active on this site. I switch back to ClikClak and search for LovelyLia. I find her easily and then follow her.

Don't ask me what is possessing this behavior, other than boredom.

And then a new video pops up. If I didn't know better, I'd think she was on her way to being thoroughly pissed. There's a slight sway to her movement that I don't recall seeing when she was at Trent's on Friday night. She doesn't speak, but graphics and words pop up, timed to the music and her dancing.

Basically, she wants ClikClak to find her the perfect guy. Requirements: not too tall, not too far away, and not too much of a dick.

Her words, not mine.

She also wants someone who's romantic and loves big, grand gestures, and who doesn't mind that she's an accountant.

Poor lass. She's going to get her heart stomped on. Again.

I switch back to Instagram and before I can analyze what I'm doing, I click on Ophelia's profile, and then "Messages."

Me: Hi there. I'm the bloke who recorded your romantic surprise video. I'm sorry you didn't realize what a wanker Trent was before, but he was and will always be a wanker. Don't take down the video. It's much too amusing to watch his face go all shades of scarlet every time someone mentions it. Hang in there.

I don't know why I do it. I don't know why I say those things, other than this poor girl wants someone to come riding in like a knight on a white steed and save her. She's going to die alone, probably with about ten more cats. The last thing she needs is a tosser like Trent.

Next, I message Claude Kenley, strength and conditioning coach for the Buzzards to tell him I'm coming to Boston and see if he has time to grab a pint. We shared more than our fair share of them the year after I moved to the States when I roomed with him. It wasn't usual for players to be staying with staff, but my situation was anything but usual.

I don't think Coach Janssen wanted me by myself all the time. Though he said he believed me, and in me, I think there was part of him that wondered what really happened. He never asked, and I never volunteered the information.

That night has absolutely nothing to do with my ability to play defender and absolutely everyone knows it. I was a scapegoat, and I refuse to give any more attention to the situation.

The shadow hung over me when I came to the Terrors, but Coach Janssen never mentioned it. He treated me like every other player. I conducted myself with honor, both on and off the field, and he never had any complaints. I started every game as if proof of his faith in me.

And then the bloody coronavirus shut down the world. Sports have long acted as the great equalizer for the world and without them, everyone seemed off-kilter. I was no exception. But I used the time to train harder than ever, turning my apartment into a gym, since the one in my complex was shuttered, like the rest of the world. I ran every day and emerged from the pandemic in better shape than I'd ever been.

Which made it hard to understand why I no longer started. Sure, I played every game, but I was no longer a starting defender. It's not uncommon for me not to see playing time until the second half. The writing's on the wall, but I still have a year left on my contract with the Terrors. Two if they extend it out to make up for 2020.

I don't think I can do this for another two years.

It's time to call my agent. "Tony, mate, I need you to work on a trade for me. I can't stay with the Terrors another season."

"I hear you, Xavier, but you're stuck. You're not eligible for a trade until March twentieth."

That's a week after next season starts, which means I'll have to do all my pre-season training with the Terrors.

"I know. I wish I could go sooner. They're going to bench me again and for no reason. I've played better this season than I ever have." I don't mention the nagging hamstring. No one wants a player with a liability.

"That's weird, and I can't get an answer as to why. Camacho isn't talking, at least not about that."

"It can't be the *thing*. I started for two years before COVID, so if he were going to hold it against me, I never would have been his starter. You've got to get to the bottom of it, so we can fix it. Either that or you've got to find a way to get me traded."

I don't love having an agent who acts as my manager, but football is a business, and I don't have the time or the finesse to make the necessary arrangements. Basically, I'm good at being a footballer and not much else.

Except for handling birds.

If I wasn't playing football, there's no doubt I'd be in the family business of wild bird rescue and rehabilitation, hence my nickname. I'm sure Mum would love it if I called right now and said I was hanging up my cleats and flying home. I'm not so sure my older brother, Philip, would feel the same, but I doubt he'd turn away the help.

Things have been very rough since the pandemic, and if it weren't for my salary, Mum and Dad would have had to close up shop. They survive, normally, on tours, birthday parties, and photography sessions. Obviously, all of those have taken a massive hit in the last eighteen months since the pandemic began.

No one cares much about a starving barn owl or a hawk with a broken wing when you can't put food on your own table.

While I'm by no means the highest-paid player in the league, my salary is more than enough to keep me comfortable while helping out the family. It's one of the main reasons why I keep my agent. Tony negotiates a much higher rate than I'm capable of, as well as endorsement deals. I had the one back home before the … incident. I've had one or two small ones here in the States. He's hoping to book more this winter while I have some free time.

I'm going to find a rescue organization here in Baltimore to volunteer at during the off-season. I mean, I'll still be doing training sessions. The schedule is simply more flexible. Most people think the off-season is a time for rest and relaxation. I look at it as a time to get into full fitness to go into the pre-season strong.

Except for today. A cursory search of flights has me getting the best price to Boston this evening.

Fine. It'll get me to town in plenty of time for the game tomorrow night. I won't mind kicking around a different city for a bit either. Doesn't hurt to do some recon, especially if I'm going to put Tony up to making a deal with the Buzzards.

CHAPTER 9: OPHELIA

I stare at the message. My fingers hover, poised over my keyboard, but totally incapable of actually typing anything.

I click on his profile. Xavier Henry.

Okay, he's hot. How did I not notice this when I asked him to record my entrance? Actually, I'm glad I didn't because if I'd realized how attractive he was, I'd probably have turned into a bumbling idiot.

But also, he's the guy with the owl in his profile picture. What is he thinking? I've got to set him straight and have him change that.

I will as soon as I take some ibuprofen. My head pounds. There's a slight—okay absolute, no pun intended—chance I overdid it on the vodka yesterday. I'll say that I deserved to get raging drunk.

Even so, I still wasn't sleeping on the bathroom floor like that loser who shall remain nameless.

Instead of responding to Xavier Henry, I text Marley.

Me: I don't know what I'm doing with my life.

Marley: Going on dates, apparently. ClikClak is trying to hook you up.

No shit! I open the app and see yet another trending video for me. Okay, maybe that was not my brightest idea. I should probably not be on this app. I can't be trusted with the responsibility of it.

Me: Make me not read the negative comments.

Marley: Like I can control anything you do. If I could, you wouldn't be in this mess in the first place.

Me: That's not untrue.

My hand shakes as I begin to scroll through the comments. There are tons that tell me about a brother/son/cousin/friend who is available. But then there are those that are downright mean. Apparently, being an accountant is not well respected, and people are not shy about telling me I should be ashamed of it. I mean, just because I help people file their taxes doesn't mean I'm the one responsible for them. There's a bunch that say I don't *look* like an accountant. I don't even know what that means. What's an accountant supposed to look like? A tight bun and glasses? No, wait, that's a librarian.

And then there are the ones that say I'm a three or a four and shouldn't expect much.

Ouch.

Or that I'm too desperate and needy and no man wants that. There's more than one "woof" comment. There is definitely a common thread that agrees I'm undateable.

People are mean, yo.

No, I have to remember that there are millions of people out there, so a few negative comments don't mean the world is mean. And that maybe, just maybe, one of the suggested brother/son/cousin/friends might actually be the guy for me.

Either that or I'm truly undateable.

Still, it's a little too overwhelming for my hungover brain to process, so I close the app. I think I've closed ClikClak more in the past five days than I ever did in the entire length of time leading up to last Friday.

I should try to focus on work.

And I will as soon as I respond to that Xavier Henry. I've had my share of impoliteness on social media. Responding to his kind words is the least that I can do.

Me: Thanks for recording the other night. I mean, I sort of wish you hadn't because, well, my life has blown up ever since. But I guess it's good to know that Trent is a ... wanker. What is a wanker even? Is there any chance you got a video of him losing his shit? It'd be epic to post that. Oh, BTW, did you see his latest Insta post to me? Next time I ask you to record me, please make me go sit in a corner and think about my actions.

I got back to his profile, click follow, and then look at his latest picture. It's a selfie ... with the Custom House in the background. At least it looks like the Custom House, which is my favorite building in the downtown skyline. Before I can stop myself, I flick back to messages.

Me: Wait, you're here in Boston? I live in Boston.

The minute I hit send, I wish I could take it back. It sounds so desperate.

This is why I'm not allowed to people.

I need to put myself in time out.

I send a quick message to Marley and my mom that I have to turn my phone off for a work thing, and if they need me, they should send an email. Then, I do the unthinkable and power off my phone.

It's for the best, really. I can't be trusted.

Why would I say that?

It's not like I'm going to meet up with him. I don't even know him. One kind message does not mean anything. Other than he probably now thinks I'm some kind of psycho stalker.

Speaking of which, I should look him up.

FOCUS, Ophelia.

Yes, I need to focus on my job that pays my physical bills but leaves a great emotional void. It's great to get lost and hyperfixate for hours at a time, but, you know, not exactly the career aspirations I dreamed about.

Here's the thing: I never wanted to do this. But with one brother in vet school and the other already through law school, the last thing I could do was tell everyone I wanted to be a writer. They would have said I was being foolish Ophelia, lost in her daydreams and out of touch with reality. Again. I'd heard that enough when I was growing up. I wasn't about to have that shoved in my face for the rest of my life.

If only I weren't too chicken to do the job I've dreamed of, instead of doing the job I'm good at.

My gaze darts to the small pile of moleskin-covered notebooks on the shelf behind my desk. They sit there, taunting me. Calling me a coward.

They know the truth.

They know I'm a coward.

I went there once, and it was a disaster.

With a Herculean effort, I force my attention back to my computer, where I crunch numbers and fill out spreadsheets for an eternity. Because I took Friday and Monday off, my to-do list seems a mile long.

The next time I look up, it's dark, which means it has to be after five. My eyes feel like I rubbed sandpaper in them, and suddenly I'm aware of how famished I am. I remove Sundance from my lap, where he's spent most of the day. It's only about ten steps to my kitchen, which isn't long enough to undo the knots in my back and legs after sitting for so long.

I should go for a run or something.

Instead, I make myself a salad. Seems like a totally appropriate compromise. After I eat, I put on a YouTube yoga video. That's about the only type of workout I like to do, which my physique definitely alludes to.

On the other hand, with so much sitting, I need to do *something*. I've often considered getting a dog if only so I have a reason to go for a walk every day. You'd think I could motivate myself without the financial commitment of an animal.

And yes, I did buy a harness and leash for Sundance early on in the pandemic to try and walk him. Unfortunately, and I still question why they even sell these, the leash was a bungee. Sundance, in typical cat fashion, freaked out and tried to run away when I put the harness on him. But since it was a bungee, he came flying back.

It was traumatic for the both of us. One of us can now laugh at it. The other may still be plotting how he's going to murder me in my sleep.

At least I feel like less of a slug having done the yoga. Then, it's a long hot shower and a bowl of ice cream while I watch last night's episode of *The Bachelor*. I don't know why I watch it. It's like the opposite of who I am and everything I want in life.

Of course, I'm the girl who asked ClikClak to set her up.

I probably should turn my phone back on and see what's going on there. I try not to see the notification along the top of my screen that I have a new message on Instagram. Once again, I'm unable to control my impulse to click away.

Xavier: I didn't realize that. I'm heading to a football game this evening, but if you want to grab a pint, I can meet you out before I head down to Foxborough.

I wrinkle my brow. I don't know tons about sports, but I'm pretty sure the Patriots play on Sundays. I remember going out to Sunday brunch that turned into an all-day affair because the Pats were on.

It is Tuesday, right?

There's a second message.

Xavier: A wanker basically refers to, well, someone who wanks off. A tosser. You know, someone who masturbates. But that's not really what it means. Basically, someone who's a jerk or arsehole. Funny thing, the English language. Even though we speak the same language, somehow, it's quite different.

Oh, he's British. I don't think I heard him speak that night at Trent's. So he doesn't mean football football. He means soccer. Which actually makes a lot more sense, with him knowing Trent and all.

I close my eyes and let out a breath, relieved for once that my imbecile thoughts were not played out on social media. Though, and I don't know why I have this thought, I could see Xavier and me laughing about it someday.

With a resigned sigh, I open ClikClak. I should probably post a video, since I haven't posted since yesterday. About what, I'm not sure. People are splicing my video left and right. I'm not gonna lie, there's a lot of eye candy here.

Like, a *lot*.

Me: Um, you gotta help me choose which one. There are too many.

Marley: Who says you gotta pick just one? Think of it like a game of Pokémon.

Me: Gotta catch 'em all? That sounds exhausting.

I could start by weeding out the ones who don't live around here. No way in hell am I doing the long-distance thing again.

I might be a slow learner, but at least I learn.

CHAPTER 10: XAVIER

I shouldn't have asked if she wanted to meet up. That was foolish. Reckless. Impulsive. And I know all too well what happens when I act like that.

There's no reason to meet up with her. The only thing we have in common is that nobhead Trent, and after bashing him for about ninety seconds, we'd be out of things to talk about.

I do have to say, her profile is refreshing, though. Mostly pictures of an overweight, yellow tabby cat. The occasional Boston picture. A selfie here and there. There are no makeup tutorials, no skin-tight dresses, and no duck lips with her fingers held up in a peace sign. It doesn't even look like she has extensions. Her profile looks nothing like the typical girl who finds me on social media. You know, the kind who are after me for my celebrity status or pro-athlete paycheck.

I sort of wish she'd replied.

I did notice she followed me on Instagram. I follow her back. She's got a healthy presence there, so maybe she won't even notice one more person. But Ophelia and my blunder slip from my mind as I approach the stadium. It's the first of the playoff games, and the Buzzards fans are out in force.

It has the vibe of a game back home. England that is, not Baltimore. Baltimore is only the place where my stuff is. But in England—home—football is revered. It is king. Well, second to the actual queen, that is. There's nothing like it here in America.

Even when I watch American football on the telly, the fans, as fanatic as they are, are nothing like ours back home. The noise in a football arena is deafening for the entire course of the game. We live and breathe the sport.

That pain in my chest is back. It's not physical. I don't need to visit a doctor for it or anything. That is, I don't have to go back to the doctor. I've been thoroughly checked by the team's physician over and over. I don't even bother to mention it anymore.

It's the literal feeling of heartbreak.

I'd only ever hoped to get signed to a team. Playing on the Bristol Bombers, practically next door to where I'd grown up in Gloucester was more than I'd ever dreamed. I never made the cuts for the National Team during my youth, but I worked hard and developed my talent. I ate, slept, and breathed football. I didn't have a life outside of the sport. The sacrifices were numerous and extreme.

And that was fine with me.

It was all worth it.

Worth it to finally see my name on the list for the Men's National Team. I had the uniform. I had the travel arrangements. I had realized my dream.

Until that night. Two nights before our first contest.

I wish I'd never laid eyes on her. I wish I'd never followed her outside. I wish I'd never gotten into the car with her. I don't know why I did. I thought I could help her.

I lied. I shouldn't have, but I thought I was protecting her. It never occurred to me that in protecting her, I was mortally wounding myself. Not literally of course. Only figuratively.

Though, the next day, when my name quietly disappeared from the National Team's roster, it *felt* like I'd been physically wounded. And when I didn't think it could get any worse, I was summarily dismissed from Bristol. No manager in all the United Kingdom would even take my calls. No one on the continent either.

I'd mucked up royally.

Tony, the agent I hired after, managed to spin my move to the US as only a sports agent can. I've no idea what he actually told people, but Camacho and the Terrors didn't seem to care about my scandalous past.

Frankly, I couldn't care less what Camacho thinks. I only ever wanted to impress Coach Janssen and Kenley. Also from the European leagues, they were right good mates. I was proud to be on their team.

And then they were dismissed without warning or explanation.

I shoot Kenley a text message. As the strength and conditioning coach, he'll be here watching the game, but not actively coaching like Bjorn is. Maybe I can stop in and greet him at the end of the game. I should have messaged him before, to let him know I'd be at the game, but I was distracted by the Trent debacle.

Seriously, I've got to stop letting these women interfere with my game.

I focus on the contest at hand, rooting for the Buzzards naturally. I recognize some of the same coaching tactics Bjorn used with us. While the Cleveland Renegades are using a traditional 3-4-3 attacking structure, the Buzzards are sticking with a 4-3-4 lineup. I know if the Renegades score more than one goal, Bjorn will switch to a 5-4-1 defense.

God, I miss his coaching.

My phone dings with an alert.

Kenley: You're here at the game? Why didn't you stop in to say hello? Come down at half-time. Head right to the field.

The first half goes by quickly, and as they head into the stoppage time, I make my way down the steps toward the field. Dressed casually in a jumper and jeans, with a cap on my head and mask on my face, no one recognizes me. A rather large security guard does, however, stop me from trying to hop over the railing to gain access to the field. In the nick of time, Kenley comes jogging up, pass in hand.

"He's with me. Here's his pass."

I hop over the barrier.

"What's with the GQ look? You going to a cover shoot after this?" Kenley ribs as we walk toward the tunnel leading to the dressing rooms.

"Not all of us live in trainers and running shorts, mate."

"What the hell are you doing here?"

I stick my hands in my pockets. I wish I knew the answer to that question. I shrug it off. "Our season is done. Might as well support my mates. Plus, I enjoy paying nine dollars for watered-down beer."

"Are you talking to our people? You should be." He's always been good at reading me.

I can only shrug again. "You know the trade status. If Bjorn is willing to wait for me until March, I'd love to play for him again. That's a lot to ask, especially when I didn't get much playing time this year to show what I can do."

I feel Kenley's eyes on me, trying to assess my physique through my street clothes.

"I'm up to a thirty-three-kilometer-per-hour sprint," I say proudly.

"That's like Rinaldo speed. Impressive. You still playing back? With that speed, they should move you to midfield."

I grimace. "Just because I *can* run that fast doesn't mean I like to."

"Nah, I'd get Bjorn to put you in at central midfield."

"Then forget you saw me here. I don't want to play for this bloody team anyway." I laugh.

Kenley chuckles. "Well, that's certainly a negotiating point for your agent." He pauses for a minute as he uses his badge to open the locked door. "It's too bad we can't get you here before March."

"That's assuming Coach Janssen wants me."

"Who'd want a stuffy old Brit like you anyway?" I would know that accent anywhere. I turn to see my former coach rounding the corner. "Good to see you, Xavier. What brings you to our neck of the woods?"

"Here to support you since my season was rubbish. Might as well root on the good guys."

"Still an ass kisser, I see."

I smile. "I'd say I'm simply trying to stay on everyone's good side. Extreme good side, that is."

Kenley says, "He's running at thirty-three kilometers an hour. Think of what you could do with that at central midfield."

"Or left back," I add quickly. It's my current position.

"An interesting thought." Bjorn is looking at Kenley. "Let's get through this season, and then we'll think about the next one." Now he shifts his gaze to me. "Maybe it's time to talk to your agent."

That's code for "I'm interested."

"You know I'm not eligible until the trading window," I remind him.

"Can you apply for citizenship?" Kenley asks. "It'd solve the problem."

Instantly my mouth goes dry. I'm a Brit through and through. I could never be an American. How very progressive of Kenley to assume I could do something like that.

On the other hand, I've been all but banned from the British Football League for life. I'll never be able to play at home again, other than kicking the ball around the schoolyard like I did when I was a tot.

"That's a thought." Bjorn nods. "Look into it. See if you can make it happen." That last statement is directed at me. He doesn't even bother speaking in code this time.

Throughout the second half of the game, I can't focus on anything but the thoughts running through my mind. The Buzzards win, advancing on to the next round.

Good for them.

As I watch them down on the field, celebrating, I'm filled with envy. The Terrors, with our sketchy management and lackluster coaching, will never get to this level. But am I willing to sacrifice my country? Even if that country sacrificed me first?

That question bounces around my brain all through the drive back up to Boston. When I'm situated in my hotel, I check my phone. Ophelia finally responded.

Ophelia: I think I shall refer to all my exes as wankers and tossers from now on. It sounds so much posher than calling them douchebags and assholes. You know, for years, I've seen it in the books I read, so I thought I had the basic emotion behind it but I didn't realize it came from like actually wanking off. For the record, almost all of my knowledge of British culture comes from romantic comedy novels. I'm starting to realize this may not be enough.

I smile at her message.

Me: I also like the term nob head. A nob is another name for a penis so I believe you can take it from there. Also, I'm thinking that perhaps, knowing at least one of your exes, that you should be looking for a different type of man to date.

As soon as I send it, I wish I could pull it back. But alas, the checkmark next to the message indicates she's seen it already. Bollocks.

Ophelia: True story. I'm trying to move on from TrentGate. Of course, I did it in probably the most idiotic way ever. Go check out my ClikClak.

I know the post to which she's referring, but I don't want to tell her that. It sounds a little stalker-ish. I do go over and check out the responses she's been getting.

Holy shite. There are a lot. Too many to even process.

Me: How are you ever going to choose?

Ophelia: <shrugging emoji> Whoever gets the most likes? Whoever looks the least likely to be a wanker? <smiley face emoji> I'm totally using that from now on.

I smile at this. The poor girl. She's got her work cut out for her.

She's not the only one. I glance at the clock and try to figure out what time it is at home. It's close to midnight here, meaning it's approaching five a.m. there. My dad's an early riser, but not that early.

I can picture him putting on his coveralls and wellies, heading out into the aviaries to tend to the birds. Checking the traps for food and the like.

Yes, he traps squirrels and rabbits and whatever other rodents may wander through to feed the birds. They are birds of prey, after all.

Then there's the never-enviable job of sweeping out the bottom of the coops. It's a shitty job. Quite literally.

But the best part is the birds themselves. Many have been injured, usually struck by an auto. Some will never fly again. Those are my favorites because they stay with us. They become like pets, in as much as a wild, predatory bird can. And while Mum and Dad take in all kinds of birds, like hawks and falcons and even the occasional golden eagle, I like the owls the best.

Homesickness washes over me. Screw COVID, I should go home for a visit. I can take my chances with having to quarantine. It's been too long since I've seen my mum or dad.

I even miss Philip, though I doubt he'd say the same about me. I can practically hear him grousing about me becoming an American citizen. *"You live there anyway. Why don't you just hang out the Stars and Stripes, Yankee Doodle?"*

He's a bitter old man, stuck in a young man's body, and has always been that way. Putting an ocean in between us hasn't improved our ability to relate to each other in the slightest. He'd be no help at all in this decision-making process, assuming it's even an option.

Suddenly, Ophelia's decisions don't seem so daunting. I can definitely relate.

CHAPTER 11: OPHELIA

To abs or not to abs. That is the question.

There are definitely some abs choices. And my lady bits are screaming to respond to those posts. My brain, however, is telling my downstairs to slow her roll and stop driving this bus, as she has a notoriously poor sense of direction.

The ongoing battle between my brain and my libido is exhausting. I should just go back to reading my romance novels and staying home. It's easier, really.

Yes, that's what I'll do. I'll become a nun. I'll take a vow of celibacy and ...

Oh, who am I kidding?

I hit the like button on a rock-hard set of abs that I could definitely scrub my laundry on if my washing machine should ever break.

I mean, if he's going to be a jerk—er, wanker—he might as well be eye candy. Right? Then, because I'm not totally unreasonable, I like a video from a much more middle-of-the-road dude. If the dad bod indicates anything, I'm quite sure he games for the entire duration of every weekend that he doesn't have custody of his kids.

Maybe I'm selling myself too short. Maybe I *should* aim high. Maybe I've always been settling and that's why I've never had good luck.

Or maybe it's because I'd rather be at home, reading and snuggled up on the couch than going out and partying.

I know, I'm a total ball of fun. The fuzzy socks and flannel pajamas are a bonus gift.

This decision is too hard. I close ClikClak before I start scrolling through for three more hours. It's decidedly less fun when your own face keeps popping up on the feed. I do have a new book to start, so I should probably read that.

Instead, I open Instagram. Xavier didn't reply, so I shoot him one more message.

Me: I think I'm going to become a nun. They have a lot fewer choices. Plus, I really want to click on the shirtless guys with the lickable abs, but I'm scared that they're automatically bad news. Why does it seem that the ability to be a nice and sweet guy is inversely related to the percentage of body fat?

I don't know why I ask him this, and I immediately regret it. It's yet another stupid thing I've done while on my quest for love. I've got so many, I could write a book. My gaze darts to the pile of notebooks on the shelf.

What's stopping me?

Oh right, the crushing fear of failure. Again. What if I do actually sit down and give it another try? What if I pour my heart and soul into it and people still hate it? Worse, what if I'm truly terrible at it?

It's been four years, but I don't think I'll ever get over that crushing first rejection.

Being five years younger than my closest sibling, people thought I didn't hear when they talked about my brothers and me. But I always heard. And I've kept it close to my heart since.

Look at Owen Finnegan. Captain of the football team and now an Ivy League lawyer. Yes, but what about Aiden Finnegan? Have you seen him with the animals? He's a miracle worker. Those Finnegan boys are so smart. Their parents must be so proud. And then there's Ophelia. She's so …

They would trail off, at a loss for words. I was too much of a lost cause, even then. It was clear I'd never measure up to Owen and Aiden. The best I could hope for was to not be too much of a screwup.

Yet I still screwed up. So much. And I'm doing it again with ClikClak. But I don't know how to function without messing up.

Those thoughts have kept me paralyzed for years. They've kept me from my dream. I tried once, and it was terrible. I'm terrible. It doesn't matter that I read tons. I've even taken quite a few writing classes. I just … I can't again. I sit down, paper in front of me, and the fear of failure freezes my hands in place. It makes the words dry up in my head and my eyes glaze over.

Marley is the only living soul who I told about my desire to write in the first place. It took me weeks to tell her what I was working on, and then even longer to let her read it. Once I started emailing her chapters, she was all Team Ophelia. She loved it, but she was the only one.

I often wonder if she read the same story by another author if she'd have felt the same way. I doubt It.

It's why I've never told anyone else that my secret dream is to become an author. Everyone will laugh. And then, everyone will be disappointed when I can't do it. I'll be the only failure in the Finnegan family. Being an accountant may not be fulfilling, but at least it's safe and honorable.

Owen is a successful attorney, and already a junior partner. He's got the Ivy League degree, the wife, the two kids, the massive house in Connecticut, and the sports car. Aiden is a vet for large animals. It's not glamorous, but he's well-respected and admired in his small Vermont town.

And yes, I have gone to visit him, hoping it will be like one of those Hallmark movies. The only thing that happened was I fell in horse poop and a crusty farm owner with about ten times more wrinkles than teeth laughed at me and told me to go back to the city.

My trip there was also another thing I could put in the "stupid things I've done in the quest for love" category. It seriously is enough to write a book.

Screw it.

I pull a purple Moleskine notebook off the shelf and write in big bold letters, "Stupid Things." I underline the title once, then twice. And then …

Nothing. All the words that are normally swirling around my brain on repeat, vanish. Hell, if I'd known that this is how to make my mind still, I would have tried writing a long time ago.

There's nothing there. How do authors come up with a story? A plot? Characters? Anything? Frankly, I'd settle for something other than, "It was a dark and stormy night" at this point.

After about thirty minutes of staring at a blank page and having it stare back, I give up and go back on ClikClak. Dad-bod has not responded. Mr. Washboard, however, responded with a few choice emojis that include a long purple vegetable and water drops.

Yuck.

I mean, it's not like I'm a prude or anything, but come on. Show me a little attention before *that*. I scroll through more of my potential suitors, but I don't trust anyone or anything anymore.

Men broke me. Maybe they're the stupid ones and not me. Maybe romance is dead and this is hopeless.

Maybe that's why I can't write.

Yet here I sit scrolling through for that *someone* who might see the real me. That they might see beyond my cluttered desk and quirky personality. But as I stare at my notebook, I'm not even sure who I really am.

I'm going to make another list about who I am and what I want from a life partner. Lists help me stay focused. Well, as much as I can.

One. I want to spend my life with someone who values me.

Two. I want someone who loves my cat as much as I do.

Three. I want someone who doesn't make fun of me and my quirks.

Four. I want someone who respects that I am a bit of an introvert, but that I also like to talk a lot.

Five. I want someone who won't laugh at my romantic notions and gestures.

The list isn't difficult. My standards aren't even that high. Maybe because I've had such low standards, I've only ever attracted the bottom of the barrel. Let's face it, the bar is pretty much on the ground at this point.

The only memorable quality I could attribute to Trent was the fact that he "wasn't too tall."

I glance at the clock. It's after one a.m., which is way past my bedtime unless I'm hooked on a great book. Luckily, I'm not, and I drift off quickly.

When my alarm goes off a mere six hours later, I start to curse myself for staying up too late, thereby setting me up for failure today. Then, I notice another message on Instagram.

Xavier: Don't become a nun. Their costumes are so drab and everyone looks the same. Be an individual. Be you. Also, sometimes people with low body fat are nice and sometimes they're not. Maybe they're just irritable from so many burpees. Burpees really are the devil.

I laugh. I don't know why he's returning my messages. Maybe I should see if he still wants to meet up. I mean, if he didn't, would he keep replying like he is?

Me: Are you still in town? Wanna grab a cup of coffee or a drink when I get out of work?

Xavier: Ah, sorry. Got a mid-day flight back to Baltimore.

Of course, I missed my chance. I check out his profile again. The owl makes me shudder, so I try to focus on him. He's really quite good-looking. Way, way, *way* out of my league. I bet he feels sorry for me, and that's why he's being so nice. I'll probably never hear from him again.

Xavier: Are you coming back down to Baltimore any time soon?

Wait, what? What does he mean by that?

Me: Yeah, no. No real reason to.

His response is immediate.

Xavier: Right. Sorry. Trent the Tosser.

My next response is critical. Like super important. I have to be funny and witty and not say anything to make myself look like a fool.

Me: Are you coming back to Boston any time soon?

Then, the messages go silent. Like dead silent. I pushed my luck. I should have played it cool. Of course, there's nothing cool about me, except the temperature of my sheets, which are flannel with pink horses on them. Like I need any help keeping a man out of my bed.

They were a gift from my brother Aiden, who only seems to give equine-themed gifts. I'm pretty sure his office manager actually does all his shopping because he's always out in a barn somewhere. Either that or he orders them from some horse catalog late at night while waiting for a foal to be born.

But the sad thing is, I love these sheets. They're whimsical and goofy, just like me. I need a man who can appreciate that.

And I bet he's out there. It's just ... I have no idea where he is. Obvlously, I'm no good at picking for myself. Maybe it's time to let the universe take over and send Mr. Right my way.

If you consider ClikClak the universe, then this is a fool-proof plan.

CHAPTER 12: XAVIER

"You could be in Boston by the new year."

I glance at the calendar. It's already the first week of November. "I highly doubt that. But enlighten me, Tony, as to how you see this happening."

"It's easy. A little paperwork, and a few phone calls. Probably some more paperwork, and then you'll be apartment hunting in Massachusetts."

"I bet it's a bit more than that."

"Xavier, my man, I looked into it like you asked. The best way to get out of the international clause is to not be an international player. Boston already has their twenty percent, and you're not eligible for trade until March. If you want to be with the Buzzards for pre-season, this is the way."

I hate this way.

"That's assuming Boston even wants me."

"They do. I heard from both the front office and Bjorn. Bjorn's the one who came up with this plan."

"So all I have to do is become an American citizen?" Saying the words leaves a bitter taste in my mouth. It's like cheating on a spouse or selling your family's secret to the competition. I'm being disloyal to my own country. My stomach roils.

On the other hand, if my own country hadn't all but booted me out, I wouldn't be in this position. I'd be happily playing in Bristol and representing England in the Global Games.

"Yup. That's all you have to do. Easy as pie." The smooth edge of Tony's voice, even through the phone, makes me wonder if he's up to something dodgy.

"How easy?" I seem to recall there's been some increased restrictions on immigration in this country over the past several years. Christ, am I really considering becoming an immigrant?

"You've been here five years, right? You have a green card. That's all you need to be a naturalized citizen."

I close my eyes. "I do have a green card." I was eligible under the clause that states I have "extraordinary abilities" in the area of employment, which in my case was athletics. "But I've only had it for four years."

"Shit. When is it five?"

"It was just four in September."

"That sucks." I hear him typing away. "Let me do some more research. But are you on board with this?"

No. "Perhaps. I need to think on it."

Even after disconnecting, that sick feeling stays in my stomach. I need to talk to someone about this. My agent isn't in a position to give me unsolicited advice. He's only going to tell me to do what makes him the most money. And if I know him, or his type, he'll be negotiating a large salary increase for me, which is cash in the bank for him.

I reach for my phone and text Alastair.

Me: My agent wants to work on a trade deal.
Alastair: For the spring?
Me: For now.

I'm not surprised when my phone immediately rings. "How's that supposed to work?" Alastair doesn't even bother with a greeting.

"He wants me to apply for US citizenship."

I hear him exhale. "Damn, that's bloody brilliant."

"You don't think it's selling out?"

"Of course it's selling out, but that's the business we're in. Do you think I really like Pro-Energy Pro-Bars? They taste like bloody wood. But they pay me to say they're delicious and not at all reminiscent of eating tree bark. That selling out paid for my car."

"I know but ..."

"No buts. We're professional athletes. We've a short shelf life. Yours is even shorter because you managed to get yourself banned at home with that Phaedra mess. If you need to improve your career by moving to Boston, and if that means you become a US citizen, then do it. The Terrors are a death trap. We both know it."

"Does that mean what I think it means?"

"I'm heading back to Bristol."

"Bollocks. I mean, good for you, mate, but I'm not sure I can stay on the Terrors without you."

"Don't. Bjorn always believed in you. You know you'll get playing time with him. That's more than you can say for the Terrors."

He's not wrong.

"Ah, I don't know if it's even a possibility. Tony's trying to work a deal, so we'll see."

"Take it. Take whatever deal you can, as long as it gives you playing time and money. Even your pretty face won't sell shorts forever."

"That's not what sold the shorts, and you know it." I laugh.

"But I don't want to be thinking about your bum, as handsome and perfect as it may be."

Without thinking, I flex a little. You're hard-pressed to meet a footballer without a good backside. However, I wasn't disappointed with that paycheck. It was the only one though, before all that stuff went down, and I've yet to secure a big American endorsement. The decreased playing time this year didn't help that either.

After Alastair and I disconnect, I call my dad. I can't make any major career decisions without running it by him. He was the one who convinced me to come to the States in the first place. *Better to play there than not at all. You don't want to waste your life sitting here forever."*

"Xavier, boy, to what do we owe the pleasure?" From the echo, I can tell Dad has me on speakerphone. My guess is Mum's right next to him.

"Eh, well, I've got some career decisions to make. I could use some advice."

"Are you coming back home? Did Jones change his mind?" I can hear the hope in my mum's voice from across the ocean.

"No, the commissioner's still got a ban on me. At least as far as I know. No one's come calling."

"Can't you ask Phaedra to talk to him?" The optimistic nature in her tone just about breaks me.

That name makes me shudder. "No. I have no call to ever speak to her again."

"But you know she could set the record straight."

She could. But she hasn't. Won't. And I won't ask either. I rub the spot between my eyebrows. "That's not what this is about."

"Well, then get to it, lad. This call isn't free, you know." Dad never was one to beat about the bush.

"Right, then. My agent is working on negotiating a deal for a trade, but it'd be better if I was an American citizen." The silence that follows stretches on for so long, I wonder if we got disconnected. "Hullo?"

Then I hear it. The faint intake of breath. Mum's crying. I know how she feels. I want to cry too. Finally, Dad speaks. "That's an interesting idea. It probably makes sense."

I nod, not that he can see me. There's a thick lump in my throat. Everything about me is tied up in my nationality. My heritage. My mum has our ancestry traced back to practically the beginning of time. At least to Henry IV. My family has worked the land and prospered when England prospered. All of my grandfather's brothers on my dad's side perished during the Second World War.

We bleed for England.

"England doesn't want me," I finally manage in a croak.

"Their bloody loss," says Dad. "America is lucky to have you."

"It's not like I'll never come home again. It's just that my passport will read something different."

"And when you stand before a game, it won't be for 'God Save the Queen,'" Mum manages.

"Mum, I stand for the American National Anthem now. I'm playing football here. This may be the best career move I can make. My days with the Terrors are limited. I'm looking to go to the Boston Buzzards. That's where Coach Janssen is. Alastair's coming back to Bristol, so I'll be losing my best mate," I explain. "They're already benching me where I am. I need to move. If I don't do this, I'm stuck in Baltimore until after the start of the season."

"Coach Janssen took you in right … after. He didn't even blink," Dad recalls. "He's a good sort, even if he is Dutch."

"Is he Dutch? Bjorn is not a Dutch name. It's Scandinavian. It means bear," Mum supplies. She's the history buff in the family. "How does a Dane get a Dutch surname?" she continues to ponder like it makes a difference in this conversation.

"You know, Mum, I've heard people from different nations can intermarry these days." This is dangerous territory, as we're bound to get an hour-long history and genealogy lesson. I can hear Dad groan.

"Xavier, don't do that. You can't afford the length of that call. Let's get back to the topic at hand. If it makes sense financially and personally for you to become an American citizen, then do it. You have your mum's and my support. You always do."

I have to smile. I'm where I am today because of that support. Not everyone is as lucky as I am to have such a great family. "Right, then, I'll tell Tony to get cracking on it."

After checking in on Philip's status, which remains as surly as ever, I disconnect, finally feeling a bit more at peace with the decision.

Me: Tony, let's go for it.

Tony: On it already. Knee deep in research.

Me: I'm chuffed to go to Boston. Let's make it happen.

Tony: The first thing you need to do is stop using words like chuffed.

Never. My passport may be changing, but I'll always be British.

At least until I'm not.

CHAPTER 13: OPHELIA

I have a date. The powers-that-be on social media thought we'd be a good match. A ClikClak guy. I'm doing it.

Well, not *it*. At least not yet. I'm putting *that* on hold until I'm very sure that the guy is not a *tosser*.

Every time the word crosses my mind, I smile. I've folded it into my repertoire, like my use of Xs and Os, feeling romantic and whimsical every time I use it.

So this guy, Jeremy, is from Lynn, which isn't too far. I'm done with the long-distance thing, so even though there are a lot of choices, once I started narrowing it down geographically, the pickings became slimmer.

The story of my life.

Jeremy is taking the commuter rail in and meeting me in the North End. That's good because it's not that close to where I live in Chestnut Hill. Several people commented on his post that he seemed like a good match for me. I'm not sure I see it, but what the hell do I know? It'll be all public, and Marley is on standby if I get weird vibes. She's going to be just down the street and with one text, she and her boyfriend will be there to escort me away.

As I stare at my closet, I've no idea how to dress. I've been inside my apartment for way too long, going practically nowhere except the grocery store and over to Marley's place. It's made me very lazy when it comes to dressing. I'm up to date on skin care, hair styling, and makeup, thanks to ClikClak, but my wardrobe ... sigh.

None of my clothes are stylish anymore.

On the other hand, what in the 1980s is up with these trends of wide-legged pants and mom jeans? I'm a size six (on a good day), but since I'm only 5'2", that means I've got some curves. Those oversized pants are super unflattering on my frame. I call them teapot pants because when I wear them, they make me look short and stout.

Do I wear jeans? Do I wear pants? Do I wear a dress?

A dress means I have to shave my legs. Shaving my legs means I'm giving myself permission to get frisky, and I've vowed not to do that.

I settle on a pair of black skinny pants, paired with my chunky-heeled black boots, a white oxford shirt, and a green sweater vest. Preppy, somewhat stylish, but still relaxed.

I look cute, for me.

It's about as good as post-pandemic fashion gets.

On the T there, I text Marley.

Me: Should I ask about his vax status or to see his card?

These are things I never had to think about before.

Marley: You didn't ask already?

Me: <shrugging emoji> Didn't know how to work it in.

Marley: <facepalm emoji> I'm not sure you're responsible enough for this.

I know that I'm not. It's why I'm still hopelessly single at the age of thirty. I could barely navigate the dating scene before COVID. Now, it's another layer that has me relegated to my apartment and contemplating adopting five more cats to round out at an even half-dozen.

Me: I know. I'll ask before we go in and de-mask.

This whole mask-no mask, vaccine-no vaccine thing reminds me of trying to discuss contraception while you're both naked. There's no way to do it smoothly, yet it has to be done.

Marley: Still going to Carmalina's?

Me: Yes. Reservations for 7

Marley: So I'll expect your text around 7:30

She's not being mean; she's being a realist. I'm the eternal optimist in the friendship because I always charge into things expecting the best. Hell, it's why I'm letting social media set me up in the first place. Also, Trent is the only person I've dated in recent history that I knew in real life and not from social media or an app, and we all know how that turned out.

The first thing I notice about the guy standing in front of the restaurant is his height. He's well over six feet.

"Oh, wow. I didn't know you were so tall. I couldn't tell that online." Stellar opening line. Score one for Ophelia.

"I like short girls."

Yes, this is our first interaction. It's not exactly romance novel material. My brain automatically rewrites the scene, including a magnetic gaze and instant chemistry. I hope I remember it when I get home.

"Well, I'm short," I say lamely. I don't know how else to respond. My head is tilted almost all the way back, just to look at him. I have a feeling I'm going to have a sore neck by the time this night is done.

"No, I don't play basketball. The weather is the same up here. Yes, my parents are as tall, and 6'6"."

That's a lot of information all at once, none of which I asked for. Okay, I was curious about how tall he was, but the other things people must ask him are just uncalled for. It's like me getting asked if I need a booster seat or if I'm a jockey.

"I understand how you feel." This could be a bonding moment. Someday we'll look back and laugh and tell our grandchildren that this was our first conversation.

"I doubt that. Short people have it easy. You have no idea how I feel."

Scratch the grandkid idea.

"Okay then. Should we go in?" I don't know what else to say.

The hostess seats us, eating up a few minutes of time. He starts talking, but I'm having trouble processing what he's saying. I resist the urge to look at my watch or phone. There haven't been any major red flags—yet—that necessitate me texting Marley, so I try to pay attention to what Jeremy is talking about.

"So then, I tell her she's gotta stop following me around. I'm not taking her back for the fourth time."

Uh-oh. I don't know what I've missed, but now the first red flag has been waved. It's still too early to tell which one of them is not stable. I should probably be paying more attention.

"Well"—I clear my throat—"what looks good to you?"

"I'm not big on Italian food, and I am lactose intolerant."

I look at all the cheese-laden options on the menu. "Okay, why did you suggest an Italian restaurant then?" There are literally thousands of other restaurants we could have picked from.

"Chicks dig the aviance here."

Aviance? What the hell is he even talking about? I keep repeating the word to myself if only so I can remember to tell Marley. Also, the fact that he actually used a sentence that began with *chicks dig*.

When the waitress comes back, the first thing Jeremy does is tell her he does not want to add the three percent kitchen appreciation fee onto the bill.

According to the fine print at the bottom of the menu, the kitchen fee goes directly to the kitchen staff to help account for rising costs, instead of raising menu prices. "Um, why wouldn't you want the people working hard to get compensated?" Having worked in a restaurant previously, what I really mean is, "Why did you just invite them to spit in our food?"

"If you want to pay that on your portion, go ahead. They get paid. At least the ones who are here legally."

Oh hell no. He did not just say that. Flags are popping up like the front of the United Nations. "That's not a fair assumption to make."

"Yes, it is. I'll take the crazy alfredo."

Didn't he say he was lactose intolerant?

I order the rollatini and hand my menu over, wishing I'd faked appendicitis before placing the order.

"I can tell you've got expensive taste."

Huh? I frown. "How can you tell that?"

"I ordered first, and you still ordered something more expensive than me."

"I didn't know there was a rule."

"Yeah, when you order second, it's impolite to order something more expensive. But seriously, let's talk about the elephant in the room."

I'm confused about which elephant he's talking about. Is it the fact that he forgot to mention he's a giant? Or the fact that he doesn't respect hard-working people? Or the fact that I'm pretty sure he's racist? Or the fact that he claimed to be lactose intolerant and then ordered alfredo? Let's not forget aviance, whatever that means. There's going to be a whole lot to unpack with Marley over a bottle of wine and a pint of Ben and Jerry's.

"Your ClikClak. I mean, were you really that stupid, or was it all staged so that you'd get famous? Like are you trying to expand your business?"

My ClikClak? That's why he's here? Oh for the love of God. If I tell him it wasn't staged, then I'm letting him think I'm stupid. I'm not stupid. I just *do* stupid things. Occasionally.

Like go out with this guy.

"And," he continues without giving me a chance to speak, "how much is this night going to cost me? I was sort of surprised that you wanted me to take you out to dinner first."

"What?" I mean, I know standards are low, but how low can they get?

"Since you're an *accountant* and all. I'm surprised you wanted dinner."

I'm not sure what my job has to do with this. "Well, accountants need to eat too."

"None of the other ones I've been with have."

Okay, the red flags are waving as if doing a color guard routine. I can't ignore them for one single second longer. Time to go.

Luckily, the waitress walks by, and I get her attention. "Um, excuse me, can I get my meal to go?" I pull my wallet out and hand her $40. "Keep the change and give the kitchen staff their three percent, please. I'll wait at the bar for my food."

She gives me a tight smile. "You got it, honey."

"Wait, what are you doing?" Jeremy asks.

"I'm paying for my food, and I'll be leaving, thank you very much." I stand up. "Good luck to you, Jeremy."

He stands up too, towering over me and the table. "What are you doing? You can't walk out on me like this. I came all the way in from Lynn!"

The manager walks over. "Right this way, ma'am. You can wait safely with me."

I don't look back, even when Jeremy yells, "You were so desperate on ClikClak. That's why millions of people watched. To laugh at you. You're disgusting. You should be ashamed of yourself."

The manager tilts his head and then squints. "Are you ..."

"Yes, surprise visit girl. I know."

"We'll make sure he leaves and then get you an Uber home. Sit tight."

While I wait for my food as well as a safe exit, I do what I do best. Pulling out my phone, I hit record.

Well, date number one was a complete and total bust. At least I'll be going home with a good meal from Carmelina's in the North End, right on Hanover Street. The staff here has been great. The date, not so much. Now, I'm gonna go block him before he can harass me here too. But I still believe love is out there, waiting for me. Kisses and hugs!

And I do block Jeremy.

Marley, on the other hand, does not, and she sends me a copy of his video, ranting about me. He also goes off about the staff at Carmelina's and how they tried to poison him because he ended up in the bathroom almost immediately after eating his food. Apparently, he doesn't understand what alfredo sauce is made of. After all, he picked the restaurant solely for the *aviance*.

I'm pretty sure he meant ambiance. At least, that's what I think he meant. Nothing else makes sense, not that the date as a whole made sense.

I'm fairly confident I'll soon be able to add "dating men I meet through ClikClak" to the list of stupid things I've done for love.

CHAPTER 14: XAVIER

I don't know if you're going to be happy with this."

When your agent starts off that way, you can almost guarantee there will be no happy endings.

"Lay it on me, Tony." If it's bad news, I want to know straight up. I stop my run, leaning forward slightly to catch my breath.

"It's five years with a green card."

I close my eyes. There won't be a trade before March. It's alright. I can tough it out. I'll hate every moment of it, but it won't be the end of me. "Well, that's that, I guess."

"Not exactly."

"What do you mean not exactly?"

"I found a loophole. It'd allow you to be naturalized after you take care of one small detail."

Something in his tone gives me pause. "How small?"

I can practically see him shrugging his expensive-suited shoulders. "Tiny. No big thing really."

The more he attempts to play it off, the more I know it's a big, huge, massive thing. "Tony ..."

"All you have to do is get married. If your spouse is American, you're eligible to apply for naturalization. Tomorrow. Or whenever the next date is. But definitely sooner than March. We could have you in Boston before the new year."

There's no way he just said what I think he said.

"Pardon me? What was that?"

"We can probably have you in Boston before the new year. It's time to get out of your lease and look for a new one."

I want to take a drink of my water, but I'm afraid I'll choke on it. "No, that's not the part I need you to repeat."

"You just have to get married. Surely you know some woman—or man—who will marry you. Love is love."

It's rare that I want to punch someone when I'm not on the field. Other than my brother and Trent, I've not had that urge since I was a schoolboy. The urge is back now. "You want me to get married. I'm not even dating anyone."

"Call up your ex. I'm sure she'd be into it. Didn't you dump her? She'd probably leap at the chance to get back together."

There were numerous and valid reasons why I'd broken up with Alycia, to begin with, the most important being I couldn't stand her. She was a fake, only wanting to be with me because of what I could do for her. What my celebrity status could do for her. "That'd be a disaster. I'd rather stick it out with Baltimore."

"The word on the street is that they're going to bench you for the season, and then not renew your contract, but that they'll probably exercise the COVID option and keep you for two more years."

This is not what I want to hear. It's the worst possible thing Tony could say. "Why would Camacho want to do that?"

Tony replies, "Who knows what he's up to? But it ain't good. You know that's like the kiss of death for any athlete. Especially one like you, who's banned by half the world as it is."

I rub my forehead. Stupid Phaedra and her stupid car. Stupid me for trying to be the nice guy. I wouldn't be in this mess otherwise.

I saw her leave the party, and it was apparent that she was upset. I didn't know she was high as a kite. If I had, I wouldn't have gotten into the passenger's side, trying to talk to her. It was only after she'd crashed her Porsche that I realized what an absolute state she was in. She begged me to say I was driving since she was in danger of losing her license and being sent to rehab. So of course, I lied.

I never expected her father, the Commissioner of the British Football League, to accuse me of trying to kill his angelic daughter and blackball me for life.

"So what you're saying is I need to get married to an American and become a citizen, or my career is essentially in the loo."

"I'd say shitter, but otherwise yes. If you need me to find a woman—or man—for you, let me know. I can take an ad out."

"First of all, it'd be a woman, and second of all, are you off your rocker? You're not placing an ad to find me a wife. I'm not that desperate."

Except I am. I don't finish my run, instead walking back to my flat, trying to figure out how I landed in this mess to begin with. Or, more importantly, how to get out of it.

But the pit in my stomach tells me this might be the only way. I text Alastair.

Me: Tony found a way for me to be naturalized so I'm an American citizen.

Alastair: Alright.

Me: There's one catch … I have to get married.

Alastair: Bloody brilliant. Who's the lucky bird? (see what I did there?)

Me: That's the problem. There's no one.

Alastair: What about Alycia?

Me: I'd rather remove my own testicle with a butter knife.

Alastair: That seems extreme.

Me: So is Alycia.

The collective opinion is getting married for citizenship is not a bad thought. I'm not sure about the legality of becoming a citizen, based on fraud, but that's far down on the list of priorities right now.

I literally don't know where I'm supposed to find someone who will up and marry me immediately. And how do I even bring this up? Hullo, my name is Xavier Henry. I'm a footballer. Will you marry me?

In my head, that plays with an Inigo Montoya Spanish accent, though I'm neither Spanish nor in *The Princess Bride*.

Though it is inconceivable how quickly my life has gone to pot.

Will this even work? Tony thinks it will, but if I'm going to make such a drastic move, I need something more. I call Bjorn Janssen. I'm sure he won't be able to take my call, but before I proceed with this cockamamie plan, I need a bit more of a guarantee.

"I've been expecting your call." As usual, Coach Janssen doesn't mess around with things like pleasantries.

"Coach, what is the likelihood that Boston will sign me?"

"In the off-season, one hundred percent. If we have to wait until the international trading block, much less. We'll already be into the season then, and we can't hold a spot, *assuming* that we'll be able to get you. We're already at our international cap."

I nod. "Right. Okay."

"Your agent told you what you need to do, right?"

I swallow the massive golf ball that seems to have lodged itself in my throat. "Yes." It comes out in a croak.

"Xavier, it's not the end of the world. Miller is excited to have you. We just need to know you're committed."

"I am."

"Then do what you need to do. If you weren't you, you'd have more options in England and Europe. This is it for you, and you have too much talent for it to be wasted. Camacho is an idiot with the direction he's forcing Masters to take the team."

I don't love the decisions Coach Masters has made for the Terrors, but I was never sure if those were his calls or if he was being directed. I guess there's my answer.

"This is coming from Camacho?"

"Word on the turf is that Camacho is trying to get in tight with Jones."

Bjorn's words hit like a punch to the gut. The owner of the Terrors is sucking up to the head of the BFL. "That explains it then."

"It'd be a penalty, and you'd have grounds for a lawsuit if they terminated your contract early, so you know they won't do that."

"So I'm benched then."

"Masters said he still put you in because it's not like he *wanted* to lose. You're one of his best players. I think it crushed him to bench you."

"Would you bench me?" I have to ask. I'm not going through with this just to end up sitting for another season.

"I've talked about it with Robert Miller. He's never been a big fan of Edmund Jones, and he doesn't intend to start now. Plus, we all know the situation with Jones and his daughter is—"

I cut him off with the need to defend myself. "Rubbish. Complete and total rubbish. I would never—"

Now he cuts me off. "We know. Both Miller and I know, which is why we want you in Boston."

"It's going to take drastic measures on my part."

"Isn't the life of a professional athlete all drastic measures? Do what you need to do."

We disconnect without much fanfare. I feel as if I've been punched in the gut. My time in Baltimore, for all intents and purposes, is over.

And the same can be said for my entire career if I don't find a wife immediately.

Chapter 15: Ophelia

I had high hopes for my second ClikClak date.

I am an optimist, after all. I figured that the first colossal failure was a fluke, and the odds had to be in my favor for something better.

We went to Carmelina's again, because it has good food, and I was impressed at how the staff took care of me. I was hopeful that I wouldn't need that kind of support tonight.

Of course, that only lasts until the moment I feel my napkin slip off my lap, about six minutes after I sit down. As I bend down to retrieve it, something catches my eye. And that something would be my date's unzipped pants and his penis sitting out on display.

I stand so fast that I'm instantly lightheaded. A hand reaches out to steady my elbow. I look. It's the same manager from the last time I was here.

"Is everything okay, miss?"

I lean in and whisper, "The snake is out."

"Excuse me?"

"There's a disco stick sighting."

"What?" The manager narrows his eyes, now clearly thinking I'm totally nuts.

In a loud clear voice, I nod toward my date and say, "He's sitting there with his penis out, in the middle of our first date."

Every single pair of eyes in the restaurant swivels toward us. But perhaps I have lost it because I point wildly. "This is our first date and Mr. Happy is apparently joining us for a bite to eat."

My date slowly slides his napkin off the table and covers his member, who must have developed a sudden chill in the November night.

"I ... I gotta go." I grab my purse and reach for my wallet to pay for the glass of wine I ordered.

The manager holds his hand up. "Don't worry, this one's on us. Oh, and wherever you're meeting these guys, you need to find a new place."

I smile tightly and walk out, holding my head as high as I possibly can in such a situation.

Did I think my first ClikClak date went well? No. Did I think it was possible for my second one to be a failure of such epic proportions so quickly? Also no.

Once I take a long and humiliating T ride on the C line home, I open ClikClak.

So the second date was worse than the first, if you can believe it.

Involuntarily, tears begin to fill my eyes.

I don't know what's wrong with me. Why are men like this? All I know is I give up, and I won't be going on any more dates. Please stop splicing and tagging me. I'm done.

Sundance comes over and headbutts me, a universal sign for "I agree, all men, besides me, suck, and you deserve so much better." Or, he just wants his ears scratched.

My phone dings. I don't have the strength to analyze my latest laughingstock with Marley. It's easy for her. She's got a great boyfriend who worships the ground she walks on. I need a Jamal for myself.

Except it's not Marley. It's Xavier Henry, sending me another DM through Instagram.

Xavier: Saw the latest ClikClak. Sorry.

Me: You and me both.

Xavier: How was it worse? The first date seemed pretty bad, but now you seem traumatized. How dodgy was he?

I sigh.

Me: Can we FaceTime? I don't want to have to commit this story to words just yet.

Xavier: Give me your number.

I type in my phone number and close Instagram. And then I wait.

A minute goes by. Then two. Then five.

I open Instagram and my digits are still the last message. He's seen it. Shit, I'm even getting blown off virtually.

Screw it. I go to the bathroom. I'm just flushing when I hear my phone ringing. I quickly run my hands under water, not for the recommended two minutes, and sprint out to find my phone. Because my hands are sopping wet, and probably still have soap on them, the phone goes flying out of my grip. I make a lunging dive for it and manage to finally answer the FaceTime.

"You alright?" Xavier asks, his brow slightly furrowed. Gosh, I'd forgotten how attractive he is, and that he speaks with a British accent. It's hot.

I'd also forgotten, in my haste to answer the phone, to think about my angle, and now this fine specimen of a man is getting a great view of my double chin, as well as my hair that seems to be rapidly escaping the messy bun I'd piled it into when I got home from my disastrous date.

Oh good God.

I sit up and tuck my chin in as fast as I can while simultaneously trying to smooth my hair. Needless to say, I'm not that coordinated. As a result, I'm not able to improve my appearance much.

"I will be someday. Maybe, in like fifty years, I'll be able to laugh about the time I went on a date and bent over to retrieve my napkin only to find out that the guy I've known for all of ten minutes is sitting in a restaurant with his dick out."

I can't believe I just said dick.

Also, I should have warned Xavier because he was taking a drink of something. I know this because it's now all over his phone screen.

"Bollocks. Hang on." The image jostles as he puts his phone down and begins wiping it off. I take the opportunity to rip my hair out of the bun and finger comb it.

It's a slight improvement.

"You're joking, right?" Xavier is back, still wiping things up on his end. "Please tell me that was a well-timed joke with the intention of making me spit out my bevvy."

I can see that his eyes are a steel-gray blue and his jaw is the type of square that romance novelists comment on. He's got a bit of facial hair—more than stubble, but not quite a beard. Whatever it's called, it works for him.

"I wish I was." I sigh. "And they say chivalry is dead."

"Was he crackers?"

I tilt my head. "What do you mean?"

"Has he lost his mind?"

I shrug. "It would appear so. And since I'm oh for two on being set up with guys from ClikClak, I think I'm going to quit while I'm ahead. I'm done. I might even take my profile down."

"Ah, but you can't let two dimwits ruin it for you. People like your content. You're funny and real, and I think that's what appeals to people on ClikClak. You know, as opposed to Instagram where you know everything is posed and filtered and fake."

I think about this. "True. Then how come you're only on Instagram? Are you fake?"

Xavier smiles, showing bright white teeth that are perfectly straight. "No, Instagram is just easier. I don't have anything really going on in my life to make videos of it."

"Wait—" I hold my hand up. "You're, like, a professional athlete. That makes you an automatic celebrity."

"A celebrity's the last thing I want to be. I'm here to play a game and that's all."

"Surely that can't be *all*. You don't play soccer twenty-four seven. What do you do for fun?"

He looks pensive for a moment. "Well, training does take quite a bit of my time, and I value my sleep."

"Understandable. I value my sleep too."

"In my off-season, which is now, I usually visit my family back home. I was thinking about it, but I get nervous that with quarantines and travel restrictions and the like, I might get stuck over in England and not be able to get back. Plus, I've got some business dealings in the works, so I need to be here to attend to those."

Sundance takes this chance to walk across my body, essentially showing his back end to Xavier. Lovely. "Don't mind that big oaf. It's Sundance. Sunny for short. He thinks he runs this place." I lean forward and whisper into my phone. "Don't tell him this, but he kind of does. Of course, I'll deny ever saying that."

"Ah, yes, I know how it can be. My brother Philip and I adopted a pet when I was about five, and now he, along with my parents, run a rescue organization. So Solomon really did take over our house."

"That's so cool!"

"Yes, but with COVID, they've had to shut down their tours and field trips. It's really cut into their income and all."

"Oh." I don't know what else to say. "That's too bad. I'm sorry."

"Ah well, it's the way things are, I guess. But I'm glad I can help them out. I mean, I can as long as I keep playing."

"Are you in danger of not playing anymore?"

Xavier sighs and he doesn't have to even say it. Something's up. Something's wrong. "What is it?" I ask. "What's going on with your career? Are you hurt?"

He shakes his head and looks off into the distance. I wish I knew what he was looking at. "It's nothing."

"It's not nothing. Look, you've been a nice guy, reaching out to me when you didn't have to. I know you don't know me from Adam, but other than my best friend Marley, you're probably the person I talk to the most. Which is totally sad, I know, but that's me. So tell me what ails you."

His gaze swivels back to the camera. "Alright, but I'm warning you now, it's messed up."

"It can't be any more messed up than Trent the Tosser or PenisGate, so lay it on me. I got you, boo."

CHAPTER 16: XAVIER

I probably shouldn't say anything to her, but getting a female take on the situation wouldn't be a bad idea. Plus, she just called me boo, which is a little adorable.

I'm used to women trying to be over-the-top sexy to get my attention. Who knew cute as a button was intriguing?

"Right, so it's long and convoluted."

Ophelia smiles. "I've got time. In case you forgot, I was supposed to be on a date. I've got no other plans, other than drowning my sorrows in this glass of wine and reading a book." She holds up her glass of wine and then takes a sip.

"Well, to start with, I have to get married."

It's Ophelia's turn to spit out her drink. A horrified look crosses her face as she hastily cleans off her phone.

"Good, now we're even."

"That was not at all what I was expecting. And this comes from a woman who discovered an exposed member at her dinner table tonight. I didn't even spit my wine out then. But go on." She waves her hand, urging me to continue.

"I guess that's not the proper start, anyway. The proper start is that I'm being benched on the Baltimore Terrors. They're looking to terminate my contract. And if I don't play, and then get cut eventually, it doesn't bode well for another team picking me up."

She nods. "Following that, but not the married thing."

"Hold on a minute. I'm getting to that. Because I'm an international player, I'm not eligible for trade until after the season starts in March. My former coach is up in Boston, and the Buzzards organization wants me. They'll trade for me. But they need me before the season starts."

"Why can't you be traded before then?"

"The USSL wants to cultivate American talent to make them more competitive on the world stage. Therefore, they're limiting the number of foreign players on any one team and limiting the trade possibilities to make American players more desirable."

"Okay, I guess. I mean, it seems discriminatory but whatever."

"The Global Games are the biggest football tourney in the world. The US Men's National Team hasn't even qualified for the past two sets. It's embarrassing for the US, really. So they've spent the last three years really building up their internal programs."

"So it's like the Olympics for soccer?"

"Exactly. In order to be traded to Boston now, the only way for me to do it is to become an American citizen."

"Okay. I mean, I'm sure it's a pain and there's a lot of paperwork, but it seems like a simple solution."

I frown.

"What'd I say that's wrong?" she asks. "I can tell from your face I said something wrong."

"I don't want to become American. I mean, no offense."

"None taken?" Her voice rises to a question. "Why not though?"

I shrug. "I'm a Brit. It breaks my heart that I can't play on my own soil, but that's a story for another day. And to have to renounce my homeland and my family, well, it's got me gutted."

"Well, why don't you go and play for England then? No one is forcing you to stay here."

Her words, though innocuous in intention, cut through me like a sharp knife. "That's not an option. So, I become an American, or my career is over."

She watches me thoughtfully for a moment. Finally, she takes a long sip from her wine glass. "But if your career is done, then you can't help your family out."

"Right." I can't believe she goes right to this. Most people would talk about losing the fame and fortune and glory. That's not what it's about for me. I love the game, and I love my family. I take my own drink. If she's going to get pissed, I might as well too. "Plus, I can't imagine my life without football. It's all I've ever wanted to do from the time I was a schoolboy."

"Okay, I think I'm following, except for the marriage thing."

"I've only been here and had my green card for four years. In order to apply for naturalization, you have to have been here five. Unless ..." I take another long sip. And then one more for good measure. "My spouse is a citizen, and then you only have to be here for three years."

The pieces click together for her. "So if you get married to an American, you can become a citizen sooner."

I nod. I'm glad we're on FaceTime, so I can see her reaction. I haven't talked about this with anyone in person, so it's nice to get someone else's take. "The only thing is, I don't have a fiancée. I don't even have a girlfriend. I'm not sure I even have a friend who's a girl. No matter how you slice it, getting married seems as impossible as walking on the moon."

Ophelia lifts her glass in a toasting motion. "You and me both, brother. Now you understand my position."

I salute her with my glass and finish it off. Yes, tonight is definitely a night for getting pissed. At least with Facetiming Ophelia, I don't have to say I'm drinking alone.

I stand up and get another beer. I see Ophelia refill her wine glass. Yes, this is good. We'll get sloshed together.

"It should be easy for you to find someone. You're totally hot." Ophelia says and then lets out a little giggle. Perhaps it's not going to take her as long to get tipsy as I thought.

I smile. "I don't know about that."

"Oh, come on. Get over yourself. You're smoking. And I bet you have like ten percent body fat or something ridiculous like that."

"Actually, it's seven and a half in season, but I might get as high as nine percent now." I'm not saying it to be boastful. It's a lot of hard work that keeps me that way.

Ophelia groans. "I probably only have nine percent muscle, so I understand why guys don't like me."

I frown at her response. Why does she say such things? She looks well proportioned to me, with the exception of her chest, which looks big for her petite frame. I'm not being a perv, but I am a man with eyes. Long brown hair and bangs that frame her dark blue eyes. Sweet nose and a wide smile. She does smile a lot. It's a good thing. "I'm sure that's not the issue. You're lovely."

She rolls her eyes. "Oh come on. But we're not talking about me. We're talking about you. You're a smoke show. You are super hot. You're a professional freakin' athlete, so you're probably raking in the cash."

I hold up my hand. "Actually, that's a misconception. Only the top players make that kind of money and most of an athlete's income comes from endorsements."

"Are you a top player?" She raises her eyebrows.

"I'm toward the top, but I haven't had an endorsement since before ... in years. My agent is supposed to be working on that, but then this bloody mess came up, and getting me on a team where I actually play is the priority."

Lucky for me, Ophelia doesn't notice my gaff, so she doesn't question me on it.

"Plus, I'm a professional athlete. That means, essentially, I'm owned by my team and my league. Work comes first. Above everything, even family. I've missed out on so much. But at the end of the day, if you ask me to pick football or a girl, the answer will always be football. That's not an easy pill for most women to swallow. They want the perks of being with an athlete, but really what they want is the lifestyle and the bragging rights without the sacrifice."

And there it is in a nutshell. Why I'm single. I'm sick of gold diggers and users. Alycia springs to mind. And I'm sick of having fight after fight about why football is more important than *she* is. It's exhausting. And why, other than this blasted stunt, I have every intention of staying single.

"So what I need, really," I continue, "is someone who agrees to be my wife but without actually needing a husband."

"IT'S MY FAVORITE TROPE!" Ophelia jumps up, screaming. I'm fairly certain she knocks over her bottle of wine in the process.

"What? And did you just spill your wine?"

She looks down. "Nah, it's empty." She sits down on the edge of her striped couch. It's rather hideous, shades of blue and orange that were never meant to go together. "No, this is like my favorite trope. In romance novels. A marriage of convenience. It's where the main protagonists have to get married, even though they're not in a relationship. It's so romantic." There's a wistful edge to her voice and a dreamy look on her face.

"How is that romantic?" I don't understand how any of this is romantic.

"Because obviously, even though they enter the marriage for business reasons or whatever, they fall in love. Duh."

"In every book?"

"Yeah." She nods. "You don't read much romance, do you?"

"Can't say I do."

"What do you do when you're traveling?"

"Listen to podcasts. Usually true crime."

"Okay, well, I'm going to get you listening to romance novels. You'll be hooked."

I have to laugh. I can only imagine being on a plane and whipping out some beat-up grocery store novel with a bare-chested pirate on the cover.

"I'm not so sure about that, but thanks just the same. Plus, if I don't figure out a way to get myself traded to Boston, there won't be any more trips for me anyhow."

"Boston?"

"Yes, all of this is so I can be traded to the Boston Buzzards."

Ophelia jumps up again. "I live in Boston."

I laugh at her enthusiasm. "I know. I asked you to meet up with me last week when I was there, remember?"

"No, let me finish." She's literally bouncing up and down. "I live in Boston. You're trying to get traded here, but you need a wife to do so. Make me your wife! Marry me!"

CHAPTER 17: OPHELIA

I'm never drinking again.

Ever.

The mere sight of the three (three!) empty bottles of wine on my floor makes me want to throw up. Again. And the rolling in my stomach is nothing compared to the pounding in my head.

Oh. My. God.

Good thing it's Sunday, and I don't have to do anything today. What time is it even?

I look for my phone. Actually, I feel around for my phone because opening my eyes hurts too much. But it's not where I expect it to be. I broaden my search, keeping my eyes tightly closed. However, when no amount of feeling around on my bed produces my phone, I'm forced to open them.

It's not on my bed. It's not on my nightstand. Shit. It's not even under my bed. It is, however, inside a wine glass on my coffee table.

At least the wine glass was empty, courtesy of my luscious—and lush-ous—self. I resist the urge to retch right here and now. Aaaand my phone is totally dead. Great.

I can't believe I didn't charge it. Wait—why didn't I charge it? I'm sort of a nut about that. A battery percentage below seventy-five percent is enough to give me heart palpitations.

I squint, not only because the overcast November sky outside my window is too bright, but also in an effort to remember last night.

I remember a penis, that's for sure. And then crying. And then …

Oh shit.

Did I *FaceTime* with Xavier Henry?

Yup. That's it. Time to empty the contents of my stomach.

Drunk texts are one thing. Drunk Facetiming? There should be a breathalyzer on the phone that prevents you from opening apps if your blood alcohol content is above a certain level.

Definitely, if you put away three bottles of wine on an empty stomach.

I hope I didn't say anything embarrassing. I mean, this is me we're talking about, so the chances of that are zero, but I can hope.

Right now, I'm happy not to have a memory of this mortification—because I'm sure I did something mortifying—at least for the time being. After a three-hour nap and a pile of greasy eggs, I start to feel a little more human.

Not enough to dry my hair after I shower, but at least I was able to summon up the energy to shower. Fine, I sat in the tub the whole time, but it still counts. I no longer smell, so that's one win for the day.

I should probably go to bed for the night while I'm still ahead. I'll ignore the fact that it's only three p.m. I check my phone, now almost fully charged.

I have text messages.

A lot of them.

I don't recognize the number. It's not a Boston area code. Probably spam looking to talk to me about my car's extended warranty or to tell me how I can lose eight inches in two weeks.

It'd better not be penis man from last night. Although I'm pretty sure I blocked him immediately after leaving the restaurant.

But as soon as I open the first message, the roiling in my stomach is back. My knees start to buckle, and I sink quickly down onto my bed. Sundance joins me, talking to me fervently about how I've neglected him all day. Absently, I pet him on the head, not wanting to believe my eyes.

I quickly open my messages on Instagram and confirm what I'm afraid is true. Yup, this number, with its 410 area code, is Xavier Henry.

That would be the same super-hot, professional soccer player, Xavier Henry, that I drunken FaceTimed with. I only have to read one message to know that whatever I thought happened last night, it was about a billion times worse.

Xavier: You okay? You seemed pretty far gone.

Xavier: Don't freak out. It's not a bad idea. Let me think it over.

Xavier: Ophelia, are you there?

Xavier: You know, and maybe I'm a bit trousered myself, but the more I think about it, the more I think it's a brilliant idea.

Xavier: I'll call my agent and lawyer in the morning. I think we should discuss the details in person. Sleep tight.

Xavier: I'm on the train up. I'll be into South Station around 5. How far are you from there?

Xavier: I can't tell you how much I appreciate this. As soon as your lawyer looks over the contract, we can go ahead and get married.

It's the last word that has me running to the toilet again.

Married.

What the hell happened last night?

And he's coming up here? I look at the clock. He's going to be here—*here!*—in about two hours. My place is a disaster. I'm a disaster. Apparently, my life is a disaster.

Married.

Every time I even think about that word, bile rises in the back of my throat. *What the hell happened last night?* I guess the good thing about him coming here is we can figure this out.

Wait—where does he think he's going to stay? I don't know this man from Adam, and *did I invite him to sleep here*?

Oh my God. I am never drinking again.

What am I going to do? I call Marley. She'll know. Dammit. No answer.

Me: Marley, call me. This is an emergency. I think I did something stupid.

Marley: Again?

Me: CALL ME ASAP

And then I wait. How dare my best friend choose to have a life when I'm in crisis because I'm a FREAKIN' idiot?

Think, Ophelia, think. What happened last night? I attempt to rifle through the alcohol-drenched corners of my brain, but I'm still coming up short. Surely—*surely*—I should be able to recall something as momentous as being proposed to. Just the fact that I've been waiting my whole life should make my synapses fire a little more.

But no. Like Taylor Swift says, "I've got a blank space, baby."

Shit.

And while this may seem like the perfect time to panic, I don't have time for that. I run around, scooping up strewn clothing and dishes. Books get piled up and the papers on my desk are quickly neatened and put into the folders where they belong anyway. I wash my dishes and wipe down the counters. A quick pass of the vacuum, much to Sunny's dismay, and then I tackle my bedroom.

Not that I'm letting him in there, but in case he peeks. My dresser, piled high with makeup and lotions and jewelry, is a lost cause. It's fine. I don't want him thinking I'm a neat freak. Next, onto the bathroom where I clean out the litter box and sweep the bathroom floor. But as I clean, the memories are slowly filtering in. Flashes of conversation. He went on about trades and international laws and needing to get married. Like in a book. Oh God, tell me I didn't.

At least I put down the toilet bowl brush before I bury my face in my hands.

I did. Obviously, I did because he mentioned it. I somehow, in my inebriated state, thought my life should be like a romance novel, and I proposed marriage. Between him and me.

And now he's coming up.

I can't breathe.

But it's not like he accepted. Or is even taking me seriously. There's no way he could. I mean, it was pretty obvious that I was hammered. He can't hold me at my word. I wasn't fit to give it in the first place.

I focus on sucking air in and letting it out slowly. Surely, he was coming up anyway. Surely he knows how drunk I was.

Surely we're not engaged.

No, of course, we're not.

He's reasonable. I'm sometimes reasonable. Marrying a stranger is not reasonable. So once he gets here, we'll talk it out, and then I'll make sure he knows this was all the product of too many assholes, too much wine, and too many romance novels. I'm willing to give up two of the three.

Okay, I'm really only willing to give up the assholes, but there's never a need for me to drink that much again. At least not any time soon.

I can breathe again. Yes, he's not expecting me to marry him. No way would he. Time to finish in here. Three disinfectant wipes later, the bathroom is in decent shape.

Now onto me.

My hair is half-damp, but the idea of blow drying it and straightening it just seems like too much. I opt for two French braids and pull on my thickest high-waisted leggings, hoping to make my lower end seem fit and toned even though running through various romantic scenarios in my brain is as active as I get. I don a crop top sweatshirt, which barely shows any skin on me because of my height, and I'm good to go.

Well, after I add hoop earrings and some makeup because I'm three shades paler than printer paper. A hangover does nothing for my complexion.

As I finish my makeup I stop and look at myself. What am I doing? Am I just going to let this random guy in my apartment? I don't know him at all.

Me: MARLEY....

But also me ... should I go meet him at South Station? It's kind of a hike down there. I've got to take the C line all the way into Park Street and then change to the red line. We're talking a good forty-five minutes, at least, so if I'm going to go, I should go.

I mean, he is on a seven-hour ride up here to see me. I wish I could remember all of the night. Like what happened after I asked him to marry me. Oh God, what if I flashed him my hoo-ha, and he's coming all this way for sex?

What if he thinks because I showed him my lady cat that I expect him to make a purchase at the pet store?

What is wrong with me?

Please don't let me have gotten naked on FaceTime.

These are things I never thought I'd pray for as a child, but I'm sure there's a patron saint for keeping your clothes on while on a video chat. Whatever that saint is, I bet they've been working overtime since COVID started.

I should go meet Xavier. That way if I get a sketchy vibe or whatever, I can take him to a hotel rather than have him here. It's definitely safer to meet up with him in a public place. I throw on my oversized coat and head for the T-stop.

I text Xavier to let him know I'll meet him in front of the Dunkin' Donuts. Then I send one last text to Marley.

Me: So apparently, I'm engaged. I don't remember all of it, but I'm on my way to meet him now. Hope you don't see me on an episode of Discovery ID. If Dateline interviews you, please talk about how much everyone loved me, and don't let them use a bad picture. I don't want to be known as a loser who talked more to her cat than to other people.

Serves her right.

CHAPTER 18: XAVIER

She's coming to meet me. That's bloody great. Despite having played in cities all over Britain and the US, I'm still not super comfortable with public transit. I'd much prefer to be in a car driving.

Fewer people, more freedom.

Plus, I'm not a big fan of being underground. I think it's because I got lost on the Tube that one time. My parents freaked out and Philip was visibly annoyed that I'd ruined the day, but it's not like I got separated from them on purpose.

Although, after seven hours on this train, I'm not sure I smell very good. As soon as I step off, I head toward the nearest loo to brush my teeth and add another coat of deodorant.

Not because I have expectations of anything. Other than her proposing, it was quite the platonic conversation. It was rather enjoyable, really. Actually, it was the best time I've had in a while. With the exception of family and friends from before my career began, not that there are many of those, people usually put on a show for me. With Ophelia, there was no show. Simply a lot of telling, not to mention laughter. Then it became apparent she was quite sloshed. I was half in the bag myself, so I'm in no place to judge.

Enjoyable times and laughter aside, it's not the purpose of my trip. With amazing speed that makes me question what exactly goes on with Tony's agency, he emailed me a rough draft of a contract. I really don't care to know how Tony drafted an entire business contract for a marriage deal in a matter of hours. Thinking about that makes my stomach churn.

Perhaps I should take some comfort in knowing that as professional athletes, we're expected to make all sorts of sacrifices for our careers. I never expected to have to marry a total stranger just to be able to set foot upon the pitch again.

At least I've talked to her a bit. It's not quite as bad as posting an ad on Craigslist or having ClikClak set me up.

Maybe I'll have Tony put in a line about how I'm not allowed to whip it out in public if only so she's reassured that she won't have a repeat of last night.

Heavens, was it only last night?

I scroll through the document Tony's sent. I guess it's pretty standard if there is such a thing. Our finances remain separate, though she will be financially compensated. The marriage has to last at least three years. We have one residence with separate bedrooms. She can still maintain her own flat if she wants, but her legal address has to be the one we share. She'll have to attend home games. She can't tell anyone, at least without having them sign a nondisclosure first.

What's not in here is that she's going to have to lie to the government and possibly everyone in her life.

No big deal really.

It was her idea.

Honestly, I wasn't even thinking about it. I was simply mooning about with this unsolvable, impossible problem when she shouted it out. It seems like as good a solution as any.

We get on fairly well if our brief text conversations and three-hour long FaceTime are any indications. There's obviously the distinct possibility that she's insufferable, which is why I hopped on a train up here.

Between seeing her in person and the surprise element, it will be hard for her to hide too many bodies in the closet, so to speak.

Though I didn't expect her to meet me at the station. It's polite of her, so that's a check in the right column. I used to be that bloke, doing the polite thing.

Doing the *right* thing.

Fat lot of good it did me.

It bloody well ruined my life.

All because I'm a nice guy.

I should probably warn Ophelia that being nice won't get her anywhere. That's not to say that I'm mean or ornery now. It's more … I keep to myself. It's easier that way. The fewer entanglements, the better.

Of course, I say this as I'm on my way to iron out the details for the biggest entanglement of my life. I reckon this won't be a big deal. I'm moving anyway, so I'll simply find a place a little bigger than I normally would. My schedule is grueling and packed anyway.

This isn't going to be that much of a change.

It'll be nice to have a friendly face to talk to outside of practice. My mates have almost always been on the team, which suits me fine since that's where I spent most of my time. However, for those rare moments when I'm not doing something team related, it can get a bit 'onely.

On the other hand, I don't want to be with someone who has a packed social calendar and expects me to be her arm candy, bankroll escort for it all.

Oh, I know it sounds like I'm complaining, which I'm not. There are plenty out there who'd sell a testicle for a chance to be a professional footballer. But there is a cost.

And with this latest venture, it seems like the cost just went up.

But all that slips my mind the moment I see her standing in front of the Dunkin' Donuts shop, just as she said she would be. She's staring down at her phone, plaits falling over her shoulders. She looks up and glances around.

She looks tired.

But then, that look fades as she sees me. She pulls her mask down. A small, tentative smile spreads, and she gives an equally small, tentative wave before replacing her mask.

I wave back. "Hullo," I say, approaching her. This time it's me with the rolling bag. I'm glad I have it in my hand. Otherwise, I wouldn't know what to do. Do I shake her hand? Hug her?

One seems entirely too formal and the other is entirely too familiar. I'm not quite sure there's a defined etiquette for how to greet your fiancée who's a virtual stranger.

"Did you have a good trip? Are you hungry? We could get something to eat down here. Do you like seafood? I do, but I'm still kind of pukey so I don't know that we want to do that. How long are you staying? Where are you staying? Why did you say we're getting married? Oh, by the way, I tend to ramble when I'm nervous. I'm very nervous."

I have to laugh.

"Are you? I couldn't tell." I tilt my head. "Pukey?"

"I may have grossly overestimated the amount of wine I can drink without getting pukey."

"Oh, that's terrible. I thought you might be a bit sloshed. Or at least I did when you rolled off the couch."

She rubs her hip. "Is that why this hurts?"

My gaze travels to the easy curve of her pelvis. I have to make an effort to drag my attention to her face if only so she doesn't think I'm a perv. "Can't say for certain, but could be. It was a slow-speed fall if that makes any difference."

Her face turns seven shade" of scarlet. "Um, I'm gonna go hide in the bathroom until after you leave, if that's okay."

I put my hand on her arm but then pull it away. "If it's any consolation, I was a bit pissed myself. But I had an enjoyable evening. I haven't laughed that much in a long time."

Ophelia furrows her brow. "I'm getting sick of being the laughingstock all the time."

This time, I put my hand on her arm and leave it there. "I believe you misunderstood. I was definitely laughing with you, not at you. I'd never do that."

She shakes me off. "Why not? Everyone does." Ophelia looks at me for a long moment, her dark blue eyes stormy. If I'm not mistaken, they're filling with tears.

"I'm sorry that I appeared to be making fun of you. I'm not. Believe me, I'm not. I understand what it's like to be the butt of the joke." The paparazzi were relentless after the incident. I don't think I got on the internet for at least a month.

My mum had to drag me out of my room and force me to answer Tony's phone calls. I think he believed the hype and thought I was really a bad boy and that managing me would be lucrative for his career.

He's been quite disappointed at my hermit lifestyle.

No one ever believed that the story wasn't true. My mum and dad said they did, but I know Philip thought it was all my fault.

"And if it's any consolation, I had a bloody good evening. Probably one of my best in a very long time."

She sniffs. "You don't look like a loser. You're too hot to be one."

I bite the inside of my cheek to avoid laughing. I don't think that would be well-received. It's one benefit of the mask, though. It gives me a moment to reset my face. "You'd be surprised. I wouldn't mind getting a bite to eat," I say, to change the topic and hopefully bring a smile back to her face. Seafood would have been great, but I'll have plenty of time for that once I'm in Boston. "What won't make you feel pukey?"

Ophelia gazes up and off into the distance. "There's the South Street Diner. It's not too far from here, maybe a five or ten-minute walk. Is that okay?" I see her looking at my bag.

"Certainly. I believe I can handle that amount of physical exertion."

Her face reddens again. "I'm sorry. I mean, I guess I know that you're like a professional athlete and all—"

"Not 'like' a professional athlete. I actually am one."

"No, I mean, I know that. I ... it's just ... I'm used to being around normal people."

"I think you'll find I'm quite normal about most things. I even put my pants on one leg at a time." Her eyes crinkle, indicating I've earned a smile. We head out into the brisk November air, the evening already dark. Once outside, we both pull the masks off. Many of the buildings look dark as well. "It seems like most things are closed around here. Is that because of the pandemic?"

Ophelia, struggling to keep pace with me, says in a breathy voice, "Some, but it's Sunday. This is more of a business district, so there's a lot not open. But the diner is open 24-7. It's been in a lot of movies and is popular with the after-bar crowd."

I slow my pace a little for her. "That's interesting. I have to say, I don't get out exploring in Baltimore much. I don't have that much downtime and when I do, I like to volunteer at a rescue facility, similar to my mum and dad's. It's outside of the city though."

"So what you're saying is you're more of a country mouse than a city mouse."

Her phrasing confuses me, but I think I get the point. "I've never heard that before, but yes, I'd prefer to be in the wide-open spaces with nature. Sometimes I feel too closed in with all these buildings around. I need room to spread my wings."

It looks as if she shudders a"bit. I wonder if she's cold. "How much farther?"

She points and I can see the large coffee cup on the roof of the building, neon lining the windows. It does look like every diner I've ever seen in a film. I pull out my phone to snap a picture. Then I turn it around to take a selfie. "Come on," I tilt my head.

"Really?" Ophelia asks.

"Yes, really. Come over here."

"I look terrible." She immediately begins swiping at her bangs.

"Nah, you look great. Come here."

She does, albeit reluctantly. I stretch out my arm and get a good picture of the two of us. I'll post it once we're inside.

We're quiet as we step into the bright, harsh lights of the restaurant. Her complexion looks a little drawn in this light, dark circles showing under her eyes. I hope she's okay with all of this.

"What looks good to you?"

"My normal diner go-to is an open-faced hot roast beef. But today, a BLT sounds like it would hit the spot. Or maybe a grilled cheese? What are you getting?"

I'm a bit more lax with my diet this week, but I still don't want to go overboard. "I think the lobster egg white omelet if the smell won't be too much for you."

"Oh, that's considerate. Don't worry about me." She shifts in her seat but doesn't say anything else.

As soon as our orders are placed, I pull up the photo of the two of us. "Do you mind if I post this?"

She shakes her head but still doesn't say anything. Perhaps she's really not feeling well. I make quick work of posting the picture with the caption, "Iconic city, iconic restaurant, incredible company. The perfect trifecta." I tag Ophelia in the post.

I look up from my phone and she's staring out the window. This does not seem at all like the vivacious, funny woman with whom I chatted last night. I wonder if something happened today to upset her.

"Ophelia," I start. Her head moves slowly, finally turning to look at me. "Is there something bothering you?"

She shakes her head, biting her lip a bit.

"Right then. It's just, well, you seem a bit off."

She stares, her eyes wide. It reminds me of the way an owl looks through you.

I'm starting to get a sick feeling in the pit of my stomach. What if she's not mentally stable? I'd better have Tony put in a clause to protect me if she goes off the rails.

And while it seemed brilliant last night, I'm wondering if marrying Ophelia is truly a terrible idea.

CHAPTER 19: OPHELIA

I'm acting weird.

I know I'm acting weird, but I don't seem to be able to do anything about it. I mean, how do you bring something like this up? It's not the easiest thing to fold into the conversation.

Are we engaged?

Were you serious about getting married? Because you know we're total strangers, right?

Did you come all this way to get married to me?

Will our babies be as good-looking as you? Please say yes.

None of those seem like good intros. Also, I have to mentally kick myself that it's not like it would even be a *real* marriage. Because, obviously, there's no way in hell someone like him would marry someone like me.

Though he did want me in his picture. That's got to count for something, right?

I'm staring out the window and Xavier's on his phone. Perhaps we have this marriage thing down already.

My phone pings with a notification. I glance down, unable to control the reflex. "@XavierHenry3 tagged you in a photo."

Quickly my eyes dart to him. Then, before I can say anything, my fingers are swiping, opening up the app. And there's the picture. He looks great, naturally. I don't look ... terrible, so that's a plus.

Iconic city, iconic restaurant, incredible company. The perfect trifecta. Thank you @opheliaxoxo for showing me around! #Boston #NewAdventures

"Incredible company? I'm over here being all awkward and weird. Definitely not incredible," I blurt.

Because why would I say anything normal?

Xavier looks up and smiles at me. "Of course, I think you're incredible. What you're doing is incredible. I'm speechless that you're helping me in such a selfless and giving way."

The pit in my stomach. At this point, it's so large, that I'm probably just a head stuck on this giant vat of dread. "What do you mean?" I ask, even though I'm pretty sure I know *exactly* what he means. My throat is dry, so I pick up my glass and take a sip.

He shifts, and if I didn't know better, I'd think now he was uncomfortable. "I guess now is as good of a time as any to discuss our marriage."

And in true Ophelia fashion, I choke on my water. At least gasping for air and attempting to calm the spasm in my windpipe buys me a few minutes. It also buys me the stares from the other diner patrons around me.

"I'm choking. It's not COVID," I assure them. "Swallowed wrong. I'm not sick. I'm vaccinated."

"I don't believe you have to justify trying to breathe." Xavier smiles.

Finally done with my fit, my face undoubtedly red and splotchy and with tears in my eyes, I lean in and whisper, "But you know, people are looking. People are thinking it. Like if they get sick, they'll blame me."

"You do what you can to keep yourself and others healthy. But you are allowed to choke every now and again. Not that I recommend it, though."

I feel the need to address his comment that nearly killed me.

"So ... you know I was drunk last night."

Xavier grins. "I believe that's been established." Then he frowns. "Do you not remember what we talked about? What you suggested?" His whole frame wilts as he slumps back.

"No, I mean, I remember. Sort of. I guess I just didn't think you took me seriously."

He shakes his head and blows out a long breath. It's his turn to gaze out the window for a moment. "No, I guess it was too bloody good to be true. I mean, you've no reason for doing it. There's nothing in it for you. I'm not wealthy, but I was planning to offer you some sort of financial compensation. Not that I think you're in dire straits or anything." He lifts his eyebrows. "But if you were, that would help tremendously."

"I'm in straits but like not dire ones." The sad thing is, it's totally accurate. I'm not wealthy, but I can make my rent—on my sad one-bedroom that's still in a college neighborhood, despite my no longer being in college. I have friends. Well, I have Marley. And ... I have a cat.

I also have a viral following on ClikClak that is setting me up with losers and keeps telling me I don't deserve anyone worthy.

Good times.

And they're probably right. It's not like I have tons to offer. I prefer a quiet night in with my cat and a good book. I'm not the life of the party, and I never will be. I'm just plain old Ophelia Finnegan. There's nothing exciting about me at all.

I look up at Xavier. He's dashingly handsome. A pro-athlete. His career might take off, and if it does, it will be because of me. Because I helped him in this little way.

Suddenly, my romantic brain takes off. I could write a book about this. *I could write a book about this!*

Fictionalized, of course, but what great material! And I'd have it all right at my disposal. I'm sure he's got to have a glamorous life with glamorous people and scandalous stories. All the pro-athletes do, right? The book would practically write itself! I feel the words starting to run through my brain. Lines. Snippets. Scenarios. It's already here.

For the first time since my story was panned, I want to write. I *need* to write. The muse is back, bitches.

"I'm not in dire straits," I continue, "but I think we should do it nonetheless. We should get married. As a business arrangement, of course. Strictly business."

My voice wobbles, even though I wish it wouldn't. My throat feels tight. Did someone shut the air off in this place?

"Are you sure?"

I nod, unable to actually say more. Oh my God, what am I doing? A small part of my brain tries to tell the rest of me to stop, but I've never been good at listening to her.

The voice I'm hearing loud and clear is that of Tosser Trent, telling me I'm not worth it. Not to mention the thousands of ClikClakers who weighed in on my unsuitable characteristics.

Let's face it, I'll probably never do better than a fake marriage anyway.

"Right then." He reaches for his phone. "It's a deal. May I have your email to send you a preliminary contract? I've briefly glanced at it, so if you have any issues, feel free to mention them. There's definitely room for adjustment, I would think."

Of course, there would be a contract. This is a business deal. But it's not like the government can know it's a business deal, right? I've seen *Green Card*, that old '90s rom-com. Though whoever thought of casting Gérard Depardieu in *anything* should be fired. But that's neither here nor there. FYI, Gerard Butler is my Gerard of choice. I mean, *P.S.-I Love You* is a definite go-to movie for me, but I've been known to watch *300* simply for the gratuitous tunic scenes.

"Okay, so like I don't know anything about this, but I'm guessing we should make this seem as 'real' as possible." I use my fingers to air quote the word real. "Like, at least in public. In case the government looks into things, right?"

Xavier tilts his head, considering my words.

I hurry to add, "I'm not saying anything over the top or anything, but like social media stuff. Staged things, just for the camera. You know, that sort of thing." I sound like I'm rambling, probably because I am. Yet I continue. "Like if INS or ICE came looking and we are both on social media, but we're never in it together, it might be a little sus."

"So that picture I posted was a good start then, I reckon."

I nod again, relieved that the waitress finally delivers our food. We eat in silence for a few minutes. I'm taking small bites, trying to look like I have manners and not tear into my food like a caveman.

I'm not saying I normally do that anyway, but suddenly I'm super self-conscious. Xavier Henry is hot and famous, and he has to pretend to be in love with me. I've got to keep my awkwardness on the DL.

In between bites, Xavier says, "Is there anything you want specifically stated in the contract? I can have Tony add it."

"Who's Tony?"

"My agent and business manager. He handles all my dealings. He's the one who sent me the draft. I'll be frank—it was shocking how quickly he produced it. I'm starting to wonder what sort of thing goes on at his agency."

"Maybe," I say, swallowing a mouthful of grilled cheese, "there's like a whole group of athletes and celebrities in the same boat. Like with fake marriages and beards and stuff. Oh!" I exclaim. "I'm your beard!"

"I think not. I'm not marrying you because I want to appear hetero when I'm elsewise oriented. I'm marrying you to make a better career move. To save my career, actually."

"Oh, right." I settle back on the bench. Mentally I slap myself for saying something so stupid. "So, then, what do we do now? I've never been in a fake marriage before. Hell, I've never been in any sort of business arrangement of any kind."

"Neither have I, so I'm not really sure. But since we'll be spending a bit of time together, perhaps we could get to know each other some?"

"I think the time for that will come, but I have other questions. Like how quickly does this marriage need to happen? I'm guessing you're on a timeline." I take a small sip of my water.

"Don't you want to look at the contract?" He nods at the phone in my hand.

I know I should. The smart, responsible, non-impulsive thing to do would be to table this discussion until I've read the entire thing cover to cover, highlighting and tabbing items for discussion and negotiation. My eyes glaze over at the mere thought. "Is it okay if I have my lawyer look at it?" It seems like a grown-up thing to say. And to do. Like, have a lawyer.

"Certainly. I'd encourage that."

I don't really have a lawyer, other than my brother. I'm not even sure this is in his area, but he's got to be able to decipher all the terminology, right?

"And yes," he continues, "I'm in a bit of a time crunch, the sooner we can make this happen, the better."

It's at this moment that I realize I know nothing about soccer, nor the structure of the league Xavier plays in. Hell, I don't even know what it's called. He did say his season was done. "Why the rush? I thought the season was over."

"Technically the regular season is done, but I'm never done. Sometimes I train more in my 'off-season' than I do during the season. It's when I get to really drill down on the things that need work and need improvement. I trained for all of the COVID shutdowns, and emerged from the downtime faster and stronger than ever." Color fills his cheeks. "I'm not saying that to be boastful. I work very hard for my sport, which is why I'm going to such drastic measures to keep playing."

I have no idea what it's like to feel this passionate about anything. Maybe, once I start writing this story, I will.

CHAPTER 20: XAVIER

This is all going too well. It's too smooth to be reality. At least in my reality.

Ophelia is adorable. She's funny and self-deprecating. She does not take herself too seriously, and she's definitely not a status seeker. I'm not sure I can even recall the last woman who chatted me up who wasn't interested in my celebrity.

She's the opposite of everyone I've ever dated, which is a breath of fresh air. She's got a bit of chaotic energy about her that reminds me of Mum, especially when she rambles. I actually think the two of them would get on famously, and I can picture them sitting at the kitchen table over a cuppa, talking for hours.

What I can't figure out, as she sits next to me on the T back to her apartment, is why she's doing this. What's in it for her?

She knows virtually nothing about football, so I don't think she's a cleat chaser. She's not a social climber. Based on what she posts on ClikClak and from our past interactions, I think she's genuinely looking for love.

And she knows that's not what this is about, so again, why is she doing this?

No sense in beating around the bush. I've got to know.

"Ophelia, please don't take this the wrong way—"

"Which automatically means I'm going to take this the wrong way, you know," she interjects. She bumps me with her shoulder.

I can't help but grin. Being in her presence makes me smile more than I have in years. "Of course. But I hope you don't. You see, I'm wondering why you're doing this. Or even considering it."

She looks down at her hands folded tightly in her lap. They seem so small. I wonder how they'd compare in size to mine. "I don't want to say."

Oh no. This is not promising.

"Right. But if this is going to work, I think we need to be honest with each other. About everything." I don't need anyone's subversive agendas interfering with my life plans again. Not that I think Phaedra planned to ruin my life, but she absolutely had her own agenda. As did Alycia. "That's pretty much all I'll ask of you."

I see her suck in a deep breath and then slowly release it. "This is my—our—stop." She stands quickly. "Come on."

I stand, throwing my knapsack on and lifting my suitcase as I walk down the train steps. It's totally dark, but the bright streetlights stave off some of that ominous feeling night usually brings.

"I'm about two blocks this way." She takes off her mask and points up the road. "Or, if you want, there are some hotels this way, but they're down a little way. Near Coolidge Corner, I think." She changes her arm in the opposite direction.

"I'll escort you to your place, and then I'll see about a hotel room. Do you mind if I work on it for a few minutes?" I remove my mask and shove it into my pocket. Then I pull out my phone and open the browser.

"Well, don't be silly. You don't need to stand here in the middle of Beacon Street. We can hang out for a while. It's only … wow, it's almost eight already. That went fast."

I too am surprised at how quickly the last three hours have passed in her presence. Usually making small talk seems much more interminable.

No one would ever accuse me of being too congenial.

As we walk up the sideway, Ophelia prattles on about this and that. "I would love to live right on Beacon, but I'm not that far off. And to save the extra thousand a month, I can walk a block or two from the main road. Plus, I don't get the noise from the T. Not to mention my building is super cool, with a turret and everything."

"If you don't mind my asking, what are you paying for rent? I mean, I don't want to pry, but more in a scouting for information way." I'm guessing Boston is more expensive than Baltimore, but they could be fairly comparable. "And you live in a turret?"

Ophelia laughs. "No, I live in the basement in the back of the building. The front has a turret. And a stone balcony and courtyard that I don't get to use.

But for the bargain price of $1,500, I can at least say I live there. Windows optional."

I frown. What does she mean? Immediately, I'm picturing a medieval dungeon.

"You'll see," she continues. "It's not bad. It's a one-bedroom, with virtually no windows, but I do have my own laundry, so that's a bonus. A similar apartment here on Beacon would be at least $2,500 and probably wouldn't have a laundry."

"I'm paying about what you're paying, but it's at least a two-bedroom and there are tons of complex amenities." We turn onto her street, and I can't wait to see it in daylight. The brownstones look old, yet well maintained, and there's something very British about the feel of this street with its stone walls and wrought iron fences. "This is quite charming."

"Isn't it? This is how I sort of picture areas of London being. At least the feel of the architecture."

"I was thinking something similar."

Ophelia lets out a little squeal, clapping her hands. "Oh, that makes me so happy. I'm totally *obsessed* with the idea of British life. It's just all so romantic."

That's it. She's not a sports fanatic, but an Anglophile.

Swell.

"So that's why you've agreed to this cockamamie plan then?"

Ophelia doesn't just stop but she actually stumbles. "What? No. I'm not looking for a romantic situation. It's all business, remember? I ... it's just ... well, you see ..."

"Did you only agree because I'm British?" I'm not sure why I'm getting upset. She doesn't have to justify this to me. And who cares if she thinks my accent or how I grew up is fascinating. "Would you still be agreeing to marry me if I were American?"

"Obviously not." She stands tall, finally with her footing secure, and puts her hands on her hips.

I knew it! She's got ulterior motives. I hope she doesn't think this is going to be a financial windfall or some short circuit to publicity. She doesn't want the type of hype I attract.

On the other hand, why else would she be doing this if she didn't have ulterior motives? Unless she was crackers, it wouldn't make sense to marry a stranger for absolutely no reason.

Yet still, I'm miffed. I don't know why.

"I see."

"Yeah." Her eyebrows lift. "Because if you were American, you wouldn't be desperate enough to ask someone like me to marry you." Her head drops, her plaits falling forward over her shoulders.

Her words stab me through the heart. What must she think of herself? And to think that I'm making her feel worse. "Don't say that." I put a finger under her chin and gently lift it up. "And remember, you asked me."

"Actually, I don't remember it at all because I was hammered. Because I'd gone on a date and was flashed within minutes of walking into the restaurant. Because I'm undatable. Unlovable." She turns away, jerking away from my touch.

Message received.

She storms down a narrow alley that may have at one time served as a drive to the carriage house. Her apartment could have been a summer kitchen that was attached to the main building. It is indeed half below ground though. There are a few square windows that dot the perimeter. They're probably not large enough to let in ample light, but plenty big enough for a burglar to crawl through. I'd ask her if she's ever thought of that, but she's already mad at me.

I don't need to evoke every single negative emotion in the span of three minutes flat.

Plus, I'm done playing the role of superhero. The last time I tried, well, we all know how that ended. In fact, it's why I'm here right now.

As Ophelia turns the key and pushes the door open, the first thing I see is a large yellow tabby cat sitting there, watching his owner come in. I'd seen the beast walking around, over, and on Ophelia during our FaceTime, so it's not a surprise.

"So this is the infamous Sundance. Should I bow to him? Offer him a can of tuna? Practice mutual ignoring? I'm not that versed in cats."

Cats and birds of prey are not compatible species. Well, not if you don't want one to end up being dinner for the other. While most of our neighbors in the country did keep a cat or six around to keep the mouse population down, we had a feathered management system.

She drops her keys in a bowl next to the door and stoops to pick up the cat. With her face nestled into his fur, she says, "He'll let you know what he wants from you." And with that, Sundance squirms in her arms, clearly indicating he's done being held.

"Wouldn't it be swell if people were that easy to read?"

I see her ugly striped couch. I didn't think it was possible but it looks even more hideous in person. I hope she's not supremely attracted to it because it's not coming into my house.

Not that I have a house. Or a home. I'm utterly displaced.

Ophelia catches me staring at the couch. "It's fantastic, isn't it? It was left here, and I simply couldn't part with it. I'm pretty sure it's vintage '60s. Think of all the memories it has. It was left to me to create even more."

It looks like something my mum would have. Another thing the two of them could bond over. "You rolled off of it while you were pissed last night. Is that the type of memory you were thinking of?" I smile as I say it. I do wonder what this upholstery has seen.

"Let's hope it's something more exciting than that." Ophelia hangs her jacket on a coat stand by the door. It looks just as vintage as the rest of the furniture around here, with the exception of the high-tech computer station, complete with dual monitors, webcam, and ring light. Though it's the most modern item in here, it's what looks most out of place.

I follow suit and hang up my coat as well.

"Right then, so should we get down to business? That way I won't keep you too much later tonight."

Ophelia sits on the ugly couch while I opt for a blue wing chair, which also looks thrifted or donated. It's not in bad shape, considering it's probably old enough to collect a pension.

"Okay, I mean, I've been trying to plan, though it's not a strength of mine. You said this has to be done quickly so you can switch teams."

I nod. "The quicker the better." My mind starts to wander, thinking about how soon I can join the Buzzards. I've got a sinking feeling in my gut though, that maybe Coach Janssen and the Buzzards are going to change their minds about me. Maybe Jones will get to them, too. Or that Camacho will be a wanker and not let me out of my contract.

He'd be an idiot to keep me, especially considering he doesn't want to play me, but no one'd ever accuse him of being Oxford material.

And then I realize Ophelia's been talking this whole time, and I've missed every blasted word.

"Small, obviously. I'll need at least a month. Will your family be coming over?"

"Come again? Coming for what?" I mean, I'd love it if my parents came to see me play here in the US, but it's too hard to get someone to take care of the birds. It's a lot for one person to handle, and heaven knows Philip would be terribly grumpy about it.

Ophelia's lips pull into a tight line. "The wedding. What else would be so important for them to fly all the way across the ocean?"

"The wedding? What wedding?" As soon as the words are out of my mouth, I wish I could pull them back in.

Of course, she's focused on the wedding.

A wedding I'd not even considered. Weddings take time and planning and money. While I can probably afford a decent shebang, I'd rather not piss my hard-earned dollars away on something like that.

Ophelia folds her arms across her chest as she fixes her gaze up on the ceiling. She's so focused that I turn to look to see if there's anything in that corner, like a spider or leprechaun scaling down the wall.

For the record, there's nothing.

But looking at her more closely, I see something much more alarming. Tears in her eyes.

Oh shit.

CHAPTER 21: OPHELIA

He doesn't want a wedding.

Of course, he doesn't want a wedding. Why would he want a wedding? It's not like he's in love with me and really wants to declare in front of all our friends and family that he can't spend another single moment without me.

Because that's not true.

Obviously.

It's not like he was going to take one look at me, hungover and pale, stupid Heidi braids in my hair, and fall head-over-heels in love. That only happens in books.

I mean, he's totally the type of person you could fall in lust with, but only one of us here belongs on a magazine cover. And it's not me.

"Did I say something to upset you?"

I shake my head, knowing if I try to speak the words will come tumbling out in a foolish, blubbering mess. You know, the real me.

It's not like I don't *know* I'm being irrational. I totally am. I just don't know how to stop my brain from speeding off down this path like Julia Roberts's horse in *The Runaway Bride*.

I keep staring at a tiny crack in my wall, just under the ceiling. I focus on that line and will the moisture to absorb back into my eyeballs. He wasn't talking about a wedding. He wanted to talk about our marriage.

The business arrangement.

God, I'm such an idiot.

I inhale deeply, letting it out over a count of six. Okay, I think I can talk now.

"Right. This isn't about a wedding. I ... I don't know why I said that. Um, I work until five, but maybe we could run to city hall on my lunch break. I mean, can it wait until Tuesday?"

Xavier's face goes pale. Shit, I've totally scared him off with my freak romantic notions. He's going to throw away his entire career rather than be attached to me.

I don't think I'll ever recover from this.

Maybe I'll buy a wedding gown and languish here like Miss Havisham from *Great Expectations*. I'd probably be really good at that.

"Well, I mean time is of the essence, but not that much so. We need to go over the contract. You'll want your lawyer to look at it, and we'll have to agree on changes. I'm sure there's paperwork and such, like a marriage license. I don't know what the turnaround time is on something like that. I've never been married before."

I swallow, finally able to look at him. He's easily the hottest guy who's ever been in my presence.

Bright blue eyes, wide grin. An ass you could bounce a quarter off of. He does not belong in my shabby apartment with its vintage—okay old—mismatched furniture. I'm going to have to move, probably to a brand new condo with glass tables and clean lines and no character. I won't fit in any more than I do now.

But at least it's a chance to do something other than collect dust and cobwebs here. "Me neither." I finally meet his gaze. "I'm sorry. I didn't mean to get upset."

Xavier leans forward. "Ophelia, you know this is business for me."

I stand up. "Of course. Me too. So, send over the contract and then let me know when you want me. Or how you want me. I'm very flexible. I mean," I fumble my words. "Where you want to do it. Me. Not do me, because, like you said it's business, and I don't do it for business. I mean, maybe I should. I'd make better money than I do now, right?"

Someone, please muzzle me.

Xavier stands as well, nervously glancing toward the door. He's probably trying to figure out if he needs to stop for his coat before running out. He doesn't need to worry. Soccer players are probably a lot better runners than couch potato accountant book nerds who hate to exercise. He wouldn't even have to try that hard to escape.

"You don't need to answer that."

"Good, because I'm not even sure what you said. Or rather, I know what you said, but I'm not sure what you meant. I know you said you had to work in the morning, but perhaps we could grab a bite to eat at some point tomorrow? Lunch or supper?"

"Why?" I'll never win Miss Congeniality at this point. Speaking of which, I wonder if I should get a glow-up like Sandra Bullock did? Maybe Michael Caine is all I need to become less of, well, me.

Xavier pauses at the door and cocks his head slightly. "We're going to have to live together. Possibly even appear in public with each other. I thought getting to know you better might help."

I let out a sigh. It's so blatantly obvious how much help I need. I'm practically a charity case. "Fine. I mean, good. You're right. How about dinner? I know this great restaurant in the North End."

Xavier nods at me and then walks out. It's only after he leaves that his words sink in.

Live together.

I mean, it's not like I didn't know it, but I can barely string three words together in his presence. I'm going to have to figure out how to be functional and normal.

Because this is a totally functional and normal thing to do.

I pick up my phone to text Marley but stop short. I'm not sure if I'm allowed to tell her. I mean, I'm going to have to, eventually, but I don't know if I can tell her the real story or what.

On the other hand, if I don't say something to someone, I'm going to burst.

Me: I'm getting married.

It's a stupid text to send, but if I don't get it out, Xavier will return tomorrow to find bits of me all over the place because I did actually spontaneously combust.

Then I wait, those three dots waving. After what feels like eons, but is in fact only two minutes, a response dings through.

Xavier: Really? Who's the lucky chap?

Me: Sorry, I just had to tell someone, and since I'm not sure who I can tell, you win by default.

Xavier: I think I win regardless.

My breath hitches in the back of my throat as I read those words. He doesn't mean anything by them, of course. He's winning because he's making the career move he wants and is going to play for a winning team.

Me: Isn't that what this whole thing is about? Making sure you win? What team are you going to be playing for? I feel like a good wife should know this.

Xavier: A good wife should. The Boston Buzzards. And where is the hotel around here? I feel as if I've been walking for hours.

Oh God, now I feel guilty for making him go.

Me: Just turn around. You can stay here. It's silly for you to get a hotel.

Naturally, I regret sending the text as soon as my thumb strikes the button. Story of my life. No, that's not going to be awkward at all.

Xavier: You sure? I don't want to put you out.

Me: <laughs nervously> It's not like you're a serial killer or anything. Right?

Me: RIGHT?????

Xavier: Not last time I checked. I'd tell you to vet me, but the only person we have in common is

Trent the Tosser, and I'm not sure he's a reliable source.

Me: He'd be a reliable source for you, just not for me. But alas, I've deleted his contact information. Please don't kill me and make a suit out of my flesh.

You know, worrying about his serial killer-ness probably would have been better before I invited him to stay. Or better yet, before I went to the train station to meet him and bring him back here. Or still better, BEFORE I ASKED HIM TO MARRY ME.

Quickly, I run over to my desk and scrawl a quick letter to Marley, naming one Xavier Henry as my killer, in the event that I go missing. On the outside of the envelope, I write, "Open in case of emergency" and before I can check myself, I run outside and place it in the corner mailbox.

I'm not sure why that brings me a sense of safety and relief. I'll still be dead, but at least justice will be served.

"You didn't have to wait out here for me." Xavier's voice startles me. It's not hard to do, considering every serial killer movie and true crime documentary I binged on Netflix is now running through my head.

"Yes, of course, that's what I was doing. Not mailing a letter to my friend in case you decide to have a perverted dark side that will end with me being dismembered and boiled." Dear God, maybe my death wouldn't be a bad thing. It'd put me out of my misery, at the very least. It may be the only thing to silence my mouth. The awkward giggle that bubbles out only makes it that much worse.

Xavier smiles though. "I promise I'm not."

"No skeletons in the closet then?" We fall in step, heading back down the driveway to my door for the second time tonight.

His smile falters and Xavier clears his throat. "Not actual humans, at least. This is an odd conversation, I must admit. Maybe we could talk about something less weird, like marrying a stranger."

It's my turn to laugh. "Right? This is weird."

Xavier reaches in front of me and pulls the door open, holding it to let me pass. A very gentlemanly thing to do.

I'm not sure anyone's ever done it for me before. Huh.

Before I can have yet another bout of verbal diarrhea, Xavier asks, "Where's the loo? If you don't mind, I'd like to freshen up a bit before I turn in. It's been a long day, and I'm a bit knackered."

I glance at my phone which tells me it's after ten already. Yikes! Where did the time go? It's time for me to sit staring at a blank notebook and then berate myself for being a failure of a writer before I've even started.

I don't know how to end my day without that. I'm nothing if not consistent in my chaos.

"Bathroom's this way." I point down the small hall. The moment Xavier's behind the closed door and I hear the shower running, I dash to my bedroom, throw on my unattractive pajama pants and oversized college T-shirt and curse myself for not having cute sleepwear.

Well, I do have that French maid outfit I bought for Trent, but I'm pretty sure Xavier *never* wants to see me in that.

And I don't know why I care about what I'm wearing. He won't. He won't even look twice. I'm the means to an end for him, and he's going to be the means to an end for me.

A perfectly symbiotic fake relationship.

I mean, he's already treating me better than my last—several—real relationships did. Maybe I should always only have fake relationships.

I have a fuzzy blanket or two already out in the living room, so all I need is my favorite pillow and my Kindle, and I'm ready to sleep on the couch. It's too small for Xavier to be comfortable on and in any case, he's a guest.

Once my stuff is situated on the couch and I've procured my emotional support water bottle, I sit down at my desk. The purple Moleskine notebook is there.

But tonight, it's not taunting me. It's calling to me. Begging me to open it and fill it with words. Words that have been flowing through and knocking around my brain since the diner.

The first page has the list of the things I want in life.

The second page has the title. I cross that out and write a new one.

And before I know it, my hand is moving quickly as words fill the third page. Then the fourth. And fifth.

Who knew writing was this easy when you had a hot soccer player naked in the next room for inspiration?

CHAPTER 22: XAVIER

I wonder what she's writing.

She's bent in half, huddled over her desk, almost like that Horton Dibble in school who was terrified that everyone was trying to cheat off him, so he had to protect his paper at all costs. He was a bit of a dunce, so no one ever wanted to copy his answers, but that's neither here nor there.

One dark plait makes a line down her back while the other is tucked in front of her shoulder. She's changed into her sleep clothes, complete with fuzzy socks that look like something my mum would wear on a cold winter night.

Instantly I'm hit with a pang of homesickness that feels as if someone has slammed into me while charging for the ball. What would Mum think of this situation? I know she'd love to have me home with her and Da, but she also wants me to play, no matter the cost.

I'm going to have to read that bloody contract to see what it says about telling our families. Not that Mum would think poorly of Ophelia for entering into this arrangement. In fact, she'd probably smother her with love for helping me out. I do think the two of them would get on famously.

It would be easy to do, smother Ophelia with love. She's earnest and open, reading like a book. She's sweet and naive almost. Maybe to a fault. She doesn't have a devious bone in her body.

Of course, that's what I thought about Phaedra too before she hung me out to dry and all but ruined my career. Hell, I'm here in this predicament right now because of Phaedra's innocent looks and her pleas for help.

But Ophelia Finnegan, in her baggy pajamas and plaits, with a mouth that rambles on saying whatever pops into it, is about the furthest thing from Phaedra Jones as you can get. Not that I'd even be tempted to be sucked in again. And I was trying to help Phaedra, a fat lot of good it did me. This is totally different because Ophelia is helping me.

There's nothing she wants from me and nothing I can do for her.

And that's how it needs to stay.

All business.

So I should probably quit standing here, staring at her like a creeper, watching her work. But she seems so absorbed that I hate to disturb her.

On the other hand, I can't just stand here forever, so I clear my throat.

"Oh!" she exclaims, sitting up quickly and slamming her notebook shut. Her blue pen skitters across the desk. She whirls around in her chair and clutches the book behind her back.

If I didn't know better, I'd say she looks guilty about something. But what could she have been up to, with paper and a pen? It's probably simply another Ophelia quirk. I have a feeling I'm about to find out that many more exist.

And each one is more adorable than the last.

I nod toward the couch as I step closer. "Thanks for getting this set up for me. If you don't mind, I'm going to turn in."

Ophelia stands up, still clutching her hands behind her back. "No, you're not staying out here. I want you in my bed."

I blink, knowing what she means, but also not able to stop my brain from going to a place that she's not referring to at all.

Ophelia squeezes her eyes shut tightly and pinches her mouth into a flat line. "That's not what I mean. I don't want you in my bed. I mean, no offense because you're smoking hot, and I bet you could squeeze a lemon with those thigh muscles." Her words stop as abruptly as they started, but it's too late. They hang in the air, like a cartoon thought bubble.

"I've never actually tried that, but the next time you get a hankering for lemonade, let me know, and I'll see what I can do." If I were cheeky, I'd wink at her.

Now her mouth flops open for a moment before she slams it shut, swallowing hard.

Right then. Perhaps that was a bit out of line. "Sorry, I'm not sure why I said that. Let's chalk it up to late-night fatigue. And I'm not taking your bed while you sleep out on the couch."

"The couch is too short for you. You'll be more comfortable in the bed, and that's final. You told me that you value your sleep, and this is the best way for you to get it. Also, I have to get up for work in the morning, so this way you can sleep in undisturbed. I'm still working from home. Right here." She points to the desk.

I don't know how to let her know that I'm usually up by five to work out. Nevertheless, I appreciate what she's trying to do for me. When you're a professional athlete, even a lesser-known one, most people think about what you can do for them. How your hard work, your blood, sweat, and tears, can be of a privilege to them.

It's probably why I don't have many people in my life, short of Tony, whom I pay to be there, and Alastair. Sure my mum and my da, but they too benefit from my career. I'm sure they'd tell me playing football doesn't matter to them, but I don't know how they'd still be in business if it weren't for me.

Ophelia doesn't seem to want anything from me. She's more about what she can do for me than vice versa. I'm going to have to make this up to her.

"That's certainly nice of you."

Ophelia slides the notebook onto her desk before taking a few steps toward me. "I mean, well, I don't know what I mean. This is weird, right?"

I smile at her. "Without a doubt."

She walks past me, motioning for me to follow her to the bedroom. Mirrors line the entire wall behind the bed. Before I can help myself, I burst out laughing. "You know, I'd have bet money that Trent was the type to have mirrors on his ceiling and everything. I didn't picture you for having a secret kinky side."

Ophelia's cheeks blush a deep scarlet. "It's because this room has no windows. The mirrors were here before I got here, I swear. I think they were trying to make it seem more open or not like a cave, which it sort of is. It's not because I'm kinky. I'm not that adventurous. I mean, I could be, if I found the right person, but we all know how that's going. I even bought slutty lingerie for someone else to appreciate."

Suddenly, my mouth has gone dry as I get a mental image of Ophelia clad in something much more revealing than she's currently wearing, staring back at me in the mirror while I hold one of those plaits.

I shake my head quickly to empty that image away.

No, I cannot be thinking something like that. Not at all. This would never work if I was thinking things like that.

Ophelia's now staring at her feet. Without looking up she says, "I'm just going to go flush my head down the toilet. If we could never speak of this again, I'd appreciate it."

Without another word, she leaves the bedroom, closing the door behind her. I stand there, unsure of what to do, but fairly confident it's going to be a long night with a host of inappropriate thoughts running through my head.

I can't even get a proper wank on because Ophelia's in the other room. Also, because this is all business, and if I were to wank off thinking about

Ophelia and these mirrors and her slutty lingerie, this whole thing might not work.

It's got to stay business. No matter what my willy is thinking about.

CHAPTER 23: OPHELIA

Did you know in Massachusetts there's a three-day waiting period from when you apply for a marriage license to when they'll mail it out to you? Then you have to wait for it to be delivered before you can get married. It's almost as if they want you to slow down and think about what you're about to do.

That's never how it is in the movies. They just run off to the courthouse. Real life can be such a buzzkill sometimes.

Lucky for me, there's also a waiver form, so you can get a marriage license issued the same day you apply for it. And if you call and tell the clerk a sob story about how your fiancé is getting traded, and he has to move and all that jazz and oh, he's a pro athlete, they're likely to grant you that waiver so you can get married right away.

And we'll be doing all that at 3:30 p.m. today.

Also, thanks to COVID, Boston City Hall only does marriages on Wednesdays and Thursdays. So here we are, getting ready to get married on a Thursday.

It's been just over a week since Xavier took the train up here and we agreed to get married. For real.

I mean, this time we were both sober and decided to move forth with the plan. I guess I didn't have any idea of how much of a whirlwind this would be. If you'd have told me ten days ago during PenisGate that I'd be standing in front of my closet on Thursday morning, looking for something appropriate to get married in, I'd have called you nuts.

Also, if you'd told me that I'd be writing thousands of words a night, I'd have asked for some of what you are smoking. Apparently, all I needed was a muse, and that muse is my soon-to-be husband. Like seriously, being around him has totally restored my flow.

It's like a river when the levee breaks.

Over the past week or so, I've come to realize the following about the man I'm going to marry: he's the complete opposite of me. Mostly because he's a man of action, yet not impulsive. He has a goal and makes a plan and then works for it. He just does it quickly.

Soccer is a speed sport, after all.

In the past ten days, he's returned to Baltimore, talked to the coaches, talked to his agent, packed up most of his stuff, researched places to live down by Gillette Stadium, and returned back here late last night.

I'm pretty sure he's worked out every day too.

I'm more the type to get a passing thought and then act before I think it through. Like posting on ClikClak to help me find dates. I had to turn off notifications for good and block people from messaging me. I even went in and deleted that video, but it doesn't matter. It's out there in the world, and by the way, people are disgusting with what they will proposition you with over the internet.

I mean, I read some pretty smutty romance novels, but these things are downright crude. Plus, it's one thing to read it in a safe, totally made-up space. I'm a real person that other real people are saying these degrading things to.

If nothing else, marrying Xavier means I don't have to deal with that anymore.

We need to move on this quickly. Because let's face it, if I have too much more time to think about this, I won't go ahead with it. I either don't look before I leap, or I think it to death. There's no middle ground for me.

Still in my pajamas, I walk out to the kitchen to find Xavier's back from his run. He didn't get here until about eleven last night, and it's only eight and he's already exercised. He's making a protein shake full of all sorts of green things I've never even heard of. I have a bowl of Golden Grahams for breakfast.

"So, I know you posted us last week, but should we make our 'relationship' social media official, seeing as how we're getting married today?" I use my fingers to bracket the word. "We don't have to post the marriage until later on, though."

He takes a sip of his health drink. "Probably. But you should also probably stop making air quotes around the word relationship. You don't want to get too comfortable with it and slip up."

I pull out my phone and open ClikClak. Without pausing to think or plan, I hit record.

Guys, huge updates since the last time I was here. And you did it! A roundabout way, but I'll have to put that in another video. But OMG, isn't he dreamy?

I step in front of Xavier, holding the phone out in front of me to get him into the frame. Xavier looks up, startled, hands still on my blender, which until this point has only ever been used to make margaritas. It's probably in as much shock from this development as I am.

So, let's just say this is not at all what I planned when I started with my hashtag surprise visit, but I'm so happy at where I've ended. You couldn't write this in a movie if you tried, right, honey?

A shy grin spreads over his face.

Well, here I am, living my own fairy tale. Thanks, ClikClak! Kisses and hugs!

I sign off blowing a kiss to the camera, and then quickly add my hashtags. #lovelylia, #liainlove, #surpriselove, and of course, #xoxo.

"That was fast. I didn't realize when you talked about posting you meant right this instant," Xavier says casually. Probably a little too casually.

"Keeping up appearances. You post on Insta, I'll post on ClikClak, and then if the FBI or ICE comes calling, we have a nice little portfolio to show them."

"Right. Good idea. Maybe we can do another one later? I've got a call with Janssen in a bit, so after that?"

"Who's Janssen again?" He said it like I should know, so I wonder if I've missed an important detail about his life. I think his agent is Tony. Other than that, I can't remember who he's talked about specifically. I have no idea if he has any family or friends.

I should probably listen more instead of daydreaming scenes for my book, and many more books to follow.

Like the one I'm thinking of now that involves the top flying off the blender, getting doused in a smoothie, wiping each other down, and then a hot steamy scene on the kitchen counter.

My mouth goes dry just thinking about it.

Focus.

"He's the coach for the Buzzards. He used to be my coach with the Terrors, but they let him go during the shutdown. He's the one I talked to last week. I want to make sure this trade is happening."

Janssen, coach. Need to remember that. It seems important. More important than defiling my counter. "Right. Because it would be totally stupid for us to get married if you don't need to." I laugh. Can you even imagine?

"Completely. I'm going to hit the shower if you don't mind. What time's the appointment again?"

Appointment. Wedding. Holy shit, we're really getting married. I'm no better than one of those people who go on a TV show and marry a complete stranger.

Suddenly, the air seems thin. Too thin.

"Three-thirty. We should leave around two forty-five to get to City Hall." I try to appear interested in some work on my desk and not at all like I'm having a panic attack.

Breathe in, breathe out.

"Right. Good." He disappears into my bathroom.

I take a moment to look around. This is all happening so fast. He's put an air mattress on my living room floor, refusing to allow me to take the couch any longer. This place is definitely too small for the two of us, and it's not like I'm trying to create a scenario for the one-bed trope.

This seems like some dream that started the moment that first video went viral. And if not a dream, surreal, at the very least.

"Hey." I knock on the bathroom door. "After we … you know … do you want to take a drive down to Foxborough and look at places?"

Xavier pulls the bathroom door open, clad in only a towel.

Jesus, Mary, and Joseph.

Check that. I'm *all* on board for the one-bed trope. We never need to move.

My mouth goes dry yet I start salivating all at the same time. Muscles ripple and cut underneath his skin. Writing in black ink wraps around his left side, just under his pec. I would like to look at it closely to see what it says. My gaze starts at his well-defined shoulders, travels down his firm pecs, continues down what has to be an eight pack, and ends on a trail of hair pointing down underneath the towel to what must be the promised land.

"Close your mouth. You're apt to catch flies."

I close my mouth but am still unable to blink at a normal speed. I'm afraid if I close my eyes, this vision of male perfection will disappear. Finally, I drag my gaze up to meet his.

"Sorry. You're naked and hot."

He tightens his grip on the towel as if I'm going to snatch it away from him. Not saying I would, but it's definitely not beneath me either. "I mean, I like *knew* you were sort of athletic and all, but …"

"I'm not sort of athletic. I'm an athlete, darling."

"Why are you fake marrying me then?" I glance down at my frumpy pajamas, oversized hoodie, and fuzzy socks. "Surely you could easily find someone who matches you better."

"I don't do drama. I'm not into that scene, and real relationships always involve drama. And you're …"

"A temporary blip on social media. I'm someone who overinvested in my last relationship because I was so afraid I'd never find someone. I want to find someone. I mean, I know you're not him, but at least I'm not alone when I'm with you. But at the end of the day, I'm still nobody. Not compared to your world."

"You're not nobody, Ophelia. I like you. You're caring and funny and …" He searches for another word.

"Impulsive, boring, introverted."

"Pretty awesome," he finishes. "Not many people would give up everything to help a total stranger out."

I look down at my feet and shrug. "That's the benefit of being a nobody with nothing. I have nothing to sacrifice. I'm not giving up anything. In fact, I'm gaining something."

"What's that?"

"For the time that we're married, I get the knowledge that people are looking at us, wondering how I was able to land you." I shrug again. "I want to be special for once. And if I'm married to you, people will think I must be special."

This pity party is interrupted by pounding on the door. I don't even need to wonder who it is because I can hear Marley yelling, "Ophelia June Finnegan, open this door this very second."

Xavier looks at me, his eyes wide.

Right. He wants a drama-free life.

Marley doesn't sound like drama-free.

"It's my best friend, who undoubtedly saw my ClikClak." I don't mention the letter I mailed to her, naming him as my murderer. "I'll pay you to answer the door like that." I nod at his mostly naked body which looks quite lickable. If nothing else, it will distract her from her rampage, which, judging from her yelling, we're going to need.

He smiles but inches toward the bedroom. "Sorry, but that's not me. I don't stir up drama."

I shrug. "Probably for the best. You should come with a warning anyway. Unexpected viewing of pecs and abs will cause spontaneous panty-dropping and immediate pregnancy."

Oh dear Lord, tell me I did not just say that out loud?

It's a good thing that we're not really in a relationship because I would never, ever survive my mortification.

"Right."

"Right then." I shift nervously. The banging at the door continues. "I'd better get that."

"And I'd better get dressed, lest you and your friend find yourself in the family way." Xavier offers a sly smile that indicates slight amusement.

I think.

I hope.

"Girl, you'd better open this door right this instant!"

I pull the door open to see my best friend standing there in an absolute panic.

"Hey," I say as blandly as I can. "What's up?"

Marley waves my letter. "Are you dead? I thought you were dead. I get this in the mail, and I don't hear from you. Then, you're posting on ClikClak with some random dude in your apartment, and you're in love? What the actual hell, Ophelia?"

"Um, I texted you. You didn't respond. This is what you get. Be nice to me or you can't come to my wedding."

Marley's brown complexion turns a shade of red I didn't know was possible. There may be steam coming from the ends of her curls. She hisses at me in a not-at-all-quiet whisper, "Wedding? Are you delusional? Has all this social media crap caused you to have a legit psychotic break? You need to pull your head out of those stupid romance novels and wake up, Ophelia Finnegan. You are NOT getting married. This is nuts."

"Who's at the door?" Xavier struts out in gray sweatpants, a skin-tight T-shirt, and damp hair.

It takes me a minute to remember how to swallow.

Xavier shoots me a grin that if I didn't know better, could be described as devilish. "Did I hear someone say something about getting married? Is your friend going to be our witness this afternoon?"

That shuts Marley up fast. Her color drains, and I'm afraid she's going to pass out. I grab her arm and drag her toward the couch as fast as I can. She's not going down on my watch.

Marley looks blankly from me to Xavier and back again. "I ... am I ... is this an alternate universe?" she finally stutters out.

"Can I speak with you for a moment?" Xavier jerks his head toward my bedroom.

"You, sit," I tell my friend. "We'll be right back."

Once behind the closed door, I raise my eyebrow and wait for Xavier to speak. He runs his hand through his damp hair, and I swear to God, I could watch him do that forever. Maybe I'll record him and make it into a GIF.

It would go viral.

Focus, Ophelia.

"I don't think you should tell your friend. Not yet."

"Um, Marley's my best friend. My ride-or-die. She knows everything about me. She's totally trustworthy."

"I don't disbelieve you, but there are legalities that we're still working out. Tony is drafting the NDAs, and until she signs one, I don't think we're allowed to tell her."

It feels wrong, like socks with the elastic broken or Pete Davidson dating Ariana Grande. Or Kate Beckinsale. Or Kim Kardashian. Seriously, how does someone like *him* land women like that? Of course, the same could be said for Xavier and me. "I don't like to keep things this big from her."

"I understand that, but I want to make sure everything is on the up and up. The very last thing I want is a scandal or something negative making the news. I cannot afford that for my career." His voice is light but there's a look in his eyes that's unsettling.

"But isn't all publicity good publicity? This seems minor, should it leak, compared to what a lot of athletes do. You're not deflating balls or stealing plays or anything like that."

"Ophelia, no bad publicity. None. I cannot afford it." His voice is grave. "We'll talk about it later, but know, for right now, this cannot blow up. It cannot end badly. My career *cannot* have another black mark."

Another? Interesting. I make a mental note to Google him, which I'm sure to promptly forget. "Right. Understood. Got it." His request should be easy, though. I'm like the least controversial person ever. I barely leave my house. I'm an accountant for Pete's sake. "But, if I can't tell Marley yet, then we have to convince her." I raise my eyebrow.

"Convince her?"

Is he going to make me spell it out for him?

"You know, convince her." I gesture between the two of us. "She knows me too well, and she knows how I act when I'm in a relationship."

"And how's that exactly?" Xavier folds his arms over his chest, which, thanks to the towel incident, I now know is chiseled and belongs on a calendar. I'm guessing there's not much on his body that's not.

I feel the heat rush my face. I can't believe I have to say this out loud. It's easier to stare at my feet than look him right in the eye when I say this. "I, um, tend to be, well, maybe, perhaps a little demonstrative." I raise my gaze slightly.

"Un-huh."

"Okay, hear me out. I'm not saying anything crazy or anything, but there'll have to be some … touching. Maybe a hug or an innocent kiss. You know, so she believes that we're, like, together."

He's going to run. Or vomit. He's going to leave me here, high and dry, and I'll spontaneously combust from embarrassment.

A girl can only stand so much.

"You're right. Not a proper snog, but we should kiss." Xavier nods. "Right then, let's go talk to Marley." He takes my hand and leads me out of the bedroom.

CHAPTER 24: XAVIER

As my hand takes hers, the thought that runs through my brain is:

Not a proper snog?

What the hell do I even mean by that? I said it so she wouldn't think I was forcing myself on her or trying to take advantage of the situation.

It's not like I find the thought of kissing Ophelia distasteful. Truthfully, it's quite the opposite. Ever since she'd talked about doing kinky things in lingerie, it's been on my mind. She's on my mind. Frequently. I can't help that—I am human after all. But I never thought about doing it for show.

I'd been so focused on the logistics of becoming a US citizen to enable the trade. On talking with Coach Janssen and packing my apartment and asking Tony for the hundredth time for the contracts to sign that I didn't think about the actual *marriage* thing. Or making people think we're married at the very least.

Ophelia and I will definitely have to have a longer conversation once her friend leaves. It's probably wise to put some parameters and stipulations in the contract that keep this a strictly business relationship, especially knowing some of the other thoughts I've had about her.

No, this shall stay strictly business.

With public displays of affection.

Her hand seems small in mine. I reckon I don't view her as overly petite, probably because her personality and spirit seem to fill any room she's in. Her whole energy is the opposite of mine. In the past, I used to find perpetually-in-motion people grating. However, with Ophelia, it's ... amusing. Entertaining. Distracting.

Attractive.

She reminds me of the way a kestrel flaps its wings to hover over prey. Still, but with a flurry of activity.

And with my life in the pot right now, I need the distraction.

"Marley, we're going down to City Hall for a three-thirty appointment. Do you want to be our witness, but more importantly, do you want to help me figure out what to wear?" Ophelia glances up at me, her hand warm in mine. "Are you okay if Marley comes with us, babe?"

Nicknames, is it? Though not one for the games typically associated with dating, it's imperative I play along. "It's fine by me, my little chickadee." It seems fitting since she reminds me of a sparrow hopping about here and there. I give her hand a little squeeze before dropping it.

If I'm not mistaken, I see her nose wrinkle slightly. I don't know why, nor do I have the energy to guess. This charade is enough for me to manage.

Marley's mouth opens and closes a few times as she looks between us. "But ... this ... this can't be real. You barely know him!"

"It is, Mar." Ophelia flops onto the couch next to her friend. "When you know it's the right thing, you know. Why wait?"

Marley takes her friend's hands in her own. "Ophelia, you've had a rough few weeks with Trent and ClikClak and everything. Are you sure?"

I see her give me the side-eye.

"Is this the safest decision? You don't have to do this."

I wander over to the other side of the room by the desk. I appreciate the care Marley has for her friend. I will not appreciate it, however, if she talks Ophelia out of this. When I talked to Tony last week, he said this was my only shot at getting traded now. I need to get traded.

The thought of staying in Baltimore has me almost as low as I was after the Phaedra debacle.

Yet when I'm in the same room with Ophelia, that feeling seems very remote.

Ophelia stands up and walks over to me, standing behind me and putting her hands lightly on my arms. "I want to do this." I turn to face her, and her hands return to my biceps.

She continues, gazing at me. "From the first message, I was smitten. How could I not be? I've never had a connection like this with anyone. Ever." Ophelia turns her head to look at her friend. "Mar, you've known me since we were little. When have I ever fallen like this? I don't believe in insta-love. Hell, you know I hate that trope. So for me to do this, you know it's gotta be big."

Ophelia, looking deep into my eyes, is so convincing that I almost forget that we're virtual strangers about to commit fraud and that there are no real feelings here. Unable to help myself, and not acting in the least, I smile at her, and she returns the expression. My hands have found their way to her waist, so I pull her closer to me, digging my fingers in slightly. She's soft and sensual without even trying.

"Ugh, get a room." Marley throws a couch pillow at us, breaking the moment. I deflect the flying object, and it bounces off Ophelia's desk, scattering papers and books.

Both Ophelia and I reach to pick up the mess. Her desk is never neat, to begin with, but now it looks as if a cyclone went through. I shuffle a pile of papers together and pick up a purple notebook.

"I'll take that." Ophelia snatches it out of my hands. I wonder if that's the book she's scribbling in whenever she thinks I'm not looking. What could be so important in there that she doesn't want me to see? "Marley, can you help me figure out what to wear?"

They dash off down the hall. I too should figure out what to wear. The lion's share of my wardrobe is activewear, and even most of that is in storage. I did have the good sense to keep my Armani suit with me in case I needed it for an interview, thus making the decision easy for me.

I text Tony again.

Me: Headed to City Hall in a bit to finalize this thing. Any progress on the paperwork?

I'm sure it's not a big deal to go forth with this project. If there was any reason why I shouldn't, Tony would've called me. It took him virtually nanoseconds to send over a draft contract. I hope the delay in the final copy doesn't indicate a complication.

I send another text to Coach Janssen.

Me: I'll have an update about the citizenship thing by the end of the week. Things are chugging along, and it should be smooth sailing.

Janssen: Good to hear. Front office is just waiting on your paperwork.

Me: Hopefully soon. Good luck next week.

The Buzzards are in the championship game. Envy floods me. Why couldn't I have been sacked with Janssen and Kenley? Then I too would be on my way to the championship, instead of moving heaven and earth to play one more game.

Janssen: We're having a small reception tonight at The Tower for the media. You should stop by.

There's so much weight to this. When someone from the organization makes this suggestion, it's not actually a suggestion. And media.

Things must've progressed faster than I'd realized. Perhaps no news is good news.

And speaking of news, I glance toward the bedroom door where I can hear Ophelia and Marley giggling. I'm sure I don't even want to take a gander at what's going on in there. My phone buzzes again.

Ophelia: I have my great-grandmother's ring if you want to use that for me. I'll get you one as soon as I can.

Bugger. I hadn't even thought about that.

Ophelia: Only because Marley will ask. I'm going to go to the bathroom in a minute. I'll leave the ring on your toothbrush.

I glance around and the inflatable mattress immediately catches my eye. That's sure to draw suspicion. I deflate it and roll it up, shoving it behind my pile of suitcases in the corner.

I hear the bedroom door open and close, and then the bathroom one. After a few moments, I hear the reverse. I call, a little more loudly than necessary, "If you don't mind, I'm going to get dressed right now. I'll just use the bathroom since Marley is here."

I see the delicate gold ring on my toothbrush, as promised. It's plain, a small cloudy solitaire on a gold band. I can do better than this. I have to do better than this. No one would believe that I would give this to the woman I love.

It's noon now. Perhaps I can make this work. Pulling out my phone, I do a quick search for jewelers near us. I find one down Beacon Street. Immediately I order an Uber. I call to the girls, "Going out for a bit, be back by two at the latest."

Once in the car, I send another text to Tony.

Me: I'm buying her a ring. You need to include in the contract that she keeps it.

It's only fair. She's doing a lot for me.

I send another text to Coach Janssen.

Me: I'd love to stop by. Is it okay if I bring a date?

I should have typed my wife, as we'll be married by then.

Wife.

My stomach clenches into a tight fist and small beads of perspiration dot my forehead. What'm I doing? This whole thing is bloody barmy.

It's my last chance to play football.

In for a penny, in for a pound.

I dash across Beacon Street, donning my mask as I walk into the store. I must look like a fool because an elderly gentleman flocks to me, ready to separate me from my money.

"What can I help you with today?"

"I'm sorry, but I need a ring. A wedding ring. Or engagement ring? I bloody don't know. I'm getting married in a few hours." The words feel like marbles in my mouth. The mask isn't helping.

"That'll be no problem. We have some in this case here that are ready to sell, but we also have estate rings on consignment. What size do you need?"

Size? This is a detail that should have occurred to me, but it didn't. Hell, I didn't even think about a ring until about thirty minutes ago. Wait! Her grandmum's ring is in my pocket. I fish it out.

"This is hers. Well, it's her grandmum's, but we were going to use it. Except, well, it's not a very nice diamond."

The jeweler, Gregory, asks to see the ring. He dons one of those eye magnifying glasses like you see in a James Bond movie. "That's because this is a white sapphire, not a diamond. Based on the age of the ring, it's definitely natural and not synthetic. Are you looking to trade this?"

"Heavens, no. I simply wanted to get her something ..." I falter. Nicer? Hers? "I'm not sure it's her style, but I know it has sentimental value."

"What is her style?"

It's a simple question. One a fiancé would know. Should know. Yet, I'm standing here like a nob. I've not seen Ophelia in anything besides pajamas and lounge clothes, other than the jeans and hoodie she was wearing that night in Baltimore. Hardly enough to tell her style. Instead, I fill the void with everything I know about her.

"She's romantic and impulsive and not too stuck on her appearance. I do believe she's genuinely a good person. Caring and giving, perhaps to a fault. But definitely romantic at heart."

That's not a whole lot to go on.

"Oh, and she loves all things British."

"Naturally," Gregory replies. "I can see why." He puts his finger up to his chin as his gaze darts around the store. "Oh wait! I've got the perfect solution." He dashes off to a glass counter on the opposite side of the store where he carefully extracts something. "Voila! This is what you need. This blue sapphire ring guard will enhance her grandmother's white sapphire, without detracting from the stone as brilliant diamonds would. These are marquis cut sapphires which tend to have a feminine and romantic feel, and they blend nicely with the original ring."

He puts the two together, and I know he's right. "Sold. That was easy."

Gregory whisks both pieces off to the back to clean and polish them. About ten minutes later, the sparkling set is nestled snugly in a ring box in my breast pocket, where it feels like ten stone against my heart.

"I hope your bride-to-be likes this. Please remember us for all your future needs."

If I weren't in this suit, I'd consider running back to Ophelia's place. I need to do something to burn off some of this feeling churning in the pit of my stomach.

I pull out my phone and call my parents. I need some sage advice. NDA or no, if I don't tell someone, I'm going to absolutely rupture.

"Hullo?" It's Philip. Great. He's not going to be of any help. Mostly because he thinks I'm a nob and the feeling is quite mutual most of the time.

"Mum or Dad in?"

"Hullo to you too. Both out," he grumbles. It sounds as if he's got a mouthful of food.

Bollocks.

"Well, I need to talk to them. To someone."

"You got me, you bloody eejit." Brotherly love at its finest.

"Do you know when they'll be back?"

"Nah. Out in the aviary. Someone brought in a barn owl with a broken wing. They're looking after it."

"Why aren't you out there? That's your specialty." My voice is rising. Why isn't Philip pulling his weight there? I'm here, literally selling my soul and country, to make sure they have what they need. And Philip is relaxing in the house while our parents are out in the cold aviary tending to an injured, and no doubt surly, bird. "This is reprehensible, Philip. You are supposed to be running the show, not letting Mum and Dad do everything while you sit back and stuff your face."

"No need to throw a wobbly. I've been out there for the better part of two days straight. I just came in to clean up and get a quick bite. Now, are you going to tell me what's got your knickers in a twist? It's obvious you didn't ring for a straight chinwag."

I exhale, covering my eyes with my hand. "Oh Philip, it's a disaster. I'm getting married in about two hours, to a bird I hardly know. She's agreed to help me out so I can become a US citizen." Saying it out loud makes me want to retch.

"Being a US citizen would be infinitely better for your career, no? You're not playing back here anytime soon, so what's the problem?"

"Right, but marrying a total stranger? Doesn't that seem extreme?"

I can hear his sigh from all the way across the Atlantic. "Brother, your whole life has been extreme. Do you think most people play football the way you do? You've given up your friends and family, your social life, and even your name and reputation for the chance to chase a ball around a field. So this is one more sacrifice in a long line of sacrifices. It would seem foolish to give it all up now. As if all of that was for nothing."

I'm speechless for a moment. Philip's never been my biggest fan. Or fan at all, for that matter. Yet here he is, giving me sound and solid advice.

"Sorry about the comments earlier. I know you work hard there. The birds are lucky you take such good care of them."

"Eh, I'd rather be with them than people anyway. Ain't got no use for most people."

"Myself included, I believe."

He ignores that comment. "As for the marriage thing, treat it like you would your playbook. You follow the script. You know the tactical moves. You know when to strike. This is another offensive move that will brush right past the defense."

Philip's words are starting to make sense. I need to do what I have to do to play, and that means having a convincing enough marriage to grant me citizenship.

There's a grunt from the other end of the line, which is Philip's usual way of dismissing the conversation. "Right then. Thanks for the advice. It's actually quite helpful."

I need to go into this marriage like I would a game. Tactical and prepared.

It's time to get my bride her bouquet.

CHAPTER 25: OPHELIA

Is it bad luck to wear black to a wedding?" I ask hopefully. My closet is not offering much in the way of a solution and the minutes are ticking by. At this rate, I'm going to show up at City Hall naked.

I can almost guarantee that'll cause exactly the kind of scandal Xavier wants to avoid.

"If you're the bride it is. Don't you have *anything* that isn't black?" Marley's rear end is only partially visible, as she's head first in the depths of my closet. "Also, I feel like I'm in some sort of alternate universe. You. A bride. I still don't know how this happened. Are you sure? Like sure you're sure?"

I lie back on my bed and cover my face with my hands. Sundance takes this as an opportunity to pounce onto my stomach and start making biscuits. Seeing as how he weighs seventeen pounds, this feels like he's trying to give me CPR or the Heimlich over and over.

"I have a light ivory cable knit, but there's a good possibility that it has coffee stains down the front of it, and yes, I'm sure, so stop questioning me. We only have about three hours to transfer me into a blushing bride."

Marley's head pops out of the closet, eying me warily. It's time to lay it on thick.

"Marl, I can't even explain how it happened. We chatted one night—all night—and the next day he was on a train to see me. You know how they say 'when you know, you know?' Well, we just *knew*. There's no sense in waiting."

Her eyes narrow, "onsidering my words.

"And this time, it's not me being impulsive and stupid. He wants to marry *me*. He sees who I am, beyond my messes, and still wants *me*. How can I not love that?"

Marley harrumphs. "You are wonderful. I don't know why it's taken someone so long to see it."

She's coming around. At least I hope she is. I stare at my ceiling and silently beg the universe to make her see it my way. I know she's turned the corner when she says, "You are *not* getting married in a sweater, let alone one with stains. How do you not have any white dresses?"

I lift my head to see her over the mound of yellow cat on my stomach. "See previous comment about spilling coffee. Also, I'm pasty white as a baseline, so white's not the best color on me. It looks so much better on you. That's why you always get white."

As soon as I say it, Marley lets out a dramatic groan. "Arrgh. Why didn't we think of it sooner? I'll be back as soon as I can. Get to work on your hair." Marley looks for her shoes, which may have disappeared into the abyss of clothes that now cover most of the bedroom floor. "And pick up this mess, because you don't want to have your wedding night in this chaos."

While my curling iron's heating up, I shove my clothes back into the closet. I'll worry about those later. It's been ages since I've curled my hair, though this is a pricey curling iron I was compelled to buy during the height of the first lockdown, mostly because everyone on ClikClak said it was revolutionary.

About every other curl is coming out well. The others, yikes. I may have to fall back on some of the other hairstyles ClikClak told me about, most of which involve flipping the hair through itself and twisting it around.

By the time Marley comes bursting back through my door, I've managed to get my hair into a purposefully messy chignon that looks elegant and romantic. A few face-framing pieces and a pound of hairspray, and I'm good to go, at least with that.

"I brought these three." Marley waves a garment bag. "I hope one will work."

I wasn't kidding when I said white was her color. It's stunning on her bronze skin.

There's a long sheath dress with a cowl neck that's too long on me. There's a lacy summer two-piece jumpsuit that looks totally inappropriate for the occasion. Not to mention the pants are about six inches too long for me.

But then I see it.

"Where'd you get this?" I can't take my eyes off the last dress.

"I wore that for a homecoming in high school. I was afraid if I left it at home, Mom would donate it to Goodwill, and it was my favorite of all my fancy dresses."

Even on the hanger, I couldn't have asked for a better dress. The top is shiny silver with spaghetti straps, while the skirt is white organza. "I hope it fits."

I don't know what I'll do if it doesn't.

"It should. I was smaller back then. Go try it on."

I rush to the bathroom, my hands shaking as I zip the zipper. It's a little snug, but I can get through the afternoon in it. The neckline plunges enough to be sexy without making me look trashy.

But the best part is that it's totally giving me Keira Knightly vibes. She wore something with a similar skirt when she got married, though I think hers was Chanel Haute Couture.

I walk out of the bathroom and twirl. "It's perfect."

Marley clasps her hands to her chest. "It's perfect," she agrees. "I can't believe you're actually getting married. I can't believe this is all happening."

While normally I'd beg her to come, I'm nervous about how it would all play out in front of her. I'm not that good of an actress. If this were real though, I'd never be able to do it without Marley by my side.

"I know. I've … I've never felt this way before." Totally insane that is. "We just knew and, I don't know, it seems like the most romantic thing ever." I work on my makeup so I don't have to look at my best friend.

Somehow it's easier to lie to her if I'm not making eye contact.

Marley finishes picking up my clothes, even going so far as to hang some up. She pulls a pair of strappy silver heels out of my closet. "I think these will work."

And suddenly, even though it's a fake marriage, I don't want to get married without my ride-or-die there. "You have to come. I want to share this with you too. You have to be there."

Marley squeals and I squeal, and then I return to finishing my makeup. We're too busy squealing to notice Xavier standing in the doorway. It's not until he clears his throat, scaring the bejeezus out of us, that we even realize he's back.

By the way, when you're trying to put lipstick on and someone startles you, there's about a one hundred percent chance you're going to end up drawing way outside the lip line.

This has never happened to Julia Roberts. Though it would totally have happened to Hugh Grant if he wore lipstick.

"Marley's going to come with us," I say, not making eye contact as I dab at the pink streak on my cheek.

"Actually, I can't. I want to, but I have to get back to work. Can you go after I get off? I don't want to miss this."

It occurs to me that it's the middle of the day on Thursday. "No, the appointments are super limited and with the holidays coming up, it was either this one or wait until January. And how did you get here now? It's the middle of the day."

"I told them I had a doctor's appointment, but I have to get back. Tessa is out sick, and I have to assist

Dr. Simmons with his in-office procedures. There's no one else to prepare his sterile fields and clean up." She sticks out her bottom lip. "If it were any other day …"

I hang my head for a moment. I know Marley can't drop everything. There are patients who have actual real needs, not just my pretend wedding. Still, I'd feel better with her there.

Marley gives me a quick hug goodbye, taking care not to mess my face or hair. "Xavier, can I talk to you for a second?" she asks, as she walks by him.

Knowing Marley, she's going to threaten him into taking care of me. I shouldn't be surprised. Marley designated herself as my mother hen when we first met. I look around the room and realize it's neater than when we started. Yup. That's Marley for you.

Xavier returns to the doorway, a slight flush on his cheeks.

He looks me up and down, and if I'm not mistaken, I see his jaw go a little slack. "You look quite smashing. Lovely. Truly lovely." He clears his throat. "Uh, are you ready to leave? There's a fee if we're late, and we're the last appointment of the day."

Heat fills my cheeks at his compliment. I don't think he's ever even commented on my appearance before. "I just need my earrings." I put in a pair of shiny cubic zirconia studs, and then I do a little twirl. "What else do we need?"

Xavier is reading from his phone. "The marriage license we'll get there, ID, money, and masks. And it looks as if your friend wouldn't be allowed in anyway. No guests."

"That stinks. I'm so over this whole COVID thing. But at least I'm not one of those brides who spent thousands on a wedding only to have it canceled. I never anticipated a wedding at all."

But as I say it, I start to think about all the wedding things I won't have. Like my dad giving me away and cake and …

"I can't say I did either. Certainly not like this. But you can't have a proper wedding without this." Xavier pulls a small bouquet of white flowers out from behind his back. The roses, lily of the valley, and greenery are absolutely perfect. I press my lips together, unable to form words.

This is the most romantic thing anyone has ever done for me.

This is *definitely* going in the book as a gesture to win over the heroine. I hurry to film a few seconds, close enough that you can't tell it's a bouquet, and post to ClikClak with the caption, "Flowers from a boy" #xoxo. If it's on my feed, I'll remember to write it down in my notebook tonight when we get back.

We're not even married yet, and the book is practically writing itself.

"We ready to go?" Xavier asks, donning a long coat over his blue suit. I'm not going to lie, I think he may look hotter in the suit than he does in the towel. Okay, not really, but the suit is a close second. Maybe I can take a picture of him to use on the cover of a book. He's totally dreamy enough.

I open the hall closet where my raspberry wool dress coat hangs. I've had it since college and hardly ever wear it anymore, but it seems wrong to put my Northface puffer on over this beautiful dress.

"Let's grab an Uber. You're too clean to ride the T. Plus those shoes don't look sensible for walking."

Once we slide into the back of the car, I look at my ClikClak to see the notifications for my last video. It's not viral—yet—but it's getting there. I should have made one of those time-lapse videos counting down the time to our wedding.

Xavier also has his phone out. "Let's do one for Instagram." He pulls his mask down and I do the same. I slide in close to him as he reaches around me to get the selfie. My flowers are perfectly blurred at the bottom of the picture. I don't look half bad myself. I mean, I'm not on his level, nor will I ever be, but I am reminded that if I put in a little effort, I'm rather pretty.

I hope he thinks so too. Not like it matters.

It's not like he's really my fiancé or anything. This isn't my real wedding. If it were, I'd have a bouquet of hydrangeas, not roses. And Marley would be here. So would my parents and brothers. My dad would be beaming with pride and my mother would be wiping her mascara away with her tears of sheer joy. My gown would be long and would not be borrowed and would not be so tight that it makes it hard to breathe.

And the man I would be marrying would actually love me.

But I don't get my dream wedding. I should enjoy this because it's all I may ever have.

Suddenly my eyes are full of tears. I pull my mask back up and stare out the window, trying to blink them back.

This is without a doubt the stupidest thing I've ever done.

CHAPTER 26: XAVIER

If I didn't know better, I'd say Ophelia is crying. Or at least trying not to cry. Bollocks.

I don't know what I did, but more importantly, I don't know how to make her stop. Marley's not-so-gentle words echo through my head.

You'd better treat her right because she is the most wonderful person on the face of the earth.

There was also a not-so-thinly veiled threat to remove my manhood from my body should I break Ophelia's heart like "all the other losers she wasted time on" did. Fine. It was an outright threat with awful details including a pair of pliers and a long needle.

I'm glad Ophelia has someone like Marley looking out for her. I'm slightly disturbed as well, but Marley's concern and caring for Ophelia came through in her threats. Ophelia needs that. She, from what I can tell, wears her heart on her sleeve way too often to avoid the heartbreak that accompanies it.

Without warning, I feel very protective of her. I want to take her in my arms and tell her not to cry. But I can't do that. That would be too real.

And all of a sudden, this has become infinitely more complicated. It did seem too easy, all of this falling into place. I've never been one to rush through things, but the past three weeks have been at warp speed.

And now Ophelia's in tears.

I reach out, my hand hovering over her bare knee for a moment, but decide that's entirely too familiar. I let my fingers rest on her forearm. "You alright, love?"

She doesn't turn back to look at me, her gaze transfixed out the window. I snap a quick picture of her. It's rare that she's not smiling.

I don't think I care for it at all.

I clear my throat. "Right, so you spoke with the clerk, and we're all set to get the marriage license immediately?"

Her hair bobs up and down, indicating a nod of agreement, but she remains silent. I put my hand back on her arm. "Ophelia, what's going on?"

Finally, she turns to face me, her eyes dull. "It's nothing. I'm fine."

"If you say so." She's obviously lying, but I'm not going to push her. God strike me down, but I don't want her changing her mind. Not with Coach Janssen wanting me at the event tonight.

I should probably mention that to her, but the Uber has come to a stop in front of a large brick plaza leading up to a cold concrete building that looks totally out of place with the historic charm of the city.

I give Ophelia my hand as she slides out of the car. Once on the plaza, I tuck her arm in mine, as she's wearing ridiculous shoes that women like to wear and that are no match for the crevices.

She's a broken ankle waiting to happen.

Though they do wonderful things for her legs. And I thought she had quite nice legs to begin with.

After a moment she says, "You know, I've walked by here and through here getting to the Government Center T stop, but I never really thought about going in this building."

"Well, I believe today will hold a lot of firsts for us." I give her a smile, hoping she'll return it.

"I just never thought this is how I'd be getting married," she says, barely audible above the din of the city.

Ah, that explains the tears.

I have to give her one last chance to pull out. I don't know what I'll do if she does, but I also can't coerce her into anything. "I do appreciate this, Ophelia. I hope you know that. I still don't know why you've agreed to help me, especially since you've dreamed of more sentimental things. You don't have to go through with this."

She stops, midway up the wide granite steps, her arm dropping from mine. "You see, Xavier, that's the problem. My whole life I've wanted it all. An exciting career and a great romantic love story. I've done tons of stupid things trying to craft it for myself. I'm thirty years old, and I don't think I've ever even been in love. I've certainly never been loved. So for once, I'm not trying to create a romance. I know that Hugh Grant or Colin Firth is not going to come swooping in and sweep me off my feet. I have to accept that my imagination wants the great adventure, but it's not my reality. So this will do. Let's face it, it's more than I'd ever get otherwise."

I feel a tightness in my chest that hasn't been there since I lost my spot on the National Team. "You can't possibly mean that. You can't give up."

She looks down and shrugs. "I make really stupid decisions when left to my own devices. Hell, that's why we're here, isn't it? I'm too impulsive for my own good. I'm much better off taking the safe route like I did with my career. You're safe. There's no risk here, and no chance to make an ass out of myself."

"You sure?" One more chance.

Ophelia nods and pulls up her mask. "Let's do this."

I pull up my mask as we walk up the rest of the stairs and into the brick lobby. "City Clerk, sixth floor," I tell the security guard as we walk through the metal detectors. Nothing says romance like being checked for weapons. I let Ophelia go first, so she doesn't see the ring box that I put into the bin with my cell phone and wallet.

After the elevator, we follow the signs to the clerk's office, which is a window separated by plexiglass. Ophelia says, "You know, early in the pandemic, they weren't even doing weddings here. And the ones that had already been scheduled, they did in a hallway. So we're lucky we can do this."

Having to marry a stranger to save my failing career doesn't feel the luckiest.

The clerk pushes a stack of paperwork on a clipboard through the slot. "You have to fill out the marriage license paperwork first. It'll be $150 to expedite this, and you both need to sign here and here that this is voluntary on both your parts. Take a clean pen."

Ophelia giggles. "I know you can't see all of his face with the mask on, but trust me, I really want to do this."

I try not to roll my eyes. We go and sit down on some chairs in the hall. "Laying it on a bit thick, aren't you?" I whisper.

"In case she gets questioned by immigration or TMZ," she says, not taking her eyes off the paperwork. Her pen is poised in mid-air, not making contact with the paper.

"Is there a problem?" She hasn't moved in at least a minute. I know she's literate. Her apartment is filled with books, most with shirtless men or cartoon people on the covers. It doesn't take a rocket scientist to know she reads a lot of romance.

"I don't know what to write here." She taps the line. I lean over her shoulder and instantly smell lilac, even through my mask. It makes me think of the hedgerows at the front of the property at home, bursting forth with pinks and purples, signaling spring. I shake my head and focus on where she's stumped.

Last name.

"What should I put?"

I pull back, raising my eyebrow. "Don't women usually take the husband's name?"

Ophelia's eyes narrow. "We don't have time for a history lesson on the patriarchal and misogynistic suppression of women right now."

I raise my hands in defense. "Right, point taken. Do what you want to do. No pressure here."

In all honesty, it's not something I've ever thought about. I'm guessing most men would say the same thing. It's not my decision to make.

"It's just, I'm Ophelia Finnegan. It's who I am."

"Then stay Ophelia Finnegan."

"But if I don't change my name, will it draw suspicion? It's so much more legit if I take your name. I mean, who would get married and change their last name if they weren't really in love?"

She seems so much more concerned about fooling the authorities than I am. I'm not the first athlete to do something like this, and I probably won't be the last. Perhaps I'm naive, but I can't imagine, with all that's going on in the world, the government spending its time and resources to track me down. It's not like I'm violating my visa or anything. I'm simply accelerating my path to citizenship.

"I can't predict whether or not we'll draw government scrutiny. I don't have a say in this matter. It's totally up to you." But even as I say it, I know I'm lying. I want her to take my name.

But I don't know why.

Nor do I have time to examine this feeling.

She sighs, scribbling what will be her new moniker. Her forehead creases into a frown as she stares at what she's written.

Ophelia Henry.

"Oh."

"What is it?"

"My initials. They're going to be O.H. Oh. O. Henry."

Like the candy bar. I haven't thought about those in years. The name makes me smile. "Those were the best."

Ophelia looks at me like I have three heads. "What? Isn't O. Henry a poet or something?"

I shrug. "Perhaps? But I'm talking about Oh Henry! The candy bar. I don't know if you can even get them anymore, but when I was a kid, I loved them. I tried to tell people they were named after my family, but then *Seinfeld* did a whole storyline with a character who was the heir to the Oh Henry! fortune, and it ruined it for me when it ran in syndication back home. But not the candy. That was still scrumptious. I mean, chocolate fudge, peanuts, and caramel, all coated with chocolate. I don't know if I loved them because of the taste or the name, but they were my absolute fav."

I should probably shut my trap. Here we are, rushing against the clock to get married, and I'm wagging on about a childhood treat.

"That sounds delicious. Okay, fine, I'll be Ophelia Henry." She wrinkles her nose as she says this.

I put my hand on hers. "Remember, it's temporary. You don't have to be Ophelia Henry forever."

She looks up at me, her eyes deep and serious. "I know. It's just …"

"I know. Not what you had planned. Trust me, this wasn't my script either. I never thought …"

"Are you two done yet?" the clerk calls, her Boston accent heavy.

Ophelia jumps up. "Yup. We're all set. We were just …" she looks back at me, "trying to process the moment."

"Process when you're not on the clock. Judge Mahoney leaves at four-thirty."

I glance at my watch. It's already ten 'til four. "Right." She processes our paperwork, takes our payment, and then points to a door at the end of the hall.

We head through the door and into an empty room. There are stacks of chairs against the wall and a white floor runner down the middle. At the end of the aisle is a large sheet of plexiglass on a stand, like a mirror, but transparent. I suppose in non-COVID times, the room would be set up to accommodate a few guests. Instead, it's rather depressing.

Ophelia is looking around, her shoulders slumped. Yes, I agree, this whole thing is a downer. Of course, that's how my life has been ever since I got into that car with Phaedra Jones. This is simply one more thing.

Judge Mahoney comes in, wearing an ill-fitting gray suit and tie, his mask down around his chin. He heads behind the plexiglass. "Okay, you're my last. Let's make this quick. You can take your masks off if you want to."

Both Ophelia and I remove our masks, and she slides out of her coat. We step to the end of the aisle and wait for Judge Mahoney to begin. He reads in a monotone voice, not looking up from his papers. "Xavier," he begins. Due to his local accent, it sounds more like Xa-vya. It actually reminds me of how my dad says my name. "And Ophelia. You come in today as two individuals but will leave as one. As you stand here before your friends and famil—Dammit, Charity, she was supposed to give me the updated version." He swears under his breath.

He continues to drone on. I should pay attention, but all I can do is look at Ophelia. Her gaze remains on the floor, and her hands clutch the small bouquet so hard her knuckles match her dress.

I'm not sure where Judge Mahoney got this script from, but it can definitely use a once-over. Or a thrice over. He speaks so fast that I can barely process his words. I'm grateful because if I could hear what he was saying about love and commitment and relationships, I'd probably bolt faster than my fifty-yard dash.

Xavier Henry, how did you break the world record for speed?

Running away from a sham of a marriage meant to ensure I can keep playing football.

"Uh, Xavier, do you take, um, Ophelia to be your lawfully wedded wife? In good times and in bad, in sickness and in health, until parted by death?"

I finally hear his words but feel as if there's a large wad of cotton in my throat.

This is bloody ridiculous. I can't go through with this.

Judge Mahoney coughs.

Ophelia is staring at me, her eyes wide and huge. I see her head nod ever so slightly. In for a penny, in for a pound.

"Right. Yes. I do. Of course."

When it's her turn for vows, I know I should maintain eye contact, but I can't seem to keep my gaze from wandering around the room. Though this has all moved faster than a forward with only one defenseman to get by, it doesn't make the situation any less serious. Philip was right. I've sacrificed so much for this sport. To feel the adrenaline coursing through my veins when I'm on the field. To push my body to the point of breaking—and beyond. To win.

And now simply, to play.

Softly, I hear Ophelia say, "I do."

Finally, I meet her gaze. Her eyes, which are normally sparkling and full of life, seem listless and dull.

This is a terrible mistake. I shouldn't make her do this.

"Then by the power vested in me by the state of Massachusetts, I now pronounce you husband and wife. You may kiss the bride."

Bollocks.

CHAPTER 27: OPHELIA

It would not be romantic if I vomited on Xavier as he leans in to kiss me.

On the other hand, there is nothing about this that is romantic. Despite the pretty dress and the flowers, this is about as romantic as dental work.

Hell, at least at the dentist, there is physical contact.

I'm not saying I want Xavier to touch me—though I might not be opposed—but there should be touching at a wedding. Or at least after.

And now we're supposed to kiss? Other than a few brief hand grabs to pull me along, we've never even hugged. I'm definitely more intimate with my dental hygienist.

This is not like any wedding I've ever imagined. No music. No family. No love. No march down the aisle or something old, something new. I mean, I guess I did borrow my dress, and his eyes are blue, a lighter shade than my own. My grandmother's ring covers the old and—hey, wait a minute!

"Hey, where's my ring?" I blurt as soon as the thought pops into my brain. If he lost it, I'm going to be livid.

"Oh, right. Right." Xavier frantically begins patting his chest. He reaches inside his breast pocket and pulls out a small burgundy box.

Where the hell did he get a ring box from?

But then he opens it. I see my grandmother's ring, sparkling in a way I didn't know possible, surrounded by a wrap of blue sapphires. They look like they were made to go together.

Immediately my eyes fill up. He takes them out of the box and looks around. The rings are in one hand, the box in his other, and there's no one to help him out. He tosses the box on the floor so he can use both hands. My left hand is shaking as I hold it out to him. Xavier slides the rings on my fourth finger.

It feels foreign, as I've always reserved that digit for *the one*.

"How did you? When did you? I—"

"Are you two going to kiss or talk all day? Fine, do whatever. You're married." Judge Mahoney turns away and begins to pack up his papers.

Quickly, Xavier leans forward, his hands still holding mine, and gives me the briefest, lightest of kisses on my lips. Just as fast, he straightens.

"Right, then. Are we all set?" he asks the officiant.

"Yep. Remember to put your masks back on. Stupid rules," he mutters before leaving the room.

I can't stop staring at my hand.

"Is it okay? Do you like it? Should I not have done that?"

Thoughts swirl through my brain as emotions fill my chest. I can't seem to come up with the words to fit how I'm feeling.

Maybe because I don't know how I'm feeling.

"It's all … a lot." I drop my hand, reaching for my coat. Once that's on, I shove my fist in the pocket. Out of sight, out of mind. Problem solved.

Xavier's on his phone, typing away. When he looks up, his brows are creased.

"Everything okay?" Somehow, it's easier to worry about how he's doing than think about the chaos in my own brain.

"Just texting Tony. You ready to go?"

As we head down in the elevator, I try to think about something to say. Something to fill this awkward void. We weren't uncomfortable with each other before the ceremony. Some dumb piece of paper shouldn't change that. But still, I just want to crawl into my bed and hide for a little while. "Are we still going to look at apartments tonight? I know we need to, but I'm not really feeling it."

By now, we're standing outside in the dusky November evening. It's closing in on five and there are flocks of people everywhere, leaving their day jobs like it's any other Thursday.

Certainly not their wedding day.

We do get a few glances from passers-by, the bouquet a dead giveaway. I'm sure they're thinking that this couple doesn't look happy. Rather than attempt to fix my face into something it doesn't feel, I put my mask back on in preparation for the T ride home.

Xavier is busy on his phone again. "Bollocks. I forgot about that," he says without looking up. "I can't make it tonight."

"Good. I know we need to figure out the living situation and all, but this is draining, you know? I didn't think I'd have any emotions about it, but unfortunately, I do."

That's enough to make Xavier look up, the color leaving his face. "Ophelia ..."

He doesn't even need to say it—I know what he's thinking. I pull my mask down. "Xavier, it's not like that. I know this isn't real and it's a business thing. I'm fine about it, really. But I just got married for all the wrong reasons, no matter how right they are, and it's nothing like I'd thought it would be my whole life. I'm okay with today, but it's just ..."

"Yeah, this is definitely not where I saw my life going either. Nonetheless, we're here, and we should make the best of it. But that's not what I was going to tell you. I can't look at flats tonight because I was invited to a reception for the Buzzards."

"Oh, did your trade go through? That's awesome. I know you said it was time-sensitive, but this is ridiculously fast. Well, you have fun. Should I expect you home tonight? I mean, not home, home. It's not like I'm keeping tabs on you. You can do whatever you want. You can see whomever you choose."

I need to shut up before I start channeling my inner Sinead O'Connor.

Xavier laughs. "No, it's not official, but this is a very good sign. I was wondering if you'd like to join me. It's not a true wedding night, but we should at least let the Buzzards give us some cocktails and hors d'oeuvres." He looks at his phone. "Actually, it doesn't start for a little while. Let's go get a celebratory drink in the meantime."

"You don't have to drag me along. I can just go home."

Xavier links his arm through mine. "Nonsense, Ophelia. I wouldn't have this opportunity, if not for you, so I'm not sending you home. Now, tell me, where should we go get a drink?"

I glance around. "We should probably just head over toward Faneuil Hall. There's plenty of places over there. Where is the reception?"

We start to walk past City Hall, up and over the steps to head toward our destination.

"The Tower. Arlington Street."

"Okay, that's Back Bay. We can take the Green Line from here."

"We can get an Uber."

"You don't like the T much, do you?" Xavier must spend a fortune on cars. I'm still living with the mentality of a broke college student, even though I'm not. An Uber or taxi is my last resort.

"Not particularly. Especially not when I have to navigate them by myself."

A pigeon lollygags around in front of me, not caring that he's in my way. As I always do, I speed up without picking my feet up, to create a loud shuffle that scares the feathered fiend into the air.

"What was that about?"

"I was afraid he wasn't going to move." It seems a better answer than telling him about my ornithophobia. He'll find out all the crazy details about me soon enough.

"I'm fairly confident he would have."

"I'm not that confident."

"Birds hardly ever run into people. Moving vehicles, well that's another story." Xavier shakes his head somberly. It's almost like he has sympathy for these harbingers of doom.

"Maybe where you're from. Here, Boston pigeons are like drivers. Full of moxie and sick of everyone's shit. Where are you from, by the way? I feel like a good wife should know this."

"A good wife should. I'm from Gloucester."

I nod like I know where that is. The only one I know about is about forty minutes north of here, and it's a good place to get lobster. I make a mental note to look up the Gloucester he's referring to later, so I don't seem like an idiot.

More of an idiot.

He continues. "I originally played football for the Bristol Bombers, which is practically my hometown team. They're part of the BFL. The British Football League. It was tremendous, being able to play for the team I grew up watching and idolizing. A real dream come true." His voice is wistful, and he looks as if he's a million miles away.

"Then how did you end up in Baltimore, and why are you so desperate to be traded to Boston?"

My words are enough to snap him out of his reverie.

"That's a story that needs to be told over a pint."

We walk the next block in silence and head to the first bar we see, which happens to be the Sam Adams Taproom. I'm not much of a beer person, so I'm thrilled to see a fruity hard seltzer on tap. Xavier orders some beer. I have no idea what he picks. He seems content with it.

"Okay, you've got your pint. Now spill the tea."

"Right." He takes a long pull from his glass and then proceeds to fidget with his phone without saying anything. As I take a sip of my drink, Xavier snaps a picture.

"What was that for?"

"Instagram. Seemed like a good candid moment." He taps away and then my phone pings with the notification.

Truly lovely. @opheliaxoxo

My heart skips a beat. Then I realize what he did. A pun on my beverage, Truly seltzer, with the location tagged. It's not a bad picture. I smile back at him. "Flattering me on social media won't get you out of the story."

"Right. Okay then." Xavier looks out the window at the busy Quincy Market as he speaks. "A little over five years ago, everything was coming together. I was a starter on the Bristol Bombers, and I think I've already mentioned how chuffed I was to be playing for the hometown team. But also, I'd been named to the British National Team for the Global Games. This was it. Everything I'd ever dreamed of. Every sacrifice was worth it because I was living it finally."

I try to mentally commit his expression to memory. I can see the hero in my book with the same look—wistfulness, pride, hurt—as he confesses something, though I don't know what yet, to the heroine.

He continues. "Edmund Jones is the president of the BFL and responsible for the National Team. You do not want to get on his bad side." Xavier raises an eyebrow.

"I'm guessing you got on his bad side? How?"

Xavier takes another sip of his beer and then offers me a weak smile. "Jones's daughter, Phaedra, was a frequent participant in official BFL activities. A real socialite if you will."

I get a pit in my stomach even imagining where this is going. Xavier's not mine, and this is all in the past anyway, but hearing about him and a woman makes me feel uncomfortable. It shouldn't, but it does.

He continues, "You know how big football is at home, so she liked having her face seen at all the parties. Perhaps a little too much. And apparently, she'd developed quite the pill problem. This was the last big party before our National Team debut. As I was preparing to leave the party, Phaedra was also leaving. She was quite despondent, not at all acting like herself. When I stopped to ask her if she was okay, she said, 'I'm leaving because no one will miss me if I'm gone.' The way she said it, I was afraid she wasn't just talking about the party."

Now, instead of being jealous, the feeling in my stomach intensifies to full-on worry. This can't be good.

"She wouldn't stop though. She got in her car, and I slid into the passenger's seat, still trying to talk some sense into her. Once she started driving, I finally realized how altered she was, but it was too late. I tried to get her to stop immediately. She finally stopped by crashing into a fence."

"Oh my God! Were you hurt? Was she? Was she killed?"

Xavier looks out the window for a moment. He finishes the rest of his beer. "Nah, we were both lucky. But after the crash, she started sobbing that she would be in big trouble if they found out she was driving, and she begged me to switch seats with her. I felt so badly for her. I had no idea that she'd had a long history of substance abuse and had several traffic infractions already. Her father'd threatened to cut her off if she did it again. So, like a dolt, I switched spots. When the authorities showed up, they called her father. Everyone in England knows who he is. He accused me of trying to kill his precious daughter and promised I'd never kick a ball in Britain again. Before dawn, I was let go from both the National Team and the Bombers. No one in the entire bloody country would even take my calls."

I reach out and put my hand on his. "I'm so sorry. And if you get cut from the Terrors ..."

"That's it. That's all she wrote. So the fact that Coach Janssen has asked me to come to this reception tonight is a bloody good sign. There will be media there, so for all intents and purposes, he's saying that the Buzzards are interested. I truly appreciate the vote of confidence. I would simply feel better if it was a firm deal in writing. Speaking of which," he pulls out his phone again, "I can't believe Tony hasn't texted me back yet. Where the bloody hell is he?"

Suddenly, Xavier notices my hand on his. He flips his over and gives mine a quick squeeze before withdrawing it. "But that's the past and this chance with the Buzzards is my last. I've got to do everything right, including staying out of even the slightest hint of impropriety."

"I'm about the least controversial person you'll meet. I mean, I'm an accountant. There's nothing exciting about that. I mean, other than my momentary status on ClikClak, but I'm sure that will die off as quickly as it started."

Xavier smiles. "As long as you're not running a pyramid scheme or anything like that."

I hold up three fingers. "I promise, Girl Scouts honor. No pyramids here. What you see is what you get. You know that. I'm not a schemer or social climber."

"I hope not. I just need to get through this without making a scene. No negative press. I can't afford it."

"I'll be on my best wallflower behavior tonight. I'm not one of those socialite girls, in case you couldn't tell." That makes me think. "Whatever happened to Phaedra?" I'm thrilled to be able to say that name out loud. It's so very British and posh, and I've never had the chance to work it into casual conversation before.

"Nothing. It was all over the news that I was driving and that I'd been drinking that night. The media had me pegged as a bad-boy party animal athlete, and if you listened to Edmund Jones spin it, an attempted murderer. As far as I know, Phaedra never went to rehab or dealt with anything. She walked away scot-free, and I lost everything."

Phaedra just became the ugly mean girl villain in my book. I will never thInk the name is delightful again, no matter how very British it sounds.

No one treats my husband like that and gets away with it.

CHAPTER 28: XAVIER

Three—or four—rounds later, and we're ready to head to The Tower. As we stand to leave, Ophelia picks up her bouquet and our waitress stops dead in her tracks, taking in the full picture of my suit, her white dress, and the flowers.

"Oh my Gawd, did you guys just get married?"

Even in the dim light of the bar, I can see Ophelia blush. She's going to have to get over that, or she's going to give everything away.

Though it is a lovely look on her. Truly lovely indeed.

The folks at the next table overhear and immediately begin clinking their beer glasses with whatever utensils are on their table. Ophelia bites her lip. I slide my hand around her waist and lean in.

"They want us to kiss."

She nods but continues to look around the bar at all the patrons who are watching us expectantly.

I pull her a little closer and turn her body so it's flush with mine. "We can do this."

"We have to do this," she whispers back.

I nod in agreement. Normally I reserve kissing for moments of true intimacy, but that's out the window now. There's no such thing as normal anymore. If there was, I wouldn't be in America, married to a stranger, and about to ditch my British citizenship.

This will be fine. I'll kiss her just long enough to satiate the crowd, and then we'll go back to how we were before.

Friends.

I lean in, feeling her warm breath before our lips meet. I close my eyes and make contact.

This is not what I expected.

Kissing Ophelia should mean nothing. It should feel like nothing. It shouldn't matter.

But in this crowded bar, egged on by strangers and fueled by the best beer that traitor Samuel Adams has to offer, suddenly, it matters.

She matters.

I put my hand on her cheek, cupping her jaw slightly to better the angle of my mouth on hers. I feel, rather than hear, her sigh into my mouth and every shred of self-control I have threatens to leap out the window.

No, this is crazy. It's only a kiss. Lips on lips. Mouths parted. Breath intermingled. Tongues entwined.

But just like that, it's done and there's cold air where her mouth should be and if it weren't for the applause in the bar startling me back to reality, I'd be tempted to do something stupid, like pull her back to me and never let her go.

That would be terribly foolish.

I barely know her. Certainly not enough to have any *feelings* like this.

It's not feelings about her. It's the beer and the adrenaline and the stress of it all. Yes, that's all it could be.

Against my better judgment, I pull her back to me.

I can almost feel her smile against my mouth. She's probably laughing at how ridiculous I am, practically jumping her bones the first chance I get. I don't want her thinking I'm a user, like Trent the Tosser. "Right, now that that's over with, shall we get our Uber?" Without looking at her, I take her hand and lead her toward the door.

I'm on my phone, ordering the car, which is convenient so I don't have to talk to Ophelia at this instant. I'm not sure what I'd even say.

The nondescript Toyota pulls up, and I open the door for my bride. She cocks her head slightly at me but then slides in without saying a word.

My phone pings.

Kenley: I hear you'll be joining us ... tonight.

Xavier: On my way now. Think this is a good sign?

Kenley: It's not a bad one.

Xavier: How can I seal the deal?

Kenley: Keep your nose clean, and show up. And agree to midfield.

I groan.

"Is there a problem?" Ophelia asks quietly.

"They're looking to move me to midfield."

"Okay. What's wrong with that?"

I look at her. She's going to be seen in public, at least a little, and I get the very real, very distinct impression that Ophelia does not know much about my livelihood. "How much do you know about football? Er, soccer."

Her expression can only be described as sheepish. "That you can't pick up the ball with your hands, and that most soccer players have really good butts."

"That's it?"

She nods. "And I only learned the second fact since you came to stay with me."

I will not think about the fact that she's noticed my posterior.

"Right, well, there are three lines, and then the keeper. Forwards, midfield, and full-backs." I can already see her eyes glazing over. "In simple terms, forwards are the offense, full-backs are the defenders. Sometimes they're just called defenders outright. That's the position I play. Left full. And midfielders play both positions. It's a lot more running."

"Who scores?"

"The forwards usually, but occasionally the midfielders."

"So you don't get goals?" Her brow furrows. "Don't you want to? Like isn't that all the glory?"

"I've had some goals. Usually, in a penalty shoot-out. I've got an eighty-seven percent success rate with penalty kicks. But it's not all about the goals. Football is truly a team effort, and we're all out there for the ninety minutes, killing ourselves for the team."

"And you don't like to run? Don't you go running, like, every day?"

"It's not that I don't like to run. In fact, I'm quite fast, which is why they want to move me to midfield. But I'm also older now, and it's a lot more wear and tear on the body."

"How old are you? I feel like I should know that."

"You probably should. I'm twenty-seven. My birthday's in May."

"Oh, does this make me a cougar? I turned thirty in August. I hope that's not too much of a scandal for you."

I laugh, glad Ophelia seems at ease again. "If that's the most scandalous thing, then I think we're all set. We just have to keep the fact that we got married for nefarious reasons off the radar."

Ophelia sighs. "Well, I think some of that might be taken care of."

I glance over to see her on her phone. She holds it up close to her face as if every detail of what she's watching is important. "What is it?"

She turns her phone to me. "Apparently, someone at Sam Adams recognized me. They tagged me in this."

It's us, kissing.

After a moment, watching the five-second clip play several times, I say, "At least it doesn't look fake."

It doesn't. Not at all, and I probably owe Ophelia an apology for getting carried away. I didn't realize I'd used that much tongue. "Look, about what happened..."

Ophelia's watching the video again. "This is perfect, really. I didn't have to post something that could be construed as being fabricated for social media, yet here it is. Do you want me to tag you in the comments?"

"I'm not sure you should respond either way. Perhaps give it a moment." The idea of getting married for the wrong reason is hard enough to swallow. The thought of capitalizing on it for social media benefits turns my stomach.

I glance over at Ophelia, illuminated by the street lights, to see she has a smug expression on her face. "What?" I ask. "What's got you so pleased?"

She looks startled as if she forgot I was sitting right next to her in the back of the Uber. "Oh, nothing, I was just thinking about my … a book. A book I'm reading."

I'm not sure what she's up to, but I'm fairly certain whatever she's thinking about has nothing to do with some fluffy romance novel.

CHAPTER 29: OPHELIA

All I need to do is commit every single moment of this night to memory so I can write it down as soon as I get home. If not the events then my emotions. I try to take occasional notes on my phone, but I don't want to draw suspicion.

I mean, how do you even begin to process a kiss like that?

For the record, it was the kind of kiss I've only ever read about or seen in the movies. I legit thought that toe-curling was hyperbole.

Now I know a toe-curling kiss is a very real thing.

The thing I can't figure out is how he could kiss me like that, so tender yet intense, without meaning it. Because, obviously, he didn't mean it. It wouldn't have even happened if the people in the bar hadn't put us on the spot.

I mean, obviously, Xavier is hot. Like, super hot. That's not even a fact one can debate. And he is actually very thoughtful. A bouquet and a ring? My heart is still fluttering thinking about that. Most guys wouldn't think of those things even with explicit directions. But he's made it clear that he's focused on his career and his career only. This is a business deal for him. The only way he can keep playing, the only thing that matters. He's not looking for more.

It's fine. I don't need more. I just need enough to write my story and get started on that dream. Xavier isn't the only one with career goals.

Out of habit, I check ClikClak again. I've long since turned off the notifications, but I can't help myself from looking to see what people are saying.

Isn't that the #romanticsurprise girl?

Well, she moved on quickly.

What do you expect from an "accountant?"

Xavier married an accountant. I guess the rumors are true.

I'm not sure what my job has to do with getting married quickly, but at least none of the comments are too horrendous.

Seriously, social media makes people mean, yo.

The Uber arrives at The Tower, which is supposed to be one of the premier event locations in Boston. From the outside, it looks like a castle. Once through the heavy oak and gold gilded doors, it's like we're transported into the past. Marble tile, cherry archways, bronze chandeliers, and candles make this easily one of the swankiest places I've ever set foot in. It looks like it could be the set for *The Great Gatsby* or *The Gilded Age*.

In reality, I'm glad I'm wearing my wedding dress, as nothing else I own would have been appropriate for this place.

"Whoa, this is nice," I can't help but whisper.

"There's a lot of money in professional sports, especially when they're trying to get more money from the sponsors," Xavier whispers back.

"The old 'spend money to make money' adage?" I grin as we approach the coat check. I hand over my bouquet as well and rub my bare arms which are now chilly.

Okay, so I might be dressy enough, but I do feel a bit foolish wearing white and silver in the middle of November, especially in the sea of black and navy that every other female here seems to be dressed in.

I'm awkward enough. I don't need any more help standing out in this crowd of highly skilled professional athletes and their supermodel girlfriends. So, in order to ease my unease, I do the most sensible thing possible: I grab a glass of champagne from the waitress passing by.

Considering I've had several hard seltzers at the bar, and the last thing I had to eat was that bowl of Golden Grahams, it's probably not the smartest decision I've ever made.

And this says a lot coming from the woman who had no idea her boyfriend was cheating on her until thousands of strangers pointed it out on social media.

Xavier is glancing around the room, looking as unsettled as I feel.

"Do you know anyone here?" I whisper. From the looks we get from the people standing around us, I think maybe my whisper wasn't as quiet and subtle as I thought it was.

Xavier nods toward a freakishly tall, thin ginger across the room. "That's Kenley. He's the strength and conditioning coach. I roomed with him when I first came to the States. He's a good bloke. I've no doubt he put in a good word for me."

Xavier starts across the room. I don't know if I'm supposed to follow him, or if I'm on my own to mingle and stuff my face. Oh, are those pancetta-wrapped scallops? I snatch one and pop it in my mouth.

It's a little bigger than I'd thought which makes it difficult to chew. Naturally, this is when Xavier turns back to see what I'm doing and jerks his head to indicate I should be coming with him. There's no way I can chew this with elegance and grace, so I do my best to keep my mouth closed and not look like a heathen.

"Ophelia, I'd like you to meet Claude Kenley."

I try to swallow what's in my mouth, so I'm much more focused on that than what I say. "You don't look like a Claude."

The words are out before I can snatch them back. I gasp, and in doing so, inhale a bit of scallop right into my trachea. Xavier turns and stares at me as if he's never seen someone have a piece of shellfish cut off their main airway before.

I may add scallops to my list of creatures I'm afraid are trying to kill me. The only difference is that this mollusk may actually be successful. I almost wish it were truly lodged so someone could Heimlich me. But no, I'm full-on coughing and sputtering.

In other words, I'm making a scene.

"I'm okay," I wheeze, red-faced and spluttering. I'm not totally sure, but there may be part of a chewed-up scallop on the floor now.

Please, dear God, let no one be filming this.

Not that having food go down the wrong pipe is the same type of scandal that Xavier was talking about, but I don't want to mess this up for him. I'm his last chance.

The weight of that realization hits me for the first time, standing in this elegant space decorated with the Buzzards colors of aqua and black. This is a really big deal.

I'm not sure how Xavier could have trusted a virtual stranger with his future like this, but desperate times call for desperate measures.

Still, it's a risk. I could be a wild card.

I mean, we all know I'm not.

I'm such an open book, except for my actual book, that someone who's barely met me feels confident that my life is so boring and safe that they put their multimillion-dollar sports career in my hands.

I start to sweat. Okay, no pressure here. "Are you alright?" Xavier asks. His hand gently rubs my bare upper back, which makes my breath—as irregular as it already is—hitch. Through another round of coughing, I give him two super cheesy thumbs up.

"I'm" —*cough, cough*— "gonna go"—*cough*—"to the restroom. Excuse me." I finish with a loud cough that draws the attention of everyone within a ten-foot radius.

I head to the restroom to regain my composure after almost asphyxiating, as well as to try and prevent the panic attack that is most definitely brewing.

The bathroom is nicer than my apartment. I can't resist. I freshen up my makeup, pull out my phone, and open ClikClak. I film myself with the camera held above and slowly turn to get a panoramic view of the most incredible bathroom this side of Buckingham Palace.

With a voice filter, my own words sound like a movie trailer announcer.

When your date takes you to one of the swankiest joints in town, but you almost die choking on an hors d'oeuvre. But at least you get to use a bathroom that's nicer than most people's homes!

I'm pleased with the results, so I finish up by adding my tags #datenight, #surpriselove, #swanky, and of course, #xoxo.

I'm about to leave when the door flies open and one of the servers rushes in. She slams the door shut and presses her back to it as if barricading out some evil force. She rips off her mask as she mutters "No no no no no," under her breath, obviously unaware that she's not alone in the bathroom.

"Are you okay?" I ask. It's stupid because she's obviously not.

Her head jerks up. "I need to get out of here. I need to leave. I need the earth to swallow me whole right this very instant." She leaves her post at the door and looks wildly around the room. She stands in front of the window, a small rectangle up by the ceiling. "Be honest, do you think I'll fit through there?"

I'm not sure anyone over the age of six would fit through that rectangle, but on the other hand, I don't want her to think I'm calling her fat.

"It can't be that bad." I put my hand on her arm. "Whatever it is, it can't be that bad. And trust me, I've done tons of super embarrassing stuff in my life. This moment will pass, and trying to squeeze out an opening the size of a vagina is not necessary." And then, because I'm a dumbass and I've had too much to drink and I'm awkward, I *keep talking*. "I mean, hell, I just married a man I barely know. But that's me, the good little wifey. Anything to support his career."

Maybe I can flush myself down the toilet.

The server looks up, her big brown eyes wide. "You got married?"

"Yeah, like literally a few hours ago. I'm not saying it was wrong or I'd take it back, but you know, we all do questionable things sometimes. You'll live."

She jerks her head toward the door. "Did you marry one of these guys? One of the Buzzards."

A growing sense of fear travels up my spine. I'm not sure if I'm supposed to say anything. Like, it's not a done deal, but on the other hand, would we be here if it wasn't?

I give the best answer I can. "It's complicated, but sort of. Why? Does your escape plan have anything to do with someone on the Buzzards?"

Any information I can find might help Xavier. I mean, it can't hurt, right?

She tilts her head. "Of course it does. I haven't seen him in a few years, but of all the banquet venues in all of Boston, he has to walk into mine."

"Did you dump a drink on him? Spit in his food? Accidentally lick him?" My mind goes through all the possible ways to make a fool of oneself, some learned from experience.

The server looks horrified. "No, nothing like that. Just, well, I ... he ... well, we hooked up. So, yes, there was licking. It was a while back, but the licking was quite purposeful. I was a soccer player too, at least I tried to be, and now he's a professional, and I'm serving canapés."

"Well, I don't know your story, but you're here doing honest work. Nothing to be ashamed of unless something happened during your time together."

Now she sighs, a million miles away. "No, it was fantastic. But there's a chance I may have freaked out and ghosted him. I wish I hadn't, but then when I tried to contact him again, he was a big star, and I didn't want to seem like a cleat chaser."

Seeing as how I've never been the ghoster, only the ghostee, I'm not sure I'm in any place to give my new friend advice. That doesn't stop me though. "I say you just get out there, do your job, and if he approaches you, be candid and honest with him. That's all you can really do, right?"

She goes over, looks in the mirror, and runs a finger under her eyes to fix her running liner. Then she re-dons her mask and washes her hands.

241

That action alone is enough for me to give this place a five-star shout-out on Yelp. Hygiene is a plus in my book.

I smile at her. "I'm Ophelia, by the way. Ophelia ... Henry." I stumble over my new name.

"Hannah LaRosa."

I open the door. "You ready, Hannah LaRosa?"

Her eyes crinkle with what I know is a smile, and she walks out. She pulls her mask down and mouths, "thanks" before disappearing down a long corridor.

Now it's time for me to find my husband.

CHAPTER 30: XAVIER

It's only when Ophelia returns that I realize she was gone a long time.

"You okay?" I inquire.

She nods. "Better now. Just chatting it up."

"You already met someone new?" I mean it as a joke, but my tone comes off dour. Perhaps because, and I haven't the foggiest idea why, the thought of her talking to any bloke in this room agitates me.

It shouldn't, I know.

It's simply because I don't want people thinking the wrong thing about my wife, and in turn, me. I can't afford it.

That's it. It's not because I'm picturing her smiling for someone else, or someone else enjoying that wide, generous mouth the way I did a bit ago. That would be ridiculous.

"Oh yes, I was off making sweet passionate love with some guy who passed me by in the hall."

"Ophelia, hush. Someone might not know you're joking. No bad publicity, remember?" I lean in and whisper into her ear. I try not to notice the pulse beating in her neck. I straighten back up. Best to put some distance between my mouth and her milky white skin before I do something foolish.

Like bite it.

That's it, I've got to lay off the liquor for the rest of the night. My inhibitions need to stay firmly in place. Before I can say—or do—anything else, I feel a firm hand on my shoulder.

"Ah, Xavier, glad you could make it. Aren't you going to introduce us to your companion?"

I don't need to turn around to know it's Coach Janssen. I stand up as straight as possible and give Ophelia a tight smile. This is it. The moment where everything either comes together or falls apart horrifically.

I turn quickly. "Yes, this is Ophelia. Ophelia, this is Coach Janssen."

Coach extends his hand. "Bjorn, please. I'm only Coach on the pitch or in the weight room. Lovely to meet you. Xavier isn't one to bring a plus one very often, so you must be quite special if he wanted to include you."

Ophelia giggles at the Dutchman, a lovely pink blush filling her cheeks. "I ... I'm ..." Bjorn takes in her appearance from head to toe, which makes me want to growl at him. Instead, I ball my fist and listen as my former and hopefully, future, coach says, "Quite special indeed." Finally, he turns his attention back to me. "I know I've asked you to a social event, but do you mind if we talk business for a moment? Is it alright to speak here, or would you rather do it privately?"

"Here's fine, I reckon." I glance at Ophelia, who gives a little shrug.

"Okay, Miller wants the paperwork this week. He wants to be able to announce plans for next season the day after our final game. He's having trouble getting in touch with your agent."

That makes two of us.

"I'm on it. I assure you, Coach Janssen—Bjorn—that this is my number one priority."

I see Bjorn's gaze dart to Ophelia, who's standing more still than I knew she was capable of.

"I need your word on that. No distractions, no bad press. Just i's dotted and t's crossed and everything ready to go."

Apparently, Ophelia hits her threshold for immobility as she leans forward, putting her hands on Bjorn's forearm. "I assure you, Mr. Coach. Um, Bjorn. I'm not a distraction. Not in the least. I'm part of the plan to make this all happen. That's why we got married. Now Xavier can get his citizenship and everything's all set." She leans over and says to me, "I figured he should know. I mean, he'd probably guess, since he knows you weren't a citizen, and then if suddenly you are? He needs to know how serious you are about being traded to the Buzzards. That playing for them means everything to you."

A small smile spreads across Bjorn's face. "You got married? You already took care of it?"

I nod, the tightness back in my chest. This is simply another thing to put on the already very long list of sacrifices I've made for football. I mean, it could probably fill one of Ophelia's many notebooks. Why stop now?

"I expect Tony to send me the final paperwork any time now." I pull out my phone and frown again, as my messages to my agent remain unread. "And as soon as possible, I'll file the citizenship stuff. This is a done deal. No problem. And for tonight, I'd just like to celebrate my bride and me."

I see some heads start to swivel in our direction, so I slip my arm around Ophelia's waist and gently tug her toward me. Somehow, she fits me perfectly, like my favorite cleats.

Good news travels fast apparently, and the only thing that could upstage my being here in the first place is the fact that we're here on our wedding night. It's as if the cocktail party to celebrate the Buzzards has become our personal reception.

This is not good.

I can see the ire forming on several faces. Not a good start. Not at all. "Buggers." I lean down and whisper into Ophelia's ear. Again. "We've got to do some damage control. I'm not the sort of wanker to come in and nab the attention. This night is supposed to be about the Buzzards and their successful season, as well as their playoff bid."

She nods, "Got it."

I want to kick myself. Showing up here with Ophelia was a stupid move. It's just going to draw attention that I don't want or need.

It's so much easier just to play the game and train and only focus on being an athlete. All of this other stuff is too complicated. For the briefest of moments, I look around this posh room, filled with talent and money and opulence, and wish for a dirty old barn filled with crotchety birds. Life there certainly is much more simple.

And it's good, honest work, saving owls and hawks and the like.

And while yes, you get bit and covered in shit, at least it's in the literal way and not the figurative way that this life I'm currently in seems to do.

"Xavier, are you okay? You don't look too good right now."

I glance down to see Ophelia staring up at me with concern. "I was just thinking about … home." I don't know how else to put it.

"Oh, did you want to go? I'm sure Sunny is wondering why we've been gone for so long."

Her vision of home is nothing like mine. This is all a terrible mistake. I can't get any air. What have I done? I'm starting to feel like I did the night of the accident, as the car was speeding down the road, knowing that Phaedra was out of control and there was nothing I could do to stop it.

Except I'm the one who's made this car veer out of control. I'm the one who makes poor decision after poor decision. I'm incapable of being smart unless it's on the soccer field. I have no business—

My off-the-rails train of thought is upended when Ophelia's lips crash into mine. Her hands, soft yet strong, hold my jaw, keeping my face flush with hers. Without thinking, my mouth parts, yielding to her. My hands seek her waist, pulling her close to me. As my fingers curl into the fluffy fabric of her skirt, I feel the panic recede, replaced by a more intense need.

"Good," she says into my mouth. "Now that I've got your attention, it's time to leave." She takes me by the hand and pulls me toward the exit. I'm barely aware of what I'm doing. I head toward the stairs, but Ophelia pulls me back. "Coat check."

Right. Of course. I nod and pull out our tickets and some cash to tip.

"Taking off so soon?" I turn to see Callaghan Entay leaning against the wall. He's the keeper for the Buzzards. He played for a few years in Manchester, one of the few Americans to play in the BFL.

"Yes, well, I didn't want to focus on us. It's your night. You should be celebrating. Best of luck to you next week."

"Are you really coming to us?"

I shrug. "Tryin' to. I'd be happy to play for Janssen again."

I see Callaghan's gaze focus on Ophelia for a brief moment, looking her up and down, before returning to me. "I hear congratulations are in order."

I have to remind myself it would not be a smart career move to growl at Callaghan simply because he appreciates a beautiful woman. I've always known she was beautiful. Now that she's dressed to the nines, she's practically glowing for everyone else to notice as well.

I'm not a fan of the Ophelia fan club.

I don't share well with others.

"Yes, well, we're going to go off and finish our celebration, if you don't mind."

Callaghan laughs. "Yeah, big night. See you soon."

He doesn't seem irritated by my presence, which is good. If the keeper likes you—and trusts you as a defender—it's a good omen for playing time.

We're relatively silent for the Uber ride back to Ophelia's. I search my phone again for some sign of life from Tony. It's not like him to be this radio silent for so long. I hope nothing's wrong. I say as much to Ophelia.

"What if he's in the hospital with amnesia and doesn't remember what he's working on for you? What if he is being held hostage in his house? What if he took off with all his clients' investments to some island nation never to be heard from again?"

I can only stare at her after that bonkers train of thought. My expression must read clearly because she immediately blushes, a bright pink stain filling her cheeks.

"I know. I'm stupid. I read all these books and watch these movies and sometimes I have trouble distinguishing real life from fiction."

I take the keys from Ophelia and unlock the door. I then step aside to let her in first. As she's talking about her fantasy life, it occurs to me that I should probably pick her up and carry her over the threshold like they do in the movies.

But I wouldn't want to give her the wrong idea.

The idea that I liked how she felt in my arms and how her lips felt on mine.

That would not be the right idea to be perpetuating.

No matter how true it is.

"Yes, well none of that's real, you know."

Ophelia flops down on her ugly couch. "I know. I think it's why I'm always disappointed. Men never live up to the movies. Love isn't like the songs."

I take off my tie and shrug out of my suit coat. My feet are pinched from my wingtips. Dressing up is for the birds. "Depends on which songs. Some songs hit the nail on the head." I listen to a lot of music while running and traveling. "Be right back, I've got to take this suit off."

I grab my shorts and T-shirt, and after a visit to the bathroom, I feel much more like myself. As I return to the living room, Ophelia's disappeared, so I set to work re-inflating the air mattress.

The first priority tomorrow, after getting ahold of Tony, is to find an apartment with two bedrooms. This is bloody ridiculous.

Ophelia returns, her hair still in its fancy style, but her face devoid of makeup and her dress replaced by her oversized shirt and ratty flannel pajamas. Somehow it does nothing to diminish her appearance. She goes into the kitchen and returns with a glass of wine and a bottle of beer. She holds the bottle out to me and I take it.

"Cheers!" I say, holding it up for a toast. "Another toast. Now it's a proper wedding. To us."

Ophelia laughs but clinks her glass against my drink. "Well, we didn't have a proper wedding. No cake, no dance, no bouquet toss."

No wedding night.

I shake my head to rid it of that intrusive thought. Ophelia, the saint that she is, did not sign on for a horndog harassing her simply because he finds her bum attractive.

It is, by the way. Cute and round. She's curvy in all the right places. Soft and feminine.

She reaches over to the flowers that lie on the coffee table. She picks them up and tosses them over her shoulder toward the kitchen. The cat scurries after them.

"There. One more thing to cross off the list, and then my dream is complete." Her voice is flat, and I can't help but feel immense regret and remorse that I prevented her dream.

"Surely, it's more about the marriage than the wedding day." As soon as the words are out of my mouth, I wish I could snatch them back in. This is reason number one why I prefer being on the field. I don't have to speak. I don't have to say the wrong thing. I just play. "You know what I mean."

"Well, no one's writing a love song about us, that's for sure." Then she looks as if she's been struck by lightning. She jumps up and scurries over to her desk where she pulls out that purple notebook and hastily scrawls something down.

When she's done, I ask, "What was that about?"

Her gaze drops to the floor. "Oh, nothing. I just thought about something and I didn't want to forget it. Something I'm supposed to do for work tomorrow. You know, work. Like a work thing."

Her babbling makes me think it's anything but work, but it's not really my business in any regard.

She returns to the couch, tucking her fuzzy-sock-clad feet up underneath her until she's folded into an impossibly small ball. "It's a good thing we didn't have to do a dance or anything. It's not like we have a song."

Ah, she's back to the wedding thing. I think this has bothered her more than she let on. "I'm sure we could come up with a proper one. What's a love song that you like?"

She takes a sip of her wine, considering my question. "Um, what about 'Need You Now' by Lady Antebellum?"

I can't remember the song so I pull it up on my phone. Sure, the piano, in the beginning, is pretty and haunting, but as soon as Hillary Scott starts singing, the song comes flooding back. "No."

"No?" she asks.

"It's not a romance song. It's a drunken booty call."

"Alright. Um, how about 'Wildest Dreams' by Taylor Swift? You can't mess with the Queen. It was good enough for Bridgerton. Surely it could be good for a couple."

I play that song as well. "It's a secret romance, and they can never be together again. Not exactly a happy ending." I shake my head. "I'll give you one more try."

Ophelia thinks for a minute before jumping to her feet, pointing her index finger in the air like an exclamation point. "I've got it, and it would be perfect for us." She reaches over and grabs my phone. In a moment, the opening chords for "One" play. "It's U2. You can't object. They're Irish."

"Well, I'm English, so that's grounds for objections right there. But aside from that, the song is about resigning to the fact that the relationship is done. Bono has given interviews about being asked to play this song at weddings and refusing because it's about splitting up." I take my phone back. "Here, listen to this."

I put on Billy Joel's "Leave a Tender Moment Alone." "Now I know it's not at pretty sounding as your songs, but listen—really listen—to what he's saying. It's real and honest." Before I know what I'm doing, I grab Ophelia and pull her into my arms, swaying to the harmonica as the bass, piano, and drums pick up.

This song reminds me of my parents, this music playing on an old radio in the barn. I'm nostalgic and homesick, and suddenly, I'm very aware that this has become my own tender moment.

With my wife.

CHAPTER 31: OPHELIA

Suddenly, I'm a Billy Joel fan.

It's always been something my parents listened to, but now I can see the appeal. Especially when a six-foot-something handsome British man is humming it softly under his breath while holding me in his arms.

I try to focus on the words to the song, but it's hard with him so near. With his hand splayed across my back and the other one clasped around mine, tucked between our two bodies.

This is not the first dance I'd dreamed of, yet somehow it seems so much more intimate.

Maybe it's because I'm not wearing a bra.

As the song fades out, we stand there for a moment, still holding onto one another.

Xavier finally looks down at me and a small smile spreads on his face. "Thanks for the dance, love. I remember my mum and dad dancing to this song. Perhaps that's why I always thought it was romantic."

I need air. Air that doesn't smell like him or taste like him. I drop my hands from his and take a step back. "Aw, that's sweet. You must miss them."

"I do. I miss everything about home." He looks out the window, though you can't see much in the dark night.

"Well, we'll do our best to make a home for you here. A home away from home. I'm sure we'll find a good place, and you'll be happier with your new team and things will work out," I reassure him. I try to commit his expression to memory, knowing full well I will want to describe it in depth. His wistfulness, his longing. I can't chance going and writing it down right now though. I did that once tonight and then had to babble on to cover up what I was doing.

Xavier looks at me for a long moment. "Yes, well I'm a player without a team, a man without a country, and a person without a home."

"But you are not without an overly optimistic wife, so at least that's something. It's like having your own personal cheerleader who knows absolutely nothing about what you do, but makes up for her ignorance with enthusiasm." So much for not babbling. I'm rambling on, making no sense whatsoever when he's very obviously on the verge of an existential crisis. "As soon as we get settled in a new place, you'll feel better. This will all be worth it."

"Right then, if you say so. Well, it's been a day, hasn't it? I'm going to turn in."

His turning-in is in the middle of my living room, so that's my cue to retire to my bedroom. I grab my purple notebook and laptop. There's no way I'll be able to sleep right away. Too many good things happened today.

Romantic things.

Book-worthy things.

There were moments that almost felt real.

They'll be real for my characters. This book is really shaping up and you know what? I don't think it sucks either. I'm considering putting up a chapter or two on Wattpad or Patreon to see if I can stir up some interest.

That's how inspired I am. I'm almost confident enough to try it again.

I'll look into it over the weekend. Tonight, my wedding night is all about letting the words flow.

I'd been working on outlines and plot points, trying to organize my thoughts, but tonight, with inspiration like I've never had before, I go right for the computer. The words spill forth, almost coming too fast to keep up with.

He couldn't take his eyes off her milky white thighs, peeking out from under her dress. Unable to resist, he slid a hand over her knee. Her skin was silky, and he couldn't help but wonder if it was this smooth everywhere ...

An hour later, I need a cold shower or a vibrator. This is one of the steamiest things I've ever read, let alone authored. It doesn't hurt that I've got the perfect inspiration on the other side of my door. And maybe, just maybe, when I picture my hero, he looks exactly like Xavier.

I bet he tastes like him too.

This thought immediately brings to mind our two kisses earlier in the day. I don't count that awkward meeting of our mouths during our wedding because that wasn't really a kiss.

Xavier showed me what a kiss was. The kind that makes your toes curl and all the blood rush to one specific part of your body. If we hadn't been in a crowded bar, I probably would have climbed him like a tree.

The second kiss, to distract him, was a moment of desperation, but it's not like it was a hardship.

Not in the least.

In fact, I'd love to waltz out there and kiss him again. Why be sexually frustrated or resort to battery-operated fun when there is no doubt that Xavier could satisfy me in a way I've never been satisfied before?

Oh right, because this marriage is a sham, and he's only here because he has to be. I am a means to an end for him and nothing more. He'd think I was some sort of unhinged or deranged person if I went out there and propositioned him.

I mean, it wouldn't have to mean anything. It'd be a release. I'm sure he could use one too. Can't he?

I push my computer off my lap and stand, taking a minute to stretch out the cramps in my legs. I make it all the way to my door before I realize this would be the most stupid thing I could ever do. Which for me, and my impressive list of stupid things, is saying a lot.

Even this would be too much for me.

It doesn't matter that we're in a fake marriage, which remains my favorite book trope of all time. It doesn't matter that there's only one bed in this apartment. It doesn't matter that he's ridiculously attractive but also nice.

Real life doesn't work that way, and it's high time I start realizing it. I sit back down and open my laptop again. It's time to focus on this book.

The next time I look up, my neck stiff and my hips cramped, it's after two a.m. My word count is over five thousand, which is impressive. I know I should be heading to bed, but I'm too excited about my writing.

But since it's also two in the morning, I can't tell Marley that I'm ready to take the plunge with writing again. So instead, I do the next best thing. I open ClikClak.

Hey everybody, I've got some big news. BIG news. It's related to my business, and let's just say I think I'm going to be on the steamy side of this app soon. Stay tuned for the big reveal! Kisses and hugs!

After a whirlwind day, the wedding day I'd never dreamed of, I finally drift off to sleep, content that at least one part of my life is finally moving in the right direction.

I stumble out of my room at seven minutes before nine, which will give me enough time to make a cup of coffee and still be at my desk for work on time. I don't think I'll ever be able to work in an office again.

That would be a great thing if I could be a full-time writer. I'd always be able to set my own schedule.

"Morning," I mumble. Xavier is again making a smoothie. It looks like he's already been out for a run. "You are up way too early for me."

"I've got to get my run in before my workout."

Seeing as how no one would ever mistake me for someone who's physically fit, the idea of working out multiple times in a day is confusing. "In theory, I understand those words, but I have no idea what you mean. Aren't you on vacation?"

"I don't have any scheduled team practices, mostly because I don't have a team. But the off-season is critical for my training. I'm currently in my hypertrophy or endurance phase. Lots of runs and endurance workouts." Xavier smiles. "It takes a lot of work to get a body that performs this way."

I reach past him and dump a spoonful of sugar into my coffee that is light with cream. "Same."

"After I shower, do you want to go look at flats? I think that should be a priority. That air mattress is killing my back."

Immediately, I feel guilty. I shouldn't be making him sleep on that $20 Wal-Mart special. His body is a temple and should be treated as such. "I have to work, but you go. I trust you. And why don't you take the bed tonight? I can sleep on the couch."

"I'm not taking your bed from you."

"Yes, but my job isn't based on my physical performance and if you hurt yourself sleeping on the floor, then you can't do your job. I understand you're trying to be chivalrous and stuff, but don't be a stubborn ass and take me to bed." The words are out before I can stop them. "I mean take *my* bed. *My bed*. Not me to bed."

My face grows hot with embarrassment. Let's hope Xavier never studied psychology and doesn't read into that Freudian slip.

A small smile spreads over his lips. "We'll see. Are you sure you can't go? I'll put a call in to the realtor."

I glance at my desk. "Yeah, I need to work. But you go. It's your place anyway. I mean, I can help with rent, but I'm fairly confident we're not in the same tax bracket. Speaking of which, we need to have Tony put in the contract about how we file our taxes. It might be better to file separately due to the disparity in our incomes, but on the other hand, it's not like I take itemized deductions. I'll have to run the numbers. Do you have your tax returns from last year so I can figure out how we want the contract written?"

See? It's not exciting to me, but I am good at what I do.

"Yes, I need to get ahold of Tony. I've got to get moving on the citizenship thing. I'm not sure what the next step is."

After Xavier leaves, I do my very best to concentrate on work. Sometimes being productive can be challenging, but I've also never had a reason to fly through things before. It's not like Sundance cared if I finished at four or seven, as long as he could sit in my lap or walk across my keyboard. I'm not sure how long Xavier will be gone, but I don't want to still be running spreadsheets when he returns.

Focus would be slightly easier if Xavier wasn't texting me pictures of the places he's touring. I appreciate the thought, I really do. But I sort of don't care. Nothing will be this place, in my funky building with a turret.

It won't be mine. It won't be home. It'll simply be a place where my stuff is for a few years.

Maybe when this marriage is over, I'll have enough saved up for a place in the Back Bay. That's always been my dream residence. However, now, the thought of my marriage one day being history makes me sad, and I have no idea why.

Me: Go with your gut about what you like. You know what I'm paying for rent now. I can't afford more for my share, but we should be able to get something decent between the two of us.

Xavier: Do you want close to the stadium or nice? We're finally getting closer to Foxborough.

Me: That's a you question. You're the one doing the commute. I only have to go to games every … how often do you play?

Xavier: I'm going to give you a study guide, and yes, there will be a test.

Me: Will you grade on a curve? Oh! Make sure the place accepts pets. Sunny is non-negotiable. Have Tony put him in the contract if you need.

Xavier: If the damn wanker ever calls me back, I will. :-/

Me: You're going to make me get rid of my couch, aren't you?

Xavier: It's an eyesore.

Me: It's got character and personality. It's not boring.

Xavier: That it's not.

Xavier: So far, my favorite is The Sylvan, but no 3 bed available. 2 bed, but it's pricey. Go check out the website.

I click on the link and can see the appeal after taking the virtual tour. There's a pool, not that we'll get to use it for a while. There is a fitness facility and everything looks new. There are even windows, so you know, it's an upgrade already. It's very posh and modern and ... cold. Sleek and stylish and everything that I'm not. Something occurs to me, so I text Xavier.

Me: Why 3 bed?

Xavier: So you can have a dedicated office.

That's so considerate. I shouldn't be surprised because Xavier is the poster child for considerate.

The messages cease for a little while. They must be in-between places. About forty-five minutes later, my phone starts blowing up.

Xavier: I've found the absolute perfect place, and I don't want to lose it. Can you come down and sign the lease today?

I look at the clock.

Me: I can probably leave by 4. With traffic should be there by 5.

I know I told Xavier it didn't matter—and it doesn't—but I wish I was there to see.

Me: Do you have a link?

Xavier: I want you to see it. Get here as soon as you can.

Google Maps tells me this place is about forty-five minutes from Brookline. While in the car, I call Marley to let her know about this development.

"Mansfield? That's so far away. I'm never going to see you again."

While forty-five minutes is certainly more than our current distance of approximately eleven minutes, it's not like it's the end of the world.

"I know, but it's close to the stadium. Like 495 can keep us apart. Xavier's going to be on the road a lot, so I'll just crash on your couch. Jamal will grow to love having me as a sometimes roommate."

"I know, it's just I feel like things are changing. Like I'm losing you forever."

I signal and change lanes approaching my exit. "Things are changing, but that doesn't mean we're going to grow apart. You'll always be my ride or die."

"Yeah, except you met the man of your dreams and fell in love without me. I didn't get to ride."

I can hear her sadness through the phone, and it breaks my heart a little. I want to tell her why. That this wasn't my real wedding, and that when it is, she'll be there.

She continues. "It all happened so quickly, and I had no idea that my best friend had all this going on. I know everything about you. I mean, I thought I did, but I didn't even know you were in love."

The guilt of the lies and the secrets presses down on me like a Mack truck, making it hard to breathe. A bed to sleep in might be the priority for Xavier, but for me, it's getting the NDAs or whatever we need from Tony so I can fess up to Marley.

She's going to be pissed.

"I know. But trust me, things will work out for the best. Xavier's good for me. He's even got my creative juices flowing."

"I bet that's not the only juices," Marley mutters.

"Marley! No, seriously, I'm writing again. And I think, this time around, it's good."

"It was good last time. I wish you'd believe me over some stupid troll on Wattpad. When do I get to read it? And don't think you can distract me from the real issue. We are going to have a long talk about all of this soon."

My exit is coming up in two miles. "Mar, I'm going to have to go, but trust me, there's more than you know. I'm fine and it's all good, but this will all make sense soon."

"What cryptic bullshit is that? Ophelia June Finnegan, tell me what's going on."

"It's actually Ophelia June Henry now."

Her silence speaks volumes.

I am a shit friend.

I want to call Xavier and tell him what's going on, but I don't want to bother him. I'll see him in about fifteen minutes anyway, and maybe he can light a fire under Tony so my life can get back to normal.

CHAPTER 32: XAVIER

She's going to love this place, and with the loft, we can even keep her minging couch. It'll be the perfect office for her.

Outside the balcony, there's a large tree—maple, I think—which is home to a bird feeder. It's a terrible place for a feeder as the squirrels probably dine there more than the birds, but to me, it's a sign that this is home.

For the first time since that night with Phaedra, I'm feeling optimistic about my life. It's all coming together. The Buzzards want me. I'm going to be playing again, and regularly too. This apartment even feels like home, already.

And it's all because of Ophelia.

This sprite of a woman with the heart of a romantic has given me my life back.

When my phone dings with a text from Ophelia that she's out front, I'm more than excited to see her.

I jog down the hall and take the stairs to the ground floor two at a time.

"You're here! C'mon. This place is absolutely smashing. It's perfect for us. You're going to love it."

When Ophelia pulls down her mask, I can see her mouth is set into a tight line, and it stops me in my tracks.

"What's up? You don't seem like a happy chickadee."

She lifts her shoulders and lets them drop, her gaze trained on the floor. "Nothing. It's fine. I'm sure it will be fine."

"No, it won't. It's more than fine." I take her hand and pull her down the hall. The rental agent is still waiting for us inside our unit. "Please trust me. I know you must on some level."

As we walk up the stairs, Ophelia says, in between breaths, "It's just I like my place. It has character and charm. I don't know if you've noticed, but I'm not sleek and stylish. I'm not put together. That one link you sent—I'd never feel comfortable there. I'd always be afraid I'd break something. But I understand, it's your place and your decision. So I'm telling myself I'll be fine wherever."

We get to the door, and I'm still holding her hand. I turn to face her, taking her other hand in mine. "This is *our* place. Not mine. *Ours*. I don't want you to be fine. I want you to be good. More than good. Bloody good. And if you don't like this place like I do, then we'll keep looking until we find something that fits us both. For better or worse, we've got a few years ahead of us, and I'm not going to make you miserable. I'll do whatever I can to make you happy. You've given me so much, it's the least I can do."

Her eyes are shiny with tears and her mouth quivers into a tight smile.

"But," I add, "I think you're going to love this place."

The moment she sets foot inside, her demeanor changes. "Look at this!" She points to the built-in desk with slate blue cabinets, nestled into an archway alcove in the living room. "It's got arches! It's not all white!"

She wanders from room to room, pointing out all the things she likes. "Wood floors that aren't gray. I mean those look nice and all, but there's no warmth. This place feels warm. Ooooh, look out the window! Isn't that the cutest little bench? I can't wait to sit outside and read a book. Oh! A balcony! A loft!"

I have to laugh, following her throughout the space. She opens every door, peers in every cabinet. "Sunny has so many windows to look out of. He's going to love it here."

Apparently, the Sundance the Cat seal of approval is all we need. It takes less than ten minutes for Ophelia to ask for the paperwork to sign. I didn't even tell her I was planning on putting her eyesore of a couch in the loft. She still thinks it's going to go to the bin.

One hour later, we're back in our future home, taking measurements. It's ours for the next twelve months.

At least that's one contract signed.

The apartment is available now, and the management company is eager to have tenants. If possible, we'd be able to move our stuff in tomorrow. It's not possible, but perhaps by next week. Certainly before the end of November, which is good because there's a fitness center for me to use when it's too cold to run outside.

"Okay, well the back bedroom seems a tiny bit smaller than the front one, but the back one has the bathroom in it. The front one has the bathroom that guests would use." Ophelia's walking back and forth between the two rooms.

"Alright." I'm not sure what her point is.

"You should have the bigger room, but it has the less desirable bathroom. The en suite really is better, but I think that room is a tad smaller. But the closet's bigger."

She's putting a lot of thought into this.

"It doesn't matter to me. Which one do you want?" I couldn't care less in all reality.

"I want you to have the better bathroom and closet. You shouldn't have to share your space with guests. Oh, and we'll probably need to have a code or policy or something for guests. I mean, for me it'll just be Marley, but if you want to bring someone back here, I can make myself scarce. You know, leave a sock on the doorknob like in college."

My head spins at the abrupt change in her thoughts. Barely able to keep up, all I manage to say is, "I didn't go to uni."

I've no idea why *that* was my response. It's neither here nor there, and it has nothing to do with the fact that she thinks I'll be bringing ladies back here to entertain in our home.

There's only one woman I want, and she's already here.

That realization hits me like a ton of bricks as I stare at said woman.

"Oh, well, you see, in college when you're sharing a room, and one roommate is having, you know, sexy time, they leave a sock on the doorknob or some other signal so the other roommate knows not to go in."

While I actually do understand the concept, as I've roomed with plenty of blokes during the junior leagues, I still can't form words realizing that she just said sexy time, and now that's what I'm imagining.

With her.

"Right. Understood. I don't think that'll be an issue. We're married so, at least for the sake of public appearance, we probably shouldn't have anyone gallivanting in or out or selling stories to the internet." Then I add, "Should we have Tony put something in the NDA about it? If I can ever get ahold of him, that is."

"It's not already in there? I assumed you'd have an entire paragraph about it. It was hard to read that draft on my phone. To be perfectly honest, I skimmed it. I just figured ..."

I shrug. "Honestly, me too. I'm not sure if it's in there one way or another. But we do want to keep this between us." Then I add quickly, "For appearance's sake."

Her lips, ones that I can still practically taste, part. "But ... but what about sexy times? How are we going to have that?"

Her use of the word *we* practically sends me over the edge. My toes grip in my trainers in an attempt to keep me from moving. Every muscle in my body contracts to keep me from taking a step toward her, and then another and another until only inches part us. The desire to touch her overwhelms me. I can practically feel my finger tracing a light line from the back of her hand, up her arm, dancing over her neck, until it rests at the corner of her jaw.

Instead of touching her, as I'm desperate to do, I clench my jaw so tightly it might shatter. As immobile as I am, my mind continues to run away. It imagines her reaction if I were to say to her, "I'm sure we can figure *something* out."

I can practically see her swallow in response to those words, those delicious lips opening and closing ever so slightly. Her pupils would be wide and dark, the blue of her irises barely visible.

"Xavier, are you okay? I'm sorry I brought it up. We … we can figure out those details later. If you don't mind, I'll take the front room, since it's obviously more of the guest room."

I blink and shake my head. Heavens, I've got to get a proper grip on myself. I don't know where these feelings are coming from. Regardless, I cannot act on them. Ever.

That would be right terrible for Ophelia, knowing she's stuck here with me, and I'm having all these *thoughts* about her. No, it wouldn't do at all for her to find out.

I can't have her thinking I'm prowling on her, or that she *has* to reciprocate because we're married. I want her to feel safe and secure around me, not like this is a con or a bait and switch. It would probably make her feel very uneasy to know that she was sharing space with someone thinking about all the things he wants to do to her body.

I might have to wank in the shower every day for the next three years—or however long this marriage has to last—but I'll never tell her. She needs to feel—and be–safe in her own home, and I'll make sure she is.

Even if it's keeping her safe from me.

"Okay, well, I doubt I can book movers tonight, but I'll work on it first thing in the morning. What furniture do you have and what do you want of mine? I know, the couch is a no-go."

"Actually," I say, glad to have something else to focus on, "I think your couch will work perfectly in the loft. It's your office up there, and there's plenty of room for your desk and that monstrosity."

This time, her lips actually do part, open for a moment in disbelief, before she breaks into a wide grin. Then, out of nowhere, she launches herself at me. Before I know it, her arms are around my neck, squeezing tight as her legs wrap around my waist.

"Xavier Henry, you are without a doubt the sweetest man ever."

I don't know what I should be doing with my hands, but it seems only natural to support under her thighs. She pulls her head back and says, "I thought I was giving up everything. But you—you knew that, didn't you? And you found this place for me. The blue cabinets, the archway, the balcony, and the loft. The loft is just for my couch, isn't it?"

I can only hold my breath and nod in affirmation, her face now just inches from mine, as I'd been fantasizing about only moments ago. I swear I feel her legs tighten around me, her pelvis tilting in and her body pressing into my own. I must be imagining this, right?

"Xavier, I can't even. I could totally kiss you right now."

I have two choices. I can put her down and put some much-needed distance between our bodies before I cross a line that can't be uncrossed.

Or, I can march defiantly across that line by claiming her mouth as my own.

But actually, option three wins as my cell phone rings. Quite unwillingly, my hands leave her thighs, and she slides down my body.

Fuck.

I turn away so she can't see my bloody arousal as I retrieve my phone to answer it.

It'd better be Tony.

Except it's not.

It's worse.

Much worse.

CHAPTER 33: OPHELIA

Saved by the bell.

Or at least the ringing of his cell phone.

While I love the often-used description in romance novels about wanting to climb the hero like a tree, I didn't expect to actually do it.

But I did.

I'm surprised he didn't toss me across the room.

I don't know what I'm thinking, other than I'm not. Typical Ophelia.

This isn't just book research, though I've got a great idea for a scene that involves a kitchen counter.

I wave at Xavier and point to the door, widely gesticulating that I'm heading out. He nods curtly, obviously irate at my ridiculous behavior. I'm really going to have to watch myself around him, otherwise the next time I have a little too much to drink, I'll be crawling into his bed, demanding my wifely rights.

That would not be good.

The moment I get back to my apartment, I pull out my laptop and start writing. Tonight, my couple is getting a love scene involving christening every room of their new place, undeterred by the pressures of their outside lives, not wanting to leave their cozy love den.

I wish.

It's after eleven and Xavier still isn't back. He's got to be home soon. To kill time, I go back and read through what I've written so far. I love every single word.

People have to read this. They're going to love this book.

Now, a normal person would finish writing the book and then edit it, and then send it out to agents. I think it's been long since established that I, Ophelia Finnegan—er, Henry—do not follow conventions like that.

Oh no, I proceed to upload the first three chapters in series on Wattpad under the author name Lia Finn. I read it. I read it again.

This is really good.

I text Marley so she can read it, but I know she's sleeping.

I need someone to read it right now, so they can tell me what they think. I go back to Wattpad. No views yet.

The need for someone else to read my story makes my skin itch. There's only one way I know to solve this problem. Naturally, I open ClikClak.

So I did a thing. I've been working on a story for a while, and suddenly my inspiration hit me just right, if you know what I mean. Head on over to Wattpad to find the first three chapters of my upcoming book! Love you all! Kisses and hugs!

I try to go to sleep, but excitement over my abrupt decision doesn't allow rest to come. As I glance at the clock and realize it's almost one a.m., worry starts to win over.

Xavier still isn't back.

Oh God, he's probably so embarrassed about what happened earlier. I don't think I could have been more desperate if I tried. And what was all that talk about sexy time? Frankly, no one else I'd ever be able to bring home would hold a candle to Xavier Henry.

Not that he'd ever look in my direction. Not for real.

I need to let him know that I know this is strictly business. I won't touch him again unless we have to for appearance's sake. No more touching when it's just the two of us.

Though *he* is the one who grabbed my hands. Repeatedly. I'll have to inform him of the no-touching rule. Yes, a list of rules is what we will need in our new place. It's the only way I'm going to keep a cool head around him. I open a document on my computer and start writing the list. Number one: no touching.

And he probably shouldn't walk around without his shirt on either. I mean, a girl's only got so much willpower, and his abs do look quite lickable. That's number two: no lickable abs on display.

Maybe I wouldn't find him so desirable if he wasn't so sweet and thoughtful. The bridal bouquet and the ring, then the loft? He's too considerate. All that kindness makes me want to bear his children. Number three: no generous gestures that make my uterus dance.

The next rule is not fair to Xavier, but it's the only way I'll make it through the duration of our sham marriage. Number four: no overnight guests. As much as I claimed to be okay with it, I'm totally not. I can't say he can't—you know—with someone else. He just can't bring her back to our place.

The last rule is for me and me alone. I should leave it off the list because it feels foolish to even type the words. Yet I know if I don't have this list to abide by, I will break this rule every chance I get. Number five: no falling in love.

Yeah, Xavier won't need that at all, but I'm a little afraid I'm already in violation of that one. It's probably because of rules one through three that Xavier so flagrantly disregards. I mean, he doesn't know about them yet, so it's not like he's doing it on purpose.

It's just him.

I glance at the clock. It's now closing in on two a.m. I call him, but his phone goes straight to voicemail. I text him asking him to let me know he's okay.

I've got a bad feeling about this.

One look at his face when he finally trudges through the door a little while later confirms it. He looks unkempt and exhausted. His blue eyes are rimmed with red, and his hair is standing on end as if he's been pulling on it.

I want to run to him and pull him into my arms, but I remember rule number one. "What happened?"

Xavier sinks down on the couch, his face buried in his hands. He shakes his head back and forth. Everything about his posture reads defeat.

"Xavier, you can tell me. Are you okay?"

He shakes his head, still not looking at me. "It's bad. Very, very bad. I'm sorry."

My skin prickles. "How bad?"

Finally, he turns to look at me, his elbows still resting on his knees. "Quite bad."

"Xavier, who called?"

He shakes his head and buries his face again. "I … I can't …"

"You can't tell me like you can't-can't or you don't want to say?"

"It's a right disaster. A bloody fucking disaster. Tony's gone."

I sit up straight. Oh no. "Like dead?"

Xavier sits up, one side of his mouth pulled up. "He's going to wish he was when I get my hands on him. No, he's gone, as in he doesn't work for the firm anymore and actually hasn't in several months. He ghosted all of his clients."

"But you've been talking to him, right?"

Xavier shrugs. "I was, until the last few weeks. He was texting and now he's not responding at all."

I'm trying to make sense of this all in my head. "But what … why? I'm confused."

Xavier stands and begins pacing around my small living room. Sundance scurries to the kitchen, jumping up to perch on top of the fridge. He can sense that something's horribly wrong.

Part of me wants to scurry and hide, but that isn't what Xavier needs right now. I'm not sure what I'm going to do to comfort him. Tossing rule number one out the window, I gently put one hand on his shoulder and the other on his forearm. "Listen, it's late. You've got to be exhaust—"

He shrugs me off. "Don't suggest I try and get some rest. Sleeping will not make this better. It's only going to, oh bugger." He looks at his watch. "I've got to make a call." He doesn't bother to leave the room before whipping out his phone and dialing.

It's two-thirty in the morning. Who's he calling?

"Mum? Is Dad there? I need to speak with him. It's quite urgent."

Xavier stands, phone pressed to his ear, his other hand over his eyes. "Fuck, fuck, fuck," he curses under his breath. "Dad? Fuck, Dad, I've gone and mucked it all up again. But this time, I did it for good. It's done. I've lost everything."

I don't understand what he's saying. I was there when he talked to the coach last night, and it was all good. So what if the agent left the agency? I'm sure that sort of thing happens all the time. Maybe Xavier can just go with another person at the firm. He's probably just panicking and didn't think about that.

"No, I'm not alone. Ophelia's here with me."

There's a pause.

"Ophelia. She's the bird I married."

There's another pause as Xavier pulls the phone away from his face and winces. Even across the room, I can hear the screaming that has eardrum-rupturing potential. Yikes.

He sighs and taps the screen. "Mum, Dad, you're on speaker. Ophelia is right here."

Oh crap. We're doing this. I didn't even have time to think about what I'm going to say to Xavier's parents. "Um, hi. I'm Ophelia."

Great. I'm not only boring, I'm restating the obvious.

"You're *married*? When did you even meet?"

Before I can speak, Xavier tries to calm his mother down. It's for the best because I don't think telling her that I've only known him for a little over a month would go over well.

"Mum, settle down. I told you about Tony's plan to have me get American citizenship. This is how I did it."

I hear a throat clear and then Xavier's dad speaks. "I guess we didn't figure this is how you'd get citizenship."

"Well, that wanker said it was the only way to fast track so I can get traded in the off-season."

"Seems drastic," Xavier's mom mutters.

Um, I'm right here, lady.

I need to defend myself. "Yeah, well, it might be drastic, but it was Xavier's last chance. It's all good. We get along fine, and we just signed a lease on our new apartment. It's right by the stadium, and it's really pretty, and—"

I'm interrupted by Xavier putting a finger over my lips. It's one hundred percent a shushing gesture, but from the instant he makes contact, all I want to do is to take his finger into my mouth.

This is neither the time nor the place, Ophelia.

I mouth "number one" which makes Xavier pull his hand back. He scrunches up his brows, trying to decipher what I was saying. I take a step back, trying to put distance between us.

"The issue is that Tony's gone. Like literally gone. He hasn't been to work in weeks, and the firm can't reach him."

"Can someone else handle your contract negotiation? You're a client of the firm, not just of Tony's."

Xavier's mom and I are on the same wavelength.

Xavier raises his gaze to meet mine, his phone held out in between us. "This is where it's all buggered up. Tony had conversations with Bjorn and Miller about the trade, but they were phone calls. There's nothing in writing. Nothing in email. There's nothing with the Terrors that we know of either. There are no contracts, and certainly nothing's finalized."

My mouth goes dry.

"I don't know that he ever talked to Camacho or Masters about the trade at all. They may not agree to it. There's certainly no indication that they're inclined to even consider it. Especially considering word on the street is that Camacho is sucking up to Edmund Jones. He definitely won't agree to a trade, if only to punish me further."

After a few beats of silence, Xavier's dad says, "Well, it must be the middle of the night there. Nothing you can do at this moment, other than get some rest so you can make a plan in the morning. Someone else must be able to straighten this muck out."

After Xavier disconnects, it's obvious there's no amount of planning that will let us sleep well tonight.

Chapter 34: Xavier

I can't even look at Ophelia.

I've ruined her life and absolutely mucked all of this up. Not to mention I've all but ended my career in one fell swoop. All because I trusted the wrong person. Again.

I was never the best in school, but I always thought it was because I was more focused on football. Turns out that I'm simply a slow learner.

Ophelia sits there, saying nothing, which indicates how upset with me she is. She's not the silent type, ever. She's the type to fill every ounce of every day with whatever thought streams through her adorable mind.

I wish she would do that now. Prattle on about nothing to push the thoughts out of my brain.

Finally, after what feels like an eternity, she clears her throat. "Okay, give me the rundown. How bad is it?"

She wants me to rip the bandage off, so I do. "Most likely the Terrors had no knowledge of a trade, so they're not going to let me out of my contract, even if the Buzzards were willing to pay for it. For some reason, Camacho is committed to sticking it to me. Robert Miller doesn't take risks. He and the Buzzards were only willing to take a chance on me if I came without drama or controversy, considering my past and my relationship with the BFL. It's all a big bungle."

"You don't know that for sure. Your brain is jumping to the worst-case scenario, but maybe it's not that bad. Maybe the Terrors will be happy to let the Buzzards buy you out. Maybe the Buzzards really want you. The coach seems to like you."

I stand up and resume my pacing. This apartment feels too small. "I can't believe Tony did this. I was apparently the last client he was in touch with. And now he's disappeared."

Ophelia frowns. "It doesn't make sense. I mean, maybe he's been in a horrible accident and is lying in a bed somewhere with amnesia."

That ridiculous statement stops my infernal pacing. "Ophelia, you've got to be kidding. This is real life, not some daytime serial. It's not a fantasy book. It's my life, and it's utterly ruined."

I should stop there, because none of this is Ophelia's fault, yet I can't. "I've given up everything just to play one more day. One more game. One more time. I've given up my home, my country, and hell, I even married you for just one more season."

As soon as the words are out, I wish I could snatch them back in so they don't land the blow I know they will. Indeed, Ophelia looks as if I've slapped her right good.

"Oh, Ophelia," I gasp, closing the distance between us. "That's not what I meant."

Her gaze is trained on the floor. Can't say I blame her.

I take her face in my hands, forcing her to look at me. "What I mean is that I've gone to extreme measures, like getting married. Not marrying *you*. Just the marriage thing. You're perhaps the only bright spot, currently." More words tumble out before I can think. What the hell is wrong with me?

"You don't have to lie. I know what you meant."

"I'm not lying. I never lie. Not anymore. The last lie I told ruined my life."

"About Phaedra not driving?" Her dark blue eyes look huge.

I nod. "Yes, and I haven't told a lie since."

She pulls out of my hands, stepping away. "Wrong. You're a liar. This whole thing is a lie. You pride yourself on being honest, but you'll lie if it suits you. If it means you can play your soccer. Apparently, soccer is worth lying for."

This time, it's her words that land like a well-timed blow. I can't say she's wrong though.

My hands fall helplessly to my sides. "You're right. I'm a liar and a hypocrite. Perhaps I don't deserve to be playing. I shouldn't be a role model, that's for sure. I wouldn't want anyone emulating me or trying to live as I do."

Ophelia looks at me for a moment before closing the distance between us. This time, she takes my face in her hands. I try to look away, but her grip is surprisingly strong. "Xavier Henry, I may not know you well, but I see your heart. You've been nothing but kind and considerate since the moment we met. Hell, the first thing you ever did was help me. I wouldn't have agreed to all this if I didn't think you were worth it. It's not like I would have married Trent or any of those guys from ClikClak. You're different. You're special, and you're absolutely someone to look up to. You're just in a run of bad luck that we'll get figured out. Somehow, someway, we'll figure this out. We'll get you playing soccer again. No husband of mine is going to sit the bench."

I want to believe her.

"Xavier, look at me. Come on, we'll figure this out, together. I know I'm your wife on paper only, but we're still a team, at least where the rest of the world is concerned."

I don't know how I ended up here, in the middle of Boston, in the middle of America, married to a stranger, with an absent agent, and the very real likelihood of no team to play for. Yet somehow, none of that matters. All that matters is the woman standing in front of me, cradling my face in her hands, telling me everything will be alright.

It'll never be alright. Never again.

"Xavier, you're starting to panic. I can see it. Look at me. Look at my eyes."

With a Herculean effort, I drag my gaze to hers. She continues, "Tell me five things you can see."

Unable to move my head—cripes, she is strong—I say, "I see your blue eyes and a smattering of freckles. The cat is staring at us. Your hair is mussed, and that couch truly is ugly."

"Okay, now four things you can hear."

I have to focus on this one. "I can hear my own heartbeat pounding in my ears. Your cell phone is constantly vibrating. The cat is now meowing at me like he's trying to tell me to leave. And I can hear your breathing. It's heavy."

Ophelia nods. "Good. Now three things you can touch."

"The ground under my feet." I raise one hand to cover hers. "I feel your smooth skin." I bury my other hand in her hair, at the base of her neck. "I feel your hair, soft and silky."

I see her swallow hard, even though she doesn't ask me for that. "Okay, two things you can smell."

"Pizza and lilacs. The two smells of you."

"Good. You're doing good. How are you feeling?"

I do feel as if my heart has slowed, and it's no longer going to burst forth from my chest. "Better, I think? Marginally better."

"Okay." Her voice is barely a whisper, forcing me to lean in even closer to hear it. "Last one. One thing you can taste."

It's been hours since I've had anything to eat or drink. I shrug. "Nothing."

"Nothing?" She raises a brow.

"Nope."

"We can't have that. How about this?"

And then her lips are on mine. I taste her, sweet and warm, like a bright spring day and stolen moments of passion all rolled into one. Even if Jones himself walked back in here right now and offered me a place on the British National Team, I don't think I could stop kissing Ophelia.

I don't want to stop.

Her hand travels up to my neck and I feel her leg wrap around me. I let go of her hand and scoop under her thigh, hoisting her up and into my body. Her thighs squeeze tight, her ankles twining behind my back. A groan escapes, I think from me, though I can't be too sure. I take a few steps to press her back into the wall. Now I can run my hand up and down her thigh, squeezing her ass.

The next moan is definitely from her as she grinds into me.

Fucking hell.

"God, Ophelia."

She pulls back slightly. "I'm sorry."

"Don't ever be sorry."

"I'm breaking rule number one."

"I don't know what you're talking about, but if this is breaking the rules, then I'm all for it." It occurs to me that she said rule number one. "What's rule number two?" I ask in between kisses.

"No licking your abs."

Now it's my turn to stop kissing. "These rules are rubbish. Throw them all out, and lick away."

The thought of her tongue on my body is almost enough to drive me over the edge right here and now, second only to the thought of my own exploration of her body.

"How about no rules for tonight?" she pants. "We can reinstate them in the morning."

"Why?"

I don't know where these rules came from, but it does seem like she wants to create some sort of boundary. Currently, clothing is the only boundary between the two of us, and if I have anything to say about it, that won't be the case for long. I lean in and kiss her neck, my hand slipping up under the back of her hoodie. Her skin feels hot under my touch. "You seem a bit warm. We should take this off."

Ophelia tilts her head back, giving me better access to that lovely spot where her collarbone hollows out.

"Oh my God, Xavier, if you don't take me to the bedroom now, I'm going to spontaneously combust." Her hands are frantically grabbing at the back of my shirt, attempting to pull it up.

I look at her. "Are you sure?"

Ophelia nods. "Please?" she whispers.

That's all it takes.

CHAPTER 35: OPHELIA

So much for the rules.

I mean, it was worth it, but I don't see how we're going to go back to a business arrangement. I'll still tell him about the rules though in case he wants an out.

I'm guessing he does.

As I glance over at his sleeping frame, I feel slightly guilty. I took advantage of him while he was in a vulnerable state. He was upset and emotional, and I pounced like a duck on a June bug.

Not that I've ever seen a duck pounce on a June bug because, well, ducks are still birds—*shudder*—but I imagine it looked something like me attacking Xavier as he was freaking out last night.

I don't know why I did it, other than he was hurting, and I wanted to make it stop, but once I started touching him, my more primitive brain took over. Yes, that's it.

It's not because I'm hopelessly attracted to him.

That would be foolish.

It's certainly not because I'm totally falling for this wonderful man.

That would be downright ridiculous.

I'm exhausted and sore. I feel my cheeks blush thinking about Xavier. Yes, rule number two was definitely violated.

By both of us.

Also, his tongue was quite generous, as was the rest of him, and my uterus is definitely dancing. Shit.

I force myself out of bed and to the bathroom where I take my birth control pill. I look at the pill pack, and I'm right on schedule. In addition to the protection we used, I should be fine. My uterus can slow her roll for right now. There is no need to complicate this already totally messed-up situation with something like an unplanned pregnancy.

I'm all in for the romantic tropes, but that would be too much, even for me. I close the toilet lid and sit down, head in my hands. What the hell was I thinking? Like I could fix his clusterfuck of a life situation with my magic vagina?

We can't do that again. It's only going to make things messier. It sounds like his life is a dumpster fire as it is. He doesn't need me to add kerosene.

At least I put him in a better mood for a while. I definitely got a smile out of him. The memory of him grinning up at me from between my legs is enough to turn my body into molten lava.

Get a grip, Ophelia.

Just because you're married doesn't give you the right to jump his bones at any given moment. That's not in the contract.

Shit. The contract. Tony. Tony's AWOL, which means there's probably not even a contract. What does this mean?

Maybe the Buzzards will still take Xavier. It's obvious they want him. So then all we need to do is draw up a little agreement between us about the marriage stuff. I can probably get my brother Owen to help. I'm almost certain it's not the type of law he practices, but I'm sure he can do something.

Sure, he'll rib me endlessly about my impulsive behavior, but I'm used to it. Isn't that the role of the youngest—to be the butt of all the family jokes?

On second thought, maybe I can figure this out for myself. Hell, the internet has a lot of contracts. I head out to my desk and fire up my computer. It's Saturday, so at least I don't have to get distracted by work. It'd be nice to have something positive to give to Xavier when he wakes up.

I glance at the clock. It's after eight. This is the latest I've ever known him to sleep. I must have worn him out. *Go me.*

Within minutes, I'm down the rabbit hole of prenups, but that's not really what I need. We need to have in there how long the marriage has to be for the citizenship thing, so I head to the government website to do a deep dive.

It's as abrupt as diving into a pool of ice-cold water.

Right there, on my screen, in black and white, point number three.

You have to be living with the marital spouse for three years immediately prior to and during the application process.

Tony is a fucking idiot.

Or are we the idiots for racing off to the courthouse and getting married and then consummating the damn thing so we can't even get it annulled?

I mean, I'm not even religious, and Xavier, if anything, is probably Protestant, but facts shall not get in the way of my righteous indignation!

This is the first thing I'm going to tell Xavier when he wakes up. Seriously, it's not like him to sleep this late. I can't believe he missed his morning run. My feelings of elation and pride drift away. I may not know him well, but I know this is not a good sign. He must be in a really bad place.

I guess my vagina isn't that magic after all.

Well, the least I can do is make him his breakfast smoothie. Naturally, I have no idea what he puts in it, so I Google recipes while I take stock of what's in my kitchen.

Look at me being a good wife and all.

If you'd told me a month ago that I'd have protein powder and kale and turmeric in my house, I'd have thought you were crazy. Of course, the health food stocking my fridge is only secondary to the fact that I married—and had my world rocked by—a super hot, super *kind* pro athlete.

The noise of the blender is enough to rouse Xavier, and he stumbles out to the kitchen, clad in only his shorts. His hair is tousled, most likely from the number of times I ran my fingers through it last night, and his stubble is thicker than normal.

And there they are. His abs.

I can confirm that they are indeed lickable.

I bite my lip to keep my tongue from taking over.

"Morning. I made you a protein smoothie. I think I did at least. I make no guarantees about the taste." I hold the concoction out to him, willing my hand not to shake.

Why the hell am I nervous now? He's seen—and explored—every inch of me. A bit of the smoothie sloshes over onto my hand. Instinctively I stick my finger in my mouth to lick it off.

I won't be craving this concoction any time soon, but it's not awful. I am glad I'm not the one who has to drink it.

But then I see it. His pupils dilate and his lips part slightly.

Maybe my lady bits did cast a spell.

Good. We're going to need it to drop this bomb on him.

"Ophelia, I wanted to discuss last night." He takes a large drink of the smoothie and then pulls a face.

"That good?"

"It's, well, no. Not good. I'm sorry. It is the thought that counts though."

My quivering quim may never quiver again. In fact, I can practically feel it shriveling up into my body, never to see the light of day.

"Too heavy on the turmeric and ginger."

I blink, trying to figure out what he means. "Oh, the *smoothie*." I smack myself on the forehead.

"It's not inedible, but I hope you don't take offense if I add some more berries to it." He brushes past me and sets about fixing my mess. "What did you think— oh, Ophelia, last night, well ..."

I turn to look at him, and I swear he's blushing. *Blushing!* He stammers, "Er, ah, it was quite lovely, in my opinion. Are you settled with it?"

Settled? What's that supposed to mean? Settled like it occurred and is in the past? "Of course." *No.*

I mean I have to be, if he doesn't want anything else to happen, then that's that. "So what now?" If he doesn't have a plan, then I'm definitely busting out my rules. We need them now more than ever.

"Well, I've got to try to set up a call with someone at the agency to see what can be done to salvage my career."

"Do you still want me to call the movers?" The place is technically ours. As soon as we can get furniture there, we could stay there. Xavier's stuff, with the exception of two suitcases, is in a storage pod in Baltimore.

"Let's hold on that to see if I'm still getting traded."

The knowledge of what I discovered sits heavy in my stomach. "Um, the trade is dependent on becoming a citizen right?"

Xavier nods. "Yes, that's why we did all this."

I blow out a small breath. "Um, we need to talk. Come here." I lead him to the couch. Once sitting, I angle to face him and take both his hands in mine. I can do this. I can tell him. "So, it's about Tony," I begin.

"When I find him, I'm going to throttle the wanker."

"I have a feeling you're going to have to get in line," I mutter.

"He always was too slick for me, but now he's slid right off the grid." Xavier shakes his head. "Bloody wanker."

It's time to pull off the Band-Aid. There's no other way. "Yeah, well, he screwed you over. Royally."

"I know, but I'm hoping something works in my favor and the Buzzards can buy out my contract for the trade."

I shake my head. "No, because you can't become a citizen. Not yet anyway. I don't know where Tony came up with this brilliant plan, but he didn't look into it. Not at all. We'd have to live together for three years prior to your application to be able to accelerate your citizenship application."

My words hang heavy as Xavier processes. His mouth opens and then closes several times. After what feels like an eternity, he says, "So then, we didn't have to—"

"Nope." I don't even let him finish. "I'm not sure if he was high or delusional or had just watched too many rom-com movies with this plot, but no. Our getting married is not going to help you become an American citizen. At least not for three years."

"I'll be eligible on my green card in eighteen months anyway."

"So we didn't need to do this." The words are heavy and hurt to say, especially after last night. "You don't need me."

Xavier sits in stunned silence.

I head back to my computer where my next search is, "how to file for a quick divorce in Massachusetts."

This cannot be real. My head hits the desk with a thump. I hear the door open and close. I'm sure Xavier needs to run or pound something. If I were the working out sort, I probably would too. I have a different sort of release. I open ClikClak.

Okay, you are not going to believe this. I live in Massachusetts, right? Did you know, according to massachusetts.gov, you can only file for divorce in this state if you've lived in the state for a year, the reason for the divorce happened in Massachusetts, or you've lived in Massachusetts as a couple. I mean, I know Boston isn't like Vegas for people eloping, but still, are they saying you have to stay married a year? That's bullshit. Kisses and hugs, I could really use some.

It does occur to me that any time I post on ClikClak there's drama and that's the last thing we need, so instead of releasing this video, I save it in my drafts. It makes me feel slightly better for ranting on camera, not that it actually solves anything. You know, like writing that scathing email but not sending it, if only to get it out of your system.

Xavier's going to need to run the entire Boston Marathon course when he finds out he's stuck with me—in this state—for a year. Of course, that's not going to work if he's playing in Baltimore.

And since the reason for our divorce is that his job is in Baltimore, we can't even use the "reason for the divorce happened in Massachusetts" excuse to end our marriage.

That's going to make him miserable if he has to go back there.

My train of thought is interrupted by the ringing of a phone. Not my phone. Xavier's cell is still on the coffee table, where he left it a few hours ago after he called his parents.

It's not my business, but perhaps I glance at the screen to see who's calling. Robert Miller. That name sounds familiar.

Last night pops into my head. Robert Miller definitely has something to do with the Buzzards. Without thinking, I pick up the phone and answer.

"Xavier Henry's phone. How may I help you?" Perhaps if I sound super professional, it'll help.

"Er, I'd like to speak with Xavier." His voice is polished and firm, and I'm immediately flustered and intimidated.

"Xavier's out for a run. He takes his training very seriously, even in the off-season. Especially in the off-season. He's in excellent shape."

I should know.

"Mm-hmm. This is Bob Miller."

"With the Boston Buzzards, correct?"

"Yes, with whom am I speaking?"

"This is Ophelia. Ophelia ... Henry. Mrs. Ophelia Henry. I'm Xavier's American wife."

So much for being professional.

"Yeah, I heard about that stunt from Bjorn."

"I suppose you're calling because you also got the news that Xavier's agent—ex-agent—is a total shyster and scammer? Xavier's devastated. He wants more than anything to come play for you here in Boston, but now he's convinced that Tony screwed him over. Please tell me there's hope?"

There's a beat of silence that's just long enough to let my heart drop to my feet.

"This is a very tricky situation now. There's no love lost between myself and Vinny Camacho, but the league has very stringent rules about trades. Not to mention they don't look favorably on pilfering between teams."

"But it's not pilfering. The Terrors guy hates Xavier, I think because of the mess with the guy and the guy's daughter back in England. But Xavier never got to tell his side of the story. He would never put anyone in danger, and there's so much more than you know. Camacho won't play Xavier, and he's trying to end his career. Isn't there anything we can do to help this trade actually happen?"

That was perhaps a bit more rambling and desperate than intended, but if this guy has a heart at all, maybe he'll listen.

"Oh, but there's one more thing you should know. Tony told Xavier to get married to expedite his citizenship. However, and it should come as no surprise at this point, Tony doesn't know his ass from his elbow, and even though we totally got married, it's not going to help. The law doesn't work that way. So Xavier's still British. I mean, he'll always be British, obviously, but he's not, like, an American citizen yet."

"Well, then my hands are tied until March. I'm not saying we won't trade for him then, but until then, there's nothing I can do."

"Nothing?"

"No. And, this needs to stay quiet. Xavier cannot handle another scandal on his sheet. Pulling a stunt like getting married and trying to orchestrate a trade with a shady agent is bad enough, on top of the Jones incident. If he *ever* wants to set foot on the soccer field again, he's got to keep his nose as clean as they come."

I'm so glad I didn't post that last ClikClak.

We disconnect, and I have the overwhelming urge to vomit. None of this is good for Xavier. I probably shouldn't have talked to Robert Miller and tried to help.

Add this to the list of stupid things I've done in the name of love.

CHAPTER 36: XAVIER

Well, I certainly have made a terrible mess of everything. It's bad enough to totally botch my own life, but now I've pulled Ophelia smack dab into the middle of it.

If the thought of never playing football again didn't make me feel like I was removing my own intestines with a salad fork, I'd pack my bags and head straight home. Not that there'd be a home for long without my financial support.

The whole thing has me gutted, and I don't know what to do. Ophelia's place is too small to get a proper mope on, not to mention I can barely look at her. I've gone and ruined her life for nothing.

But I had to go jump the gun and give up my Baltimore place as well. My eagerness has always been an issue, on and off the field. It's led to more than a few yellow—and even red—cards as I've been too excited to charge a player for the ball.

I did the same thing now.

This time, a red card won't suffice. My career is done. My parents are probably going to literally lose their farm. All their birds will probably die because they can't survive in the wild. I'll be responsible for a mass avian execution. But worst of all is that I conned Ophelia into marrying me. I know it was her idea and all, but she did it for me.

Forever, she'll have to explain to someone how she married a bloke she didn't even know and that it wasn't a real marriage.

But of course, we did have to go and sleep together, so she can't even say there wasn't anything between us. Not that there is.

But not that there isn't, either.

And now my head is pounding.

It's been pounding for the past week since I left Ophelia. Every time I looked at her, I felt sick. What was I supposed to say? How exactly does one apologize for ruining one's life?

Flowers don't seem to say enough.

There's not a proper greeting card to express this sentiment either.

She's been a rock star though, researching law and loopholes. She's found no answers yet, but I appreciate her effort. She texts me frequently, often with pictures of the cat.

I've resorted to responding with emojis, as I can't always come up with the words right now.

"Still nothing yet?" Alastair asks. I've been crashing on his couch since returning to Baltimore. Camacho is being shady and evading my calls. I've half a mind simply to storm into his office and demand he trade me.

"Bloody crickets. He's being a wanker on purpose." I've no doubt he's trying to make me squirm. The Terrors grapevine confirmed he's trying to get in good with Edmund Jones, possibly to work a telly deal between the leagues. Also, I came down here at the worst possible time. It's Thanksgiving week, so there's the *slight* possibility the office is simply closed, but I'm not giving him that much credit.

"No doubt. But you've got to do something. The movers are coming in an hour."

"I can't believe you're actually leaving me."

Alastair shrugs, continuing with the last of his packing. Boxes surround me. Ophelia and I should have spent this week doing the same so we could move into our new place. A place that will never be "our" home now. There's no reason for us to be married, so certainly no reason for us to live there.

That thought is taking up more emotional room than I'd anticipated.

"I wish you could come home with me." Alastair is leaving for England in the morning. He'll be training and playing with the Bristol Bombers before Christmas.

"If things don't take a turn for the better soon, I'll be sitting in the stands for your home opener." I don't even want to picture it. I cannot imagine life back on the farm, sleeping in my old room, cleaning out the aviary every morning, and never playing football again.

Not being able to see Ophelia either. I shake my head, trying to get her image out of it. It's not right how much I miss her. Why does she have to be so damn perfect?

"The first thing I'm doing is heading to a proper chip shop."

"That would be one benefit of having to return to England, tail between my legs. At least I'd get proper chips. And bangers. Even the so-called British pubs here don't do it right." My stomach growls.

"Aye. And a good cuppa." Alastair sinks down on the couch next to me. "But I'll miss ya, mate. It doesn't seem right to be playing at home without you."

I shrug. "What's done is done. Now I've got to figure out this mess. Ophelia's working on it from her end, but neither of us has come up with anything."

My phone pings with a text. My fingers fumble, trying to open it quickly.

Ophelia: Marry You *by Bruno Mars. That would be the perfect wedding song. Obv.*

In spite of myself and my current predicament, I smile. In addition to copious pictures of Sundance, she sends at least one text a day on the quest to find our perfect wedding song.

The woman has atrocious taste, as every song she's suggested is not actually about love.

Me: Try again. He's basically saying they're bored and doing a dumb thing, like getting married.

Ophelia: Maybe it fits more than you think. <winky smiley face emoji>

"Good news, mate?" I glance up to see Alastair grinning at me.

"Ah, no, it was just Ophelia."

"Mmm-hmm. *Just* Ophelia."

I tilt my head. "What do you mean by that?"

"No one who puts a smile on your face like that should have the word 'just' before their name."

I attempt to lower the corners of my mouth. "I'm not smiling."

"Right. Anything you say." He stands. "I'm not trying to give you the bum's rush, but you either need to help or get out of the way. I've only a little bit left before the movers come."

I stare at my hands, still gripping my phone.

"Where ya goin'?" Alastair's voice is soft, and if I'm not mistaken, filled with pity.

Slowly, I stand. "Not sure. I've no place to go. I need to settle things here, but there's probably no sense in hanging around this week." Stupid holiday. "Seriously, why do they have turkey now? Don't Americans know that should be reserved for Christmas, and how are you supposed to eat it again in a month? Also, what's with all the American football? It's on for approximately seventeen hours straight, and I'm sorry, but our game is much superior." I nod triumphantly.

"I agree, mate, but if you're here, then you roll up to the table and eat. But in all honesty, I don't believe I'll ever understand the obsession with sweet potatoes covered in sticky marshmallows."

I give my friend a hug and show myself to the door. My duffle is there, packed and ready to go.

Go where is the question.

Ophelia: Stay with Me *by Sam Smith*

It's not a love song, more a breakup song, but it gives me the answer I need.

She's all I need.

I drive for hours, sitting in traffic on I-95, cursing this infernal country the whole time. I should chuck it all and go home, but I'm not ready to quit.

Not yet.

The drive that should take just over six hours takes closer to ten, thanks to this day being the busiest travel day of the year. It's well after midnight when I pull up in front of Ophelia's flat.

As soon as I put the car into park, I realize that I probably should have texted or called her to see if it was alright for me to crash with her, at least for a few days. I'll knock lightly and if she doesn't answer, then I'll text her.

Unfortunately for me, neither method gets an answer. I'm already wearing a jumper, so I pull my anorak out of the back seat and don it as well. I've got gloves and a cap, and what I wouldn't give for a muffler. The temperatures dip low, and it reminds me of being out in the aviary in the dead of winter.

This is ridiculous. I should check into a hotel. My whole life is ridiculous at this point, and without a doubt, I'm at an all-time low.

Yet I don't move, and eventually, I shiver myself to sleep.

Zero stars, do not recommend.

The sky is just beginning to show signs of light when my phone rings, waking me up.

"Xavier! Where are you? What are you doing?" Ophelia whispers.

"I'm outside in the car like I texted. Can you let me in and why are you whispering?"

"I'm whispering because my mom is next door and if she hears me talking at 6:30 in the morning, she'll get all up my grill about what I'm doing, and no I can't let you in because I'm not there. Have you been in the car all night?"

I shift and turn the car on, desperate for a little heat. My neck is stiff and my knee screams at me. Also, I've really got to use the bathroom.

"Yes. Alastair is leaving Baltimore, so I ..." I shrug, not that she can see it. "I've nowhere to go. I can't get through to the Terrors, and I'm sure they're all on holiday for the next several days. Where are you?"

"I'm at my brother's in Connecticut for Thanksgiving."

Bollocks.

"No worries. I'll figure something out." I run my cold fingers through my hair, pushing the cap off my head. *Shit. Shit. Shit.*

"Come down here. You can't be alone on Thanksgiving."

I have to laugh. "It's not like I celebrate the holiday, you know."

She continues to whisper. "Oh yeah. Duh." She pauses before continuing. "I don't want you to be alone."

Something rolls over in my chest. "How far is it?"

According to the address Ophelia texts me, I should be there in just under two hours. After stopping to fuel and take care of my most pressing biological needs, as well as grab a cup of Dunkin', I'm driving again, this time west on I-90. I wish I could shower before I have to meet Ophelia's family.

Her family.

My head starts to pound. This is going to be a right disaster.

CHAPTER 37: OPHELIA

I probably should have thought this one through.

I know, the story of my life.

I'd texted him nearly non-stop since he left, trying to cheer him up if nothing else. I know he didn't leave because of me. I've wished he would come back, but it didn't seem fair to ask that of him.

While I'm one of his problems, he doesn't need me tossing my emotional demands on him. So instead, I kept it light and funny with pictures of Sunny and song suggestions for us.

He never said we didn't need a song, but I've forbidden myself from reading into that. Still, when he said he came to see me in Boston, my heart leapt.

My girl bits did a little too, but I'm trying to calm *all* my organs down as I try to figure out how to drop this bomb on my family, including my sister-in-law who's running around like a chicken with her head cut off, trying to cook a meal worthy of Martha Stewart.

Yes, I know this is in poor form.

"Hey, Owen, can I talk to you for a minute?" I ambush my brother as he's carrying a large stainless steel feeding trough out to the back deck. Xavier should be here in less than an hour, so no time like the present.

"Only if you get the bags of ice out of the garage freezer and help me fill this up." It's about forty-five degrees, so it shouldn't take too much ice to keep some bottles of soda and fancy sparkling water cold. I grab a bag with each hand and waddle my way upstairs, thinking that I probably should start working out with weights.

"Carolina is going nuts. That's why I hate hosting anything."

I scrunch up my brow. "When you bought this house, you literally said it was for entertaining. It's why we had to schlep here, instead of home to Mom and Dad's for Thanksgiving."

"Yeah, but that was before I knew how fanatic Carolina gets. She's a total perfectionist and thinks that every person who sets foot in the door needs a three-star Michelin experience and that every single nook and cranny of the house will end up on Instagram or *Better Homes and Gardens*. We basically have to lock the girls in their rooms for two days so they don't touch anything. I'm surprised she even let you and Mom and Dad stay here."

This news about my sister-in-law is not surprising. Owen himself is big on appearances, always sharply dressed and perfectly groomed. Even now, he's wearing designer jeans, a button-down shirt, and leather oxford shoes that probably cost almost a month's rent. This is all while he's getting the house set for company. "When's Aiden getting here?" I'm not sure Aiden is allowed to be an overnight guest at Casa

Carolina. Our middle brother, no matter how much he tries, always has some bit of farm on him.

Sometimes I like Aiden to be around, if only so people don't focus on what a mess I am.

"He's going to be cruising in at the last minute. He had to deliver … something." Owen shrugs. "You know."

Yup. As our brother is fond of saying, "Mother Nature doesn't make dinner plans." That's the line he used when he almost missed Owen and Carolina's wedding. Needless to say, I'm Carolina's favorite in-law. Sure, I win by default, but I'll take it where I can get it. Though what I say next may cost me that standing. "So, like, it looks like there's a lot of food. And your dining room is really huge. You could probably fit more chairs at the table." I turn to survey the room like it's the first time I've ever been here. "And—"

"Cut the bullshit, Ophelia. What do you want?" Owen has reverted to scary lawyer mode.

"I may have a friend who's suddenly without a place to go, and I may have extended an invitation here."

Owen slams down the tub. "Jesus Christ, Ophelia, could you have waited any longer? When are you going to grow up and start acting like a responsible adult? You can't live your whole life flitting about, making rash decisions without any regard for how it affects everyone else."

You mean like marrying a stranger in response to accidentally going viral? I feel my face flush. "I just found out!"

"And did you tell them yes?"

I roll my eyes. I don't even need to answer that question. Owen knows.

"Carolina's going to shit a brick, you know that, right? You know how uptight she gets when her sister is coming. She feels so inferior to Georgia, God knows why. It turns her into an absolute monster, trying to one-up her sister."

I can sort of relate. At least to the inferior thing.

"So is it okay?" I give my older brother my best puppy dog eyes. It's never worked on him before, but I'm an eternal optimist.

Owen shakes his head. "I hope your friend doesn't eat much."

I glance toward the kitchen where there are piles upon piles of food. No one's going to starve. "Is that a yes?"

Owen doesn't have time to answer, as the doorbell chimes. He looks at me and narrows his eyes. If we were still kids, I'd undoubtedly be on the receiving end of a punch by now. "Unbelievable," he mutters before storming off to answer the door.

I'm at his heels, attempting to get around him. He tosses an elbow out, blocking me. "It's my house, dammit, even if you do consider it yours to invite any random person off the street."

In a further unfortunate turn of events, Xavier, standing on the other side of the door, happens to look terrible, bearing a striking resemblance to some random person off the street. Incredible stress and temporary homelessness will do that. He looks awful, and my heart breaks a little.

Apparently, my efforts at cheering him up failed miserably.

But also, I'm glad Owen answered rather than Carolina. There'd be no recovering from that.

I mean, it's Xavier, so he's still the hottest guy I've ever met, but his clothes are rumpled and mismatched, he hasn't shaved, and I would guess he doesn't smell the freshest.

He looks like he needs a hug.

I step past my brother. "Hey, you found us! Xavier, this is my brother Owen. Owen, Xavier." Considering the tongue lashing I've already received from my eldest sibling, I don't bother with qualifiers like friend, husband, or guy I'm maybe sleeping with. I don't want to muddy the water.

"Pleasure to meet you." Xavier extends his hand. Owen, big on formality and appearances, has no choice but to take it.

"Ophelia said you've no place to go for the holiday?" Owen doesn't exactly say Xavier's welcome, but he at least steps aside to let Xavier in. I put my hand on Xavier's arm. "Do you want to get cleaned up? I can show you to my room."

"Right. I'm sorry I'm afraid I'm a bit of a wreck. A hot shower'd be heavenly."

Xavier runs out to the car and grabs his duffle. Owen eyes it suspiciously. "Planning on staying a while?"

Xavier offers a wry smile. "I'm in a bit of a transition currently, and I didn't do a fantastic job packing. I'm used to life on the road, but when I have to plan something outside my uniform, cleats, and trainers, I tend to bring too much."

I put my hand on Xavier's arm and show him to my room. He looks exhausted. "Is there anything you need? Towels are in there." I jerk my head toward the bathroom. I start toward the door and then stop. "Are you okay?"

He gives me a weak smile. "I'm afraid not. I ..." He shrugs. "I don't know what the future holds, and that scares me. I have no idea who I am without football, and frankly, I'm not ready to find out yet. I may not have a choice though."

I step toward him and wrap my arms around his waist. "If it's any consolation, I have no idea who I am either." We hold each other for a moment before Xavier releases me.

"Thanks for that. I'd better get cleaned up." We stand there, inches apart. He's only been gone a few days, but I've missed him. I should tell him that, but I'm not supposed to miss him. This is bonus time with him. Gravy.

Let's face it, Thanksgiving is known for its gravy.

"Ophelia, can you come down here?" Owen bellows.

"You're in trouble, I believe." Xavier turns toward the bathroom.

Feeling like my feet are made of lead, I trudge downstairs to find my parents with Owen and Carolina in the kitchen. The kids are running around with their iPads in hand.

There are a lot of scowls.

"Carolina, I'm sure Owen told you, but I invited a guest for dinner. Thank you for opening your lovely home to not only me but him. You know, my parents always had room for one more at their table."

Dad puts his arm around Mom. "Aw, hon, it's nice to see Owen and Ophelia carrying on our tradition to make sure no one is alone on Thanksgiving."

This, of course, gives Carolina and Owen no choice but to be gracious a few minutes later when a clean and freshly groomed Xavier makes his way into the kitchen. It's disappointing that I won't get to see him walk around in various states of undress post-shower.

Maybe I'll ask him to do it one more time, just for posterity.

I make the introductions, and Xavier is cordial, yet reserved.

I wish my mother was so reserved. She's gushing and fawning, making a big deal out of his accent, asking him to say different words and what he calls different things. I guess we know which side of the family I inherited my awkwardness from.

Also, if my life were a rom-com movie, this is the part where the audience would be shifting in their seats from their second-hand embarrassment.

"Carolina, is there anything I can help you with?" I don't know what else to do.

"I think you've done enough, but I suppose you can add one more place setting. He won't have a place card. And then make sure people have drinks."

I turn to the dining room table, easily ten feet in length. I don't even know where you'd buy one that big or that they made tablecloths that long. The sheer expanse of it makes me think of The Last Supper, and I wonder if I can convince everyone to recreate that famous painting after dinner. "I'm sure that won't matter. He'll be sitting next to me."

The doorbell starts ringing and my mom and I are tasked with greeting the guests and getting drinks. I lose track of Xavier for a bit until a red-faced Owen enters the sitting room to announce that dinner is ready.

The table is full of the usual suspects. In addition to my parents, Owen, Carolina, and their two daughters, Savannah and Kennedy, Carolina's sister and her family are here. Georgia's daughters, one in her late teens, the other in her early twenties, each have a significant other with them. I didn't catch their names, so in my mind, they're Dude Number One and Dude Number Two. Aiden walks in without a moment to spare. Owen's client and his wife round out our party of seventeen.

I've never had a date for a family function. At least this year, I'm not the single spinster loser who has to sit with the kids because she doesn't have a grown-up relationship.

Why is it that Aiden gets to be the funcle, but I'm a spinster? He's thirty-five and not married. Societal roles are stupid.

Dinner is about as New England as you can get. Turkey, oyster stuffing, cranberry everything. It's all delicious and flawless, as is everything my brother and sister-in-law do. Even their children are well-mannered and impeccably groomed.

Georgia's girls are less so, obviously bored and talking only to their dates. When they're not on their phones, that is.

Owen's client—I've already forgotten his name as well—asks Xavier, "What part of England are you from? I'm having difficulty placing the accent."

Xavier swallows what's in his mouth because of course he'd just taken a bite. "Just outside of Gloucester, toward Bristol. It's southwest England."

"What brings you to the states?"

"Football." Xavier takes another bite, probably because he doesn't want to have this conversation.

"Soccer football, not American football. Xavier's a professional soccer player. He's totally awesome. He used to play in England, but now he's here."

Owen's head turns toward Xavier. "Oh? What team? Anyone I've heard of?"

I wish I could stick my foot in my mouth if only to shut me up. Instead, I shovel in another mouthful of mashed potatoes, which sits like lead.

"Currently, I've a contract with the Baltimore Terrors, but I'd been pursuing a trade to the Boston Buzzards."

"I didn't know we even had a soccer team here." That helpful—and mortifying—contribution is from my mom. "Did you know that?" she asks my dad.

"What do you do besides play soccer?" Owen asks. "Surely you must have other ventures for when your career ends. You know, you're only ever one slide tackle away from being done."

I'm not sure where this colossal bunch of assholes came from. I'm starting to think that Xavier and I would have been better off sitting in his car and eating turkey sandwiches from Subway.

Aiden chimes in, "Oh—isn't that true of all of us? You're only one lost trial away from failure. I'm only one bad horse delivery away from getting a bad rep. We're all only ever one mistake or unfortunate event away from disaster at any given time." He looks at Xavier. "Sorry, didn't mean to interrupt."

"When my career is finally done"—he gives me a sideways glance—"I'll return home and help with the family business. Currently, I financially support them, but when I can't do that, I'll contribute in person."

Even though I sort of knew this, my chest tightens at his words. If he's in England, he'll never text from my doorstep again. I'll never see him again. The food in my mouth turns to sawdust.

"And what exactly does your family do?" Carolina gently places her fork down.

"We run a wildlife rescue center."

"So cool," Aiden says. "What type?"

It's my turn to look at Xavier. "Why'd I think it was a farm?"

"We have land, naturally, and barns, in addition to the aviary."

"The what?" He did not say what I think he said.

"The aviary. We rescue birds of prey and rehabilitate them. We're all falconers by training."

I feel the color drain from my face.

Birds.

Big birds. Scary birds. Birds that could kill me.

My husband is a bird man.

CHAPTER 38: XAVIER

If there's one thing I like talking about more than football, it's falcons. And owls. Owls are my favorite.

I announce this to the table, telling the story of how I found an owl on the side of the lane, and how Philip and I researched how to care for it. "And what's not to love? Have you ever seen an owl walk? It's the best thing ever. Really. Google it. Also, most people think an owl can turn its head one-hundred and eighty degrees, but it's actually more like one-hundred and thirty-five," I babble. Aiden is rapt with attention, and he and I talk for several minutes before I realize everyone is staring at me.

And not in the good, "oh wow, we're in the presence of greatness" kind of way. Moreso in the, "what is this freak rambling on about" way.

"Right. Sorry. Apologies for rambling." Apparently, not everyone wants to know about the life cycle of owlets.

Ophelia lets out a small, strangled noise and then Owen bursts out laughing. A loud guffaw that seems out of place in this posh home. He's laughing so hard that his face turns red. If I'm not mistaken, there are tears in his eyes.

Ophelia, on the other hand, is not laughing. She's pale. Whiter than the dinner plate pale. I put my hand on hers and she pulls it back. Leaning in, I whisper, "What's wrong?"

She shakes her head, lips pressed tightly together.

"I'm not sure where she found you, but this is the best thing I've ever heard." The brother keeps laughing. "Ophelia finally brings someone home and not only does he not even live in this country, but he's into birds. My sister really does know how to pick 'em."

"I'm sure they're just friends," the sister-in-law interjects.

I stiffen, my molars grinding. I glance over at Ophelia, whose eyes are now as wide as a barn owl's. I look around the table. The younger couples are on their phones, not paying attention. Ophelia's dad is still stuffing his gob. Her mother is tut-tutting.

Somehow, somewhere, this entire conversation has gone completely awry. It's probably because people don't expect someone like me to be passionate about something other than football. And for a long time, I think I too forgot that there's more to life than kicking a ball around a field.

Ophelia pushes back from the table, dropping her napkin over her plate as she stands. She dashes out of the dining room, I imagine upstairs.

"Well, I don't quite know what is going on," I mumble, not sure what to do with myself. "I need to go. Excuse me." I stand up as well and head upstairs to find Ophelia.

She's sitting on the bathroom floor, knees to chest, back to the bathtub. Her hair is again in plaits, cascading over her shoulders as her forehead rests on her knees, and she looks young and sweet.

And sad.

Like someone broke her favorite doll.

That someone is me, but I don't know how or why. And it occurs to me that the mere thought of causing Ophelia pain causes me as much distress as my football career ending.

As if Ophelia means as much to me as football does.

I slide down next to her, wrapping my arms around my knees. There's a lot more of me than of her, and I don't compact as well. "I feel as if I should be apologizing, but I don't know what for."

Her head shakes back and forth.

I wait a moment before continuing. "No, really. I don't know what I said or did, but I'm sorry. I thought I used the correct fork."

"I don't know you at all." Her voice is so hushed I can barely hear it.

I'm in a stranger's house, eating dinner with people whose names I can't even remember. I'm not even sure what state I'm in. "True. We didn't get the time we thought we would, I guess."

Ophelia sniffs and finally looks at me. "We … I don't think we should have slept together. It was a mistake."

Ouch.

Rather than let her know her words hurt, I shrug it off like I would if I were in the middle of a game and just received a cleat to the shin. "Probably not. Obviously, this whole thing was quite foolish."

"Quite," she murmurs quietly.

Now it's my turn to bury my head in my hands. "This whole thing has gone off the rails. Tony ..." The mere mention of his name fills me with rage. "If I ever see that wanker again ..." I clench my fists. I'm not a violent man, but thoughts of pummeling him into the ground are soothing.

"Xavier, this is serious. Birds? Like actual birds? With feathers and everything?"

Birds? That's what she's gone bonkers over? I must be misunderstanding her. It must be a language barrier or something akin to a cultural divide. "Um, right. We run a rescue operation for birds of prey. We do get mostly owls and hawks, but we've had the occasional falcon, and even a golden eagle once. I'm sure I've mentioned it."

Ophelia sits up ramrod straight. "No, no you have not. I would have remembered such an atrocity. Birds are ... evil and I'm confident one will kill me someday."

This explains why she chased that pigeon. "Ah, you have ornithophobia."

"It's not only a fear. It's a true hatred. Every time one is near me, I just *know* it's out to get me."

While I've certainly encountered people with this fear before, I've never seen it to quite this extent. After a few moments of silence, I say, "Perhaps it's a good thing that this isn't a real marriage. Now you won't have to deal with my family and their love of birds."

She nods silently.

I continue. "Seriously though, virtually every bit of decor in the house is some form of bird or another. It's all people seem to give my parents as gifts. There are bird pictures and bird pillows and bird blankets. Even the bin and the bog roll holder are birds. The whole thing is like one giant Alfred Hitchcock movie set."

"That sounds terrible. Perhaps I can get a divorce on those grounds alone. By the way, we can't officially dissolve our marriage in Massachusetts for one year."

Right. It's not surprising Ophelia looked into it. The whole point of this charade was to help me get traded. That seems like such a fantasy now, it might as well have some Fantastic Beasts in it. "I'm sure we'll figure it out. We have time. Frankly, it's the only thing I have."

Ophelia looks at me. "Birds? You really love birds?"

I laugh. "I do. I don't suppose you want to hear how at times you remind me of a kestrel, flapping and hovering, moving yet still all at the same time."

She shudders. "I know you mean that as a compliment, but please don't ever say that out loud to me again."

"I won't. I suppose you don't want to be called 'chickadee' either?"

Ophelia tips her head so it's leaning on my shoulder. "Not really." She lets out a sigh. "What are you going to do now?"

I'd shrug, but I don't want to disrupt her or break our contact. I like it when she touches me, even though I've no right to. "Not sure. I'm basically homeless, so I'll kick about for a bit, I suppose."

"You're not *homeless* homeless. You do have our apartment. Why don't you move in there? You know you're not going back to Baltimore, so you might as well be here. I mean, in Boston. Then, maybe if you wanted to hang out every now and again, we could. As long as you don't talk about birds, that is."

"It would be nice to have a friend. My best mate, Alastair, went back home."

There's silence, as neither of us knows what to say next. I'm absolutely pitiful.

Finally, she says, "I didn't text you today. What about 'When a Man Loves a Woman' by Percy Sledge? That's a good love song."

I shake my head. "Oh darling, he berates himself and totally gives everything for someone who doesn't love him back."

She laughs. "I don't think I'm ever going to find a song for us. Not one that's really about love. Maybe it's a sign because we're not really anything. Or perhaps I don't know what it is." Her voice drops low and thick.

Her words tug at my heart. I want to tell her I'll show her, but it seems too soon. Or too out of place. Or too … something. Instead, I say, "And if you even say, 'I Will Always Love You' by Whitney Houston, I'm going to disown you right now."

This time, Ophelia laughs, and it's music to my ears. "Even I know that's about loving someone who's better off without you and you can't be together." Ophelia straightens before standing up. She extends a hand down to me and pulls me to my feet. "We're going to figure this out. We're going to get you a new agent, and make this trade happen, come hell or high water. Now, let's go talk to Owen. He's got to have some lawyer-y contacts who can help. Somehow."

I smile down at her, still holding her hands in mine. "You're right. It may not be ideal, but some of the best things in life don't start as you planned them to be. So maybe I don't get traded until March. If I put my work in and show Janssen I'm worth it, then perhaps it'll work out."

"That's the spirit."

I nod, feeling a surge of energy I haven't felt in a while. "All I need to do is train my arse off and keep my nose out of trouble."

"The Buzzards would be fools not to put you on their roster." Ophelia shudders. "Buzzards. More birds. I'm never going to escape them with you, am I?"

CHAPTER 39: OPHELIA

I've never actually walked into a firing squad, but I feel as if I'm doing that now, returning to face my family following my post-bird revelation meltdown.

You laugh, but you have no idea the anxiety that runs through me when I think about birds. And the thing is, they're *everywhere*. Unless they're cooked and on my plate with a side of mashed potatoes and gravy, I want nothing to do with them.

But to my family, as with so many other things I do, it's just Ophelia being ridiculous.

You know, I did tell them about wanting to write once. I put it in my fifth-grade "All About Me" Essay. I believe my dad's comment was, "Why would you waste your time on something so trivial when you're so good at math? You need to do something that really matters."

I remember that moment. It felt like a heavy steel door slammed around my heart. I'm sure he doesn't even remember making the comment, but it was a core memory for me.

Before we get to the bottom of the stairs, I stop, tugging on Xavier's hand. And yes, I know we're breaking rule number one. "Just so you're prepared, I think you should know if you couldn't tell already, that my family thinks I'm ridiculous, and they're going to give me nothing but endless shit about my fear of birds."

Xavier tilts his head slightly. There isn't much room between us, and my body is responding to being so close to him. It really shouldn't, but he doesn't know that. "You can be a tad rash, and your energy has a bit of chaos to it due to your enthusiasm. But if they can't tell the difference between exuberance and ridiculousness, then that's *their* fault, not yours. I appreciate your energy. It's breathed some much-needed life into my stingy, rigid soul."

His words turn my inside to mush. Dammit, he just broke rule number three.

I squeeze his hand and then let go. If I maintain physical contact with him for one-second longer, I cannot be held responsible for my actions.

Also, because I'm definitely afraid I've broken rule number five.

There's a very good chance I'm in love with Xavier.

We manage to slip back into the room. Thanks to the open concept of the kitchen-dining-family room, the entirety of the dinner party, regardless of location, turns to look at us. Most of them have migrated to the family room portion by now.

My dad, true to form, laughs from his place in the armchair. "Leave it to Ophelia to make a scene about something so silly. I mean, one goose chased and bit her once, and you'd think all birds are ax murderers."

"What?" I ask. "When did this happen?"

My mom laughs from the kitchen, where she's working at the island, scooping leftovers into storage containers. "Oh, you couldn't have been more than one and a half or two. I know we've told you this. We'd taken the three of you to feed the ducks on the pond. The Canadian geese were about as tall as you, and one was definitely as fast as you."

I don't have any recollection of this event, but even as she says it, I can feel my blood grow cold in fright. Well, damn. It's not an irrational fear. I was literally attacked. I'm about to say as much in defense of my behavior when a loud laugh arises from the couch.

"Ahhhh, I *knew* it! I knew you looked familiar!" It's Dude Number Two. "You're romantic surprise girl."

Makayla looks up from her phone, squinting at me through her oversized clear glasses. "Oh my God, that is you. You're a disaster."

Carolina marches across the room toward her niece, demanding to see the phone. Owen's client and his wife come trailing after. Awesome. A larger audience. "What exactly have you been up to, Ophelia?" my sister-in-law demands.

I look at Xavier and then back to her. The whole crowd of them are gathered around Makayla's phone—Carolina and Owen, the client and wife, Georgia and Thomas, Madyson, and Dude Number Two, and of course, my mom.

God forbid she be left out of my complete and total mortification.

Aiden's disappeared. Most likely he's on the phone about an animal or something. It's fine. I don't need one more person to witness my complete and utter humiliation.

Makayla's date—Dude Number One—is scrolling through his phone at the opposite end of the couch as if there's nothing amiss.

Xavier and I stand in the middle of the room until my dad tells us to move because the Lions are driving and might actually score for once. It's good to know football—the American kind—keeps Dad's attention.

What do I do? Do I storm out—again? Do I see what they're looking at? Do I try to explain?

I can't stop thinking about the bird thing. "Wait, so my whole life, as I've panicked about birds, you knew there was a logical reason? That I wasn't just acting out or doing it for attention?" I don't know who I'm speaking to, but someone has to take ownership. "I can't believe you've all made me feel like I was crazy. That's gaslighting!"

My mom looks up. "Oh, Ophelia, I thought you knew. We've told the story before. It wasn't a big secret. It was just another thing ..."

"What's that supposed to mean?" Xavier asks.

The football game is at halftime, enabling my dad to join the conversation. "Oh, you know, typical Ophelia. She was a ball of energy from day one, and it usually got her into trouble. She never sat still, was never quiet, and never did what we expected her to."

I know what's coming next. Aiden walks into the room, and he knows too. I see him standing behind Mom, mouthing and mimicking her as she says, "Everything about Ophelia is spontaneous and unplanned, right down to her conception."

Aiden rolls his eyes, which makes me smile. It's not the first time I've heard these things, and I doubt it will be the last.

It's not like I don't understand these things about myself. It wasn't like I didn't try to sit still or be quiet or not do stupid things. Sometimes—a lot of the time—the action part of my brain fires before the rational part does. Trust me, I'd like it if they worked together more often. My life would be a lot easier.

Aiden flops down on the arm of the chair that Dad is sitting in. "Yeah, but God certainly gave her tons to make up for that. She's by far the smartest of the three of us."

I want to hug him.

This time Carolina looks up and then looks at me in disbelief. "What? Owen went to Yale."

"Yeah, but Ophelia has a higher IQ than either one of us. We were tested when we were kids. Mom has the reports, right, Mom?"

Wait, I'm smarter than my brothers? There's no way. They're put together and accomplished and …

Before I can process this Earth-shattering bit of news that will forever give me bragging rights over my brothers, it happens. If my life was a movie, it would happen in slow motion. Instead, everything comes rapid-fire and from all directions at once. "Jesus Christ, you're Xavier Henry." Dude Number One is apparently on his own internet deep dive.

"Who's that?" Owen asks.

"Him," Dude Number Two says, pointing at Xavier. "He's an actual soccer player."

"Duh." My witty retort is all I have time for before chaos ensues.

"You went viral because you didn't know your boyfriend was cheating on you."

"You asked ClikClak to set you up."

"You're married."

"He almost killed a woman drunk driving and left her to die."

"You're a prostitute."

It's a lot all at once, but the last statement is so random and outrageous that it's enough to spur me into a reaction. I wave my hands. "Whoa, that's enough. What did you say? Did you call me a prostitute?" I glance at Xavier. He didn't pay me to marry him—not really—and he certainly didn't pay me to climb him like a tree.

I did that all on my own, thank you very much.

"I'm sorry, do you prefer sex worker? Are you in film or an escort or what? It's fine. You do you." Makayla nods.

On the other hand, my mother does not have such a sex-positive view. "It's not fine. She can not do her. Nor anyone else, and definitely not for money! Ophelia June Finnegan, what are you thinking?"

"Actually," Owen adds dryly, not looking up from his own phone, "It is apparently Ophelia June Henry. They are married."

"Why would you marry a porn star?" Dude Number Two asks Xavier. "Don't you have to sign like morality or behavior clauses? You're just supposed to bang those chicks. Not marry them. That's the point. They'll do you anyway."

I think I'm going to vomit. This is about seven billion times worse than the bird revelation. I'd walk through an entire cage of birds if I didn't have to be a part of this barrage right now.

"Why on earth do you think I'm a prostitute?" I say at the same time my mother says, "Married? You're married? You can't be married."

Mom is growing a teensy bit hysterical. "There was no wedding. We've never met him before. Last we knew your boyfriend was Trent. You are not married."

Voices rise, trying to outdo each other. Mom is yelling. Owen is yelling. Carolina is yelling. Aiden's telling everyone to calm down. The client and his wife are looking around, clearly embarrassed at this fiasco. Makayla and Madyson are cackling and shrieking. The Dudes are still scrolling and calling out embarrassing things from my ClikClak, like the PenisGate date.

I'm pretty sure Dad is still watching football.

Xavier looks at me, his eyes growing wild. "What's happening?"

"Apparently I'm not the only one in my family with chaotic energy?" I offer, shrugging.

"Why is he saying you're a prostitute?" Xavier hisses at me in a loud whisper. Then he says, in a much louder voice, to Dude Number One, "Why do you keep calling her a prostitute?"

Dude Number Two chimes in, "It's right here. In her ClikClak." He waves his phone.

It is indeed my profile, a cute picture of Sundance and me. Under our photo, it says, "Book Lover, Cat Lover, Accountant. #XOXO."

"Yeah." I nod. "What about it?"

"You put that you're an *accountant*." Madyson says the word like it's vile, complete with a disgusted nose wrinkle. I mean, it's not the world's most glamorous job, but it's not *that* bad.

"Eh, it's a living."

"Um, Ophelia, here on ClikClak, when people say they're an accountant, they actually mean they're a sex worker. Like a prostitute or they run an internet porn site or they—"

Owen starts bellowing, "That's enough! We get it. I don't know what all this other shit is about, but I can say that my sister is actually an accountant. An accountant-accountant. She's done my parents' taxes before."

Georgia, who's had to have had at least two bottles of wine by now, looks up through slightly crossing eyes. "Are you sure though? I mean, look at her. Look at him. One of these things is not like the other."

Xavier's face is like steel. He puts his hands on my shoulders and says, "Thank you very much for your hospitality, but the way you treat Ophelia is frankly shocking. It's clear you neither know nor appreciate who she is. No, we're not like each other, but that doesn't matter. She's amazing and beautiful, inside and out, and I'm lucky to be her husband."

His defense of me 'ives me the strength to finally move. Without a word, I storm up the stairs and hastily throw everything I have into my bag. Approximately sixty seconds later, I'm stomping back down the stairs and out the front door without a word to anyone in there.

I get in my car but can't actually leave because there are two cars behind me. So I sit in the driver's seat, fuming.

Owen's client and his wife come out and look at the car at the end of the driveway. I stare straight ahead, unwilling to make eye contact with anyone. A moment later, Xavier walks out carrying his bag. I watch in the rearview mirror as the mortified client leaves. Good. As soon as Xavier moves, I can finally get the hell out of here. I hit reverse and am about to peel out when I realize Xavier's hasn't gone anywhere. I slam the car into park and get out.

"What the hell do you think you're doing? Get out of my way or I'll drive right into your car. I need to go. Now," I bellow.

"Ophelia, calm down. I can't let you go. Not like this." Xavier approaches swiftly, and before I know it, he's enveloped me in his arms. "I've got you, chickadee. You're safe with me, and I'm not going to let anything happen to you."

CHAPTER 40: XAVIER

I want to bash all their faces in. Maybe not Aiden who tried to calm everyone down, because he seems like an alright bloke, but definitely everyone else. I want to hug Ophelia and kiss her hurt away. Then I want to bash some more.

How dare those twats attack her like that? They wouldn't even let her get a word in edgewise, jumping to conclusions and taking every opportunity to insult her. No wonder she dated wankers like Trent and losers from ClikClak.

I'll never, as long as I live, forget the look on her face when they started saying all those *things* about her.

"Even though I did marry you without knowing you, and there may have been talk of financial compensation, that's not why I married you. It's definitely not why I slept with you. I'm not that kind of girl."

"I know," I murmur into her hair. "I've seen your desk. I've seen your spreadsheets. I know you're an accountant. An actual one, not a euphemistic one. You're not hiding your profession from anyone."

Ophelia makes a strangled sound, a cross between a whimper and a cry.

"Ssshh," I say again. "I've got you. I'm here for you. Let me help you."

She pulls back, looking up at me. Her eyes are wide and wet with tears. "Why? Why would you help me? Can't you see what a disaster I am? Can't you tell I make a mess of everything?"

I give her a small smile. "No, you're perfect the way you are. Don't you see that?"

It hits me like a ton of bricks that I mean every single word.

"Go ask the mob in there if I'm perfect, and they'll give you a list a mile long of all the ways I've screwed up in my life."

"Ophelia, this entire situation is a bin fire. You had nothing to do with that. It's not your fault, and I'm sorry your family can't see. I'm sorry they didn't even give you the decency of hearing you out."

Seriously, they're a bloody bunch of wankers, the right lot of them.

All I want to do is make her hurt go away. Brush those harsh words off her like crumbs. Wrap her in my arms and protect her.

I could do that.

I should do that.

I do that.

I was defenseman of the year the last year I played in Bristol. It's how I earned my spot on the national team. I can defend the hell out of Ophelia like she's the goal. Just as I wouldn't let a ball pass, no longer will the hurt get through to her. She's my goal and I will defend her with every ounce of energy I have.

And I'd like to start with some definite man-to-man coverage.

Her body trembles against mine. I'm not sure if she's cold or simply upset. It doesn't matter. I want to soothe her, as she did me.

Exactly like she soothed me. Maybe with a few new things we could try.

I don't know where these thoughts come from, but it's all I can think of. Making Ophelia feel better. Making her smile and laugh. Making her moan.

Making her see how incredible she is. "We should go far away from here, where it's just the two of us."

I feel her nod against my chest.

"How far is your place?"

"Over two hours."

Bollocks.

"How far is our place?" I look down at her. My eyes must be full of want and longing.

"About the same."

"Drat. I don't want to wait that long."

Ophelia pulls back. "That long for what?"

My hands slide down and tighten, lifting her up against me. Her legs wrap around my waist. I move one hand up to grip the base of her neck and kiss her. There's no hesitance on her part. Her mouth is warm, tasting vaguely of the wine she'd been sipping before all hell broke loose.

"Ophelia," I groan into her mouth. "Let's. Get. Out. Of. Here." I pepper each word with a kiss along her jawline and to her neck. She moans softly when I get to the soft spot behind her collar bone.

"Hotel?" she breathes as she tilts her face up to meet my gaze.

I nod, letting her slide back down me. Christ, her body feels incredible rubbing against mine. I can't wait to do it without clothing.

Ophelia pulls out her phone. "I've got one in Avon that doesn't look too seedy. I'll text you the address. Follow me there, so we don't have to come back here for our cars."

I smile. "You know I'm from Avon County, right? It's where my home is."

"Then this was all meant to be," she says with a wink.

Driving the nine or so kilometers to the hotel takes just under ten minutes. The GPS said eleven, but she's obviously as anxious for this as I am. We stand, antsy and impatient, at the check-in counter of the Avon Old Farms Hotel while the clerk painstakingly clicks through screens on the computer.

"Luxury King or Traditional King?"

"What's the difference?" Ophelia asks. I don't care personally, as long as it has plenty of room for me to shag her senseless.

"The Luxury is on the second or third floor and features a two-poster bed for $169 a night. The Traditional will be located on our first floor and features a four-poster king bed for $149 a night."

"The Traditional," Ophelia answers before I even have time to process the choices. I may run a thirty-three-kilometer-per-hour sprint, but I can't keep up with her right now. Her credit card is out and in the clerk's hands before I can protest.

As soon as the keys are presented, she snatches them and starts power walking down the hall. I adjust my stride to keep up.

"What's the hurry?" I want her to say it. I want her to say she wants me the way I want her, and nothing but our bodies pressed together, hot and sweaty, will make things right.

"Four-poster bed," she pants.

We get to the door and I put my hand over hers on the knob. "Yes, so?" I'm right behind her, so she turns, hand still under mine, to face me.

"Four-poster bed," she repeats, raising her eyebrows.

I tilt my head, still not getting what she's attempting to communicate.

"Think of all the things we could do."

My mouth goes dry as my pants become unbearably tight. I grip the door handle, pushing the door open as my mouth crashes onto hers. I back her through the door, and as soon as our bags clear the threshold, I pick her up and carry her directly to the bed.

It's a good thing it's a long weekend here in America. I plan to use every second wisely.

CHAPTER 41: OPHELIA

I'm exhausted, but in the best possible way.

If you've never spent two days in a hotel room with a professional athlete, let me tell you, five out of five stars, highly recommend. Will do it again.

And again.

And again.

In fact, some of what we did was so magical that I want to write about it. Not like the actual details, but some of the sensations, definitely. Who needs to invent your own spice when you have a real-life Adonis showing you things you didn't know your body could even do?

Xavier is going to get something to eat. We've lived on room service for the past two days, and I really wanted bagels this morning. Xavier agreed that we needed some carbs to replenish our energy.

Swoon.

I pull out my laptop and plug it in. Without distracting myself with the internet, I open my book document and continue typing. The words flow fast and free, and my face burns with the memories of the things we did and the passion we shared.

I have to stop and fan myself more than once. Who am I? I don't even know anymore. I might have to add another item to the list of things you should know about me. I'm Ophelia, and I love kinky hot sex with my husband.

Perhaps that's not something I should share on a LinkedIn profile or even ClikClak.

ClikClak.

Shit. I should probably update my profile to indicate my actual profession. This might need a video to clear it up that I'm a boring accountant, not a sex worker one.

I haven't thought of that app since the whole debacle at my brother's house. I push the events of that day out of my mind until I finish my steaming hot love scene. After running it through a grammar program to check for errors, I'm content that it's enough to leave my readers hot and bothered, wanting to come back for more. I upload it to Wattpad and check the views on my project.

It's number forty-five in the romance category with over twenty-five thousand views. How? Why? It's not even done yet. I only ever mentioned it on ClikClak that once.

My mouth goes dry.

I need to figure out what I'm doing here. This … could be huge. I could be one of those indie authors who hits a homerun on their debut novel and a career is made.

It's already tearing up Wattpad, and I haven't really even started talking about it on ClikClak. Quickly, I run to the bathroom, brush my hair, and put on makeup. I record a video on my phone, so I can post it to Instagram as well when it's done.

> *Hi everyone! Sorry, I've been on a little social media break. I've been … busy with some other projects. I just put the hottest chapter ever up on Wattpad. Check out* Stolen Stars *by Lia Finn. Kisses and hugs!*

I add my hashtags, including #XOXO and #StolenStars. At the last minute, I add #LiaInLove.

I am. I know I am.

It's what's made the last two days so incredibly magical. I've never felt this kind of earth-shattering connection with someone before. Does he feel it too?

He must. This can't be a one-sided thing. There's too much here for him not to have some sort of feelings.

We've definitely progressed from a fake marriage to something more.

So, I sit there in bed, clad only in Xavier's T-shirt, grinning like an idiot. Things are actually falling into place for me. Back in October, when my first video went viral, I had no idea the path my life would take me on.

It's been a whirlwind, but I wouldn't trade it for anything.

Now I just have to convince Xavier that we're worth fighting for. We'll figure out how to get him traded to Boston, and we'll live happily ever after.

This hotel, charming and luxurious all at the same time, is the setting for our grand finale, closing credit music over our laughing yet passionate embrace.

Except the moment Xavier walks back into the room, I know we're not there. Oh, we might be at the end all right, but there's no happily ever coming after.

I close ClikClak instead of making my second video about not being a sex worker. I jump out of bed, tangling myself in the white sheets and duvet. "What's wrong?"

He all but drops the cardboard drink carrier on the desk, coffee sloshing over onto the glass-topped cherry surface. He lets the bag of bagels drop as well. Xavier doesn't turn and look at me. Instead, he stares out the window, hands balled into fists at his side.

I've spent the last forty-eight hours exploring every inch and nuance of his body, so it's quite obvious that the tension and anger rolling off him in thick waves has something to do with me.

Gently I put my hands on his shoulders. He still doesn't turn to look at me. Ever so slightly, he shrugs me off.

Message received.

But I don't know why.

"Xavier, what's wrong?" I ask again. "Did something happen with Tony or the trade? Whatever it is, I'm sure we can figure it out."

He shakes his head almost imperceptibly. "No, *we* won't. There is no we."

I suck in a gasp, his words slicing through me like a razor. I put my hands back on his shoulders and try to turn him to face me. "Xavier, look at me. Xavier, tell me what's going on."

"God, I'm such a fool. You must all see it. Do I have a bloody fucking target on my head? Do I have a tattoo on my back that reads 'world's most gullible eejit' or something? First Tony, then you. Or perhaps it was you, and then Tony. Hell, for all I know, the two of you are thick as thieves and working together to ruin me. Jesus, did Edmund Jones put you up to this? Some elaborate plan to ruin me? He's always been good at playing a long game. I thought you were different. I thought I could trust you."

I'm totally lost as to what he is ranting about. I've never seen this side of him, not even the night he found out that Tony screwed him over. "Xavier, I don't know what you're talking about."

"No, of course not. You don't know anything about lying to me about what you do."

If he believes that whole "an accountant is a sex worker" bullshit, I'm going to scream. "Come on. You know I'm an accountant. You said it yourself. You've seen my spreadsheets."

He turns, glaring. His eyes are cold and hard, like blue ice. "But that's not all you do, is it?"

I open my mouth to defend myself and then immediately close it. Weakly, I offer in defense, "It's all I get paid to do."

"Fucking hell, Ophelia. Or should I say Lia? Lia Finn, is it?"

He knows. He knows about the book.

Oh God, I just wrote the smuttiest chapter ever, and he knows.

I might be sick.

"Xavier, let me explain." I hold up my hands. He's got to hear me out.

"One thing. That's all I had to do was one thing—stay out of trouble. Keep my nose clean. *Avoid scandal*."

I'm not following him. "What does my writing have to do with you?" I mean other than the obvious not-safe-for-work content and candid descriptions of the male member, possibly inspired by the one I'm so intimately acquainted with. It really is a sight to behold.

Focus, Ophelia.

Xavier whips out his phone and pulls up a screen. "I don't even know how you orchestrated this. Diabolical, really. And the best part is, I didn't see it coming at all. You blindsided me with it. Well done."

I take the phone from him, unsure of what he's accusing me of.

It's the ESPN site. I may not be a sporty person, but even I know what ESPN is. It didn't occur to me where it's located. Or that it would not be unfathomable that one of the guests at my brother's house in West Hartford is employed there.

Specifically Dude Number One.

I know because his picture is next to his name on the byline. Chassen Donato. Douche name. Seems appropriate. I read the article aloud.

Curse of the Birds
Chassen Donato, reporting for ESPN.com

Some say birds are bad luck. USSL soccer player Xavier Henry would disagree. His family owns and runs Henry Hawkery in Avon County, England, where they provide rescue and rehabilitation for birds of prey, specifically owls, hawks, and falcons, according to the family website.

"This is good so far. Maybe it can get your family some business and attention."

"Keep reading," Xavier growls.

Folklore has it that birds, especially owls, can be bad luck. While Xavier Henry may disagree, it's time for him to rethink his position.

Ouch.

Xavier was a rising star in England, named Defenseman of the Year in the British Football League in 2016. The same year, "Bird Man" was named to the BFL National Team, earning a starting spot representing England for the Global Games. You may not remember him from that stellar tournament in which the Brits came from behind to win the entire thing. That's because the night before the team announcement, Xavier did the unthinkable.

The pit in my stomach plunges down to my toes as I read the recap of the accident and the accusation that Xavier was drunk driving and almost killed Phaedra Jones.

Since then, Xavier hasn't been able to set a cleat on a British football pitch. Hiring super slick agent Anthony Bardolello, Xavier negotiated a position starting for the Baltimore Terrors in the USSL in 2017. As reported previously on this site, Anthony Bardolello is the sports agent accused of falsifying contracts, misrepresenting clients, and embezzling almost half a million dollars from his firm, Fast Feet, PLLC, before disappearing a month ago.

At the time of his disappearance, Bardolello was said to be working on a large trade deal with his number one client, Xavier Henry. Following the return to play after the COVID-19 hiatus year, the Baltimore Terrors had the worst record not only in their division but the entire USSL. Xavier Henry, said to be quite upset with the leadership and direction of Baltimore under owner Vincent Camacho and head coach Ted Masters, saw little playing time this past season.

However, because of his English citizenship, Xavier Henry isn't eligible for trade until the international window in March. This is where it gets interesting and like something out of a tabloid or made-for-TV movie.

Enter viral ClikClak star, Ophelia Finnegan. You may know her by the handle @LovelyLia. She rose to social media notoriety in early October (pay attention to the timeline here, because it's important), when she filmed a series of ClikClak videos in which she supposedly staged a surprise visit to her boyfriend, Trent Carlson, who, coincidentally, is the athletic trainer for the Baltimore Terrors. The #romanticsurprise hashtag went viral, propelling LovelyLia to internet fame. Other ClikClak videos from that same event show an interesting twist: the entire thing was recorded by none other than Xavier Henry. A mere week or so later, Ophelia Finnegan (LovelyLia's real name) and Xavier Henry were posting together in Boston. About the same time,

Xavier was spotted at a Boston Buzzards game and was rumored to be in trade negotiations with Buzzard's owner, Robert Miller and former coach, Bjorn Janssen.

Throughout the article, words are hyperlinked. I don't even need to click on them to know they will take the eager reader to our social media.

A mere three weeks after the #romanticsurprise viral video, another ClikClak video of Xavier Henry and Ophelia Finnegan surfaced, indicating that the couple is married. While this may not be a big deal in and of itself, Ophelia Finnegan, up to this point, had been publicly posting about her career as an 'accountant' and asking the whole of ClikClak to set her up on dates. Due to content restrictions on the app, users on ClikClak will substitute terms so posts don't get flagged for violating community standards. A well-known substitution is to use the profession of accountant in place of sex worker.

I have to put my hand over my mouth to avoid throwing up.

It appears that Ms. Finnegan, or should we say, Mrs. Henry, conspired to commit fraud against the United States government in an erroneous attempt to help Xavier Henry gain accelerated citizenship. Financial details of this arrangement have not yet been disclosed, but Ms. Finnegan's family knew nothing of the relationship or the marriage.

However, candid, sordid, and sexually graphic details are available from Ms. Finnegan's own hand. Writing under the nom de plume of "Lia Finn," Ms. Finnegan is publishing serial chapters to her forthcoming novel, Stolen Stars, *on the Wattpad website. She has made ClikClak videos about her debut smutty novel, which is basically mommy porn.*

Vincent Camacho, Baltimore Terror's owner, said he's "very disappointed in the actions and associations Mr. Henry has chosen to align himself with, including Mr. Bardolello and Ms. Finnegan." Boston Buzzard's owner, Robert Miller, declined to comment other than, "Mr. Henry is not on our roster, and he has no formal business dealings with the Boston Buzzards."

I can't even finish the closing paragraphs. I run to the bathroom and vomit the bile in my stomach.

I've ruined Xavier's last chance.

CHAPTER 42: XAVIER

I listen to Ophelia retching in the bathroom, knowing I had a similar experience when I read the article myself.

And to think that I shared a meal with the tosser who penned it.

Tosser isn't strong enough. Bloody fucking wanker.

Who knew he was a journalist for ESPN?

And what a juicy story it is. Granted, except for the Phaedra bit, it's not untrue. That's the terrible part. He didn't come right out and say that Tony and I were in cahoots, but it's implied.

And as damaging as if it were actually true.

I can't be sure if Ophelia and Tony are working together. The rest about her is certainly real, right down to the fact that she's writing a book.

I haven't stopped to read it yet, but I've seen what she reads. She's undoubtedly writing about us. Will she describe it as "pounding, railing, and ravishing," like they so often do? I shudder as those words dance through my memory, seared into my brain. Her body, her sounds, her taste in my mouth. But now it's out there for the entire bloody world to read as if they were voyeurs in our bedroom.

This is it. My career is done.

In the blink of an eye, all because of Ophelia.

When Phaedra Jones royally rooked me, I could feel some semblance of compassion. She had a lot of problems. It wasn't personal. I was simply the dumb sap who tried to help.

But Ophelia ... it's like a career-ending slide tackle that I never saw coming. Of course, I didn't, because I was too busy memorizing every facial expression and the sound of her laugh.

I was too busy falling in love.

I think I'd rather have my knee blown out by a dirty play than this. At least then people would understand the pain. There's no amount of paracetamol—or hell, even morphine—that will ever make me feel better about this.

I shove my clothes into my bag. My shaving kit is in the bathroom, but I can always buy new supplies. I have to get out of here now. Without a word, I leave. If I never have to see Ophelia Finnegan again, it will be too soon.

I drive away from the hotel, not even sure of where I'm going. Eventually, and because this is New England, I come upon a Dunkin' Donuts. I turn into the parking lot and pull out my phone.

It's hard to ignore the notifications which are lighting it up, but I do. I apply the same laser-sharp focus I use when I'm going through a grueling training circuit. I focus on my end goal.

Going home.

My initial instinct is to hop on a flight today, but it is the Sunday after Thanksgiving, which is one of the busiest travel days of the year. Not to mention I've got business to wrap up here seeing as how I'm never coming back.

And that's the plan.

I need to do something, focus on *something*, other than this pain in my chest, threatening to rip me apart from the inside out.

I pause for a moment to take stock of my life. It's rather depressing.

I've got two bags of clothes in my trunk. I don't even have a toothbrush since I left it behind in the hotel. I have an apartment, which I'm paying for, that has no furniture. I've got furniture in storage four states away. My best mate is back in England. I've got a wife I hate, an agent who screwed me over, and the American sports media thinking I'm the world's biggest nob.

What I don't have is a career or options.

My phone buzzes and reflexively I look. It's Kenley. This should be interesting.

"Hullo."

"Holy fuck, Bird Man, what the hell?"

I shake my head, though he can't see it. "I dunno. I ... I don't know what happened."

"The media has been all over central office, looking for a statement."

"I saw what Miller said to ESPN." I cover my eyes with my hands. I just want this all to go away.

"Jesus, that article was brutal. What the hell? Where did it even come from?"

I explain the coincidental circumstances that led me to that ill-fated dinner. "I didn't even plan on being there. I … I had nowhere else to go, so I called Ophelia."

"But you did really marry her to try to get citizenship for the trade."

Shame fills me. "I'm not a cheater. I never have been, and I don't like people who play dirty. I don't know why I thought it would be okay."

"Desperate times call for desperate measures. We all saw the writing on the wall with the Terrors. Another season of riding the bench, and you might as well hang up your cleats."

Kenley knows me well. Apparently better than I knew Ophelia.

"What are you doing now?"

"Right now? Sitting in a Dunkin' Donuts parking lot with no plan and nowhere to go. I've got to get tickets back to England, but there are some loose ends I should tie up here first."

"You're quitting?"

"I don't want to, but I'm out of time and luck. I was treading on thin ice before this, and now I don't see how I'll ever rebound. It's like a permanent red card."

"It's not looking good for you, man. Why don't you come up here and crash with me for a few days? At least give you a quiet place to get things sorted out."

Kenley's generosity shocks me. "Why? Won't Janssen be upset? Harboring a fugitive, and all?"

"Nah, we're friends. It's not business. But also, he was looking forward to having you on the roster again. I'm sure he's disappointed at this turn of events."

Disappointed is the understatement of the year.

Everything I've worked my whole life for, plus more, is gone with the publication of one stupid article.

Disappointed? No. Devastated is more like it.

CHAPTER 43: OPHELIA

I know the knocking on the door isn't Xavier. He's not coming back. Yet I'm still disappointed to open my front door to see Marley standing there.

I mean, she told me she was coming over, even though I'd told her not to. I'd also told my mom not to come, and also that I never wanted to speak to anyone in my family ever again.

I'm sure I don't actually mean it, but for right now, I need some hard and fast boundaries, since my family—and their guests—see nothing wrong with complete and total violations of my privacy.

Maybe I'd let Aiden in, but he's back in Vermont, so it's not like he's going to hang out here and cheer me up.

My mother actually tried to defend Carolina's niece's date by saying if I didn't want the details of my life public, then I wouldn't have been on ClikClak in the first place, and I certainly wouldn't have written about them in a book.

I guess she doesn't understand what fiction is.

Sundance looks at me with the judgment only a cat can. He really doesn't care that my life has imploded. He's still harboring resentment that I left him alone for the weekend.

Wanker.

The word makes me think of Xavier, and my heart breaks all over again. I can't believe I lost him so quickly. I can't believe my foolishness cost him everything.

I can't believe I was so stupid.

This certainly takes the cake in the "dumb things I've done" column. Mic drop, I'll never top this.

From here on out, I will be a hermit and only compute numbers all day, every day. It's hard to get into trouble or ruin someone's life doing that.

"Ophelia June Finnegan, I have no words."

I turn away, also bereft of words, and faceplant on my couch. Landing on my nose hurts, but at least it's physical pain, rather than the emotional pain that's been ripping me apart for two days.

"I screwed up." I finally manage.

Marley plops in my armchair, scrolling away on her phone. "Yes, you did, girl. You most certainly did."

I lift my head. "What's the world saying?"

She laughs nervously. "You don't want to know."

I sit up. "You know what makes me the most angry about this? My family. They rag on me endlessly about being impulsive and silly and frivolous, but then they take something and blow it so out of proportion, and then it causes real damage. I mean, all Owen had to do was tell his nieces to rein it in. Put a stop to it."

Mom could have done that.

Xavier could have done that.

Hell, I could have done that.

But I didn't. I chickened out and ran away, and now it's cost Xavier his career.

And cost me the man I'm in love with.

I didn't even get to tell him. Not that it would matter now anyway.

I flop back down. "You know I'm actually an accountant."

"Yeah, I know that. I'm just surprised you put your writing out there again. I'm happy you're back to it. It always pissed me off that you let one or two stupid people influence your decision."

"Don't you watch my ClikClaks?"

"You know how the app is. It's random what it pushes out. I missed the first one where you announced it. And then, everything was blowing up. But damn, that's some spicy shit there. I didn't know you had it in you."

I sit up. "That's what she said." I can't help myself.

"I like this story. You should always write romance. You're good at it. But seriously, how did you come up with some of that shit?"

"A lady doesn't kiss and tell."

"Good thing you're not a lady."

I throw my pillow at her. I have half a mind to throw the cat at her as well. "Xavier was the inspiration, certainly, but mostly for how I felt with him. Not the literal blow by blow."

Pun intended.

"Um, obviously. Anyone who's actually taken the time to read it can tell that."

As long as I'm being honest I add, "I love him, Marl. I really do. He's the most thoughtful and caring person. He doesn't think I'm silly or trivial. He said he likes my topsy-turvy energy. To him, it's a plus, not something I should try to change."

"He likes you just as you are?"

I sigh. "Oh, that line from *Bridget Jones* always makes me melt. But it's even more than that. He's like a real-life Mr. Darcy. Mark, not Fitzwilliam."

"This is real life, Ophelia, not a movie. Don't you understand that? You're not guaranteed your happy ending just because you want one."

"You mean I can't write my way out of this one? I'm not Joan Wilder?" I reference Marley's favorite old movie.

She sighs. "Dammit, now I'm going to have to watch *Romancing the Stone* again. You know I have a weird thing for Michael Douglas."

She does, and we're friends anyway. She leaves the Brits to me.

"Ugh, that movie is so old. You need a newer favorite movie. I vote that you become obsessed with *This Means War*." I admit I have ulterior motives with this one. If it's her go-to movie, then I still get to watch Tom Hardy—another Brit.

In a book or movie, this would be the sweeping grand gesture time. But Marley's right. It's not a work of fiction—it's my real life. And Xavier's too. I messed up royally in so many ways I could make a list.

One: I suggested we get married under false pretenses.

Two: I used his energy as my muse.

Three: I didn't tell him I was writing a book and publishing it online.

Four: I didn't stand up to my family and shut it down before this all got out of hand and caused a career-ending scandal.

Five: I didn't tell him I loved him when I had the chance.

I don't know that the last one matters to anyone but me, but I wish he knew.

It may not be possible to fix this situation, but the least I can do is try. Xavier deserves someone to stick up for him. He needs someone to defend him for once, the way he defends and protects not only the soccer ball but the people like me in his life.

"Marley, I've got to try and help. Somehow. At least get it out there that he's not a drunk driver, and he's not in cahoots with Tony. He deserves to play soccer. It's all that matters to him, and he's had nothing but the raw deal. That includes me."

"What are you going to do?"

That's where my bravado starts to falter. "I have no idea."

If my life were a movie, this would be the montage scene showing Marley and me in various positions, sprawled about my apartment, trying to come up with the world's most brilliant plan. There'd be snappy music playing in the background until one of us sits up, points skyward, and exclaims they've figured it out.

Seeing as how my life is not a movie, Marley eventually leaves, and I try to distract myself by scrolling on ClikClak. I don't go to this app like I used to. As soon as I started going viral, it got a little—a lot—overwhelming, so I'd post, but not scroll.

It's not possible to keep track of my followers or those who like my posts either. Especially not now, as there are several videos circulating rehashing the current scandal.

You know, this social media thing is wild. I'm probably one of the most boring people you've ever met, and now I'm bordering on celebrity—or at least notoriety—for no reason, other than my ex was a cheating louse.

But when a video pops up with Chassen Donato—aka Dude Number One—talking about it, I know I've seen enough. My first phone call is to Owen.

"Listen, you know this is all complete and utter bullshit, and I'm going to go Johnny Depp on his Amber Heard's ass and sue him for defamation." I lead with that. As an afterthought I add, "Hello Owen, it's your sister."

"Yeah, I got that, Ophelia. Your name comes up. Who are you trying to sue now?"

"Dude Number One. Chassen, what's his name? You know, your *guest* who completely ruined my life. Xavier's too."

"Your *husband*?" I can practically hear my brother's sneer through the phone.

"Yes, your brother-in-law. His career is finished because of that article."

"I think his career is finished because he almost killed a woman, conspired with a thief, and committed fraud."

"But that's the thing. He did none of those things, and it is irresponsible journalism to print them. Or publish them. Or report them. Whatever online news is called these days."

There's silence on the line, and I'm pretty sure my brother is about to blow me off. I'm totally surprised when he says, "Do you have any proof?"

"Any proof of what?"

"What you claim the truth to be."

I run a mental inventory, but of course, my brain is like the attic on an episode of *Hoarders*. The only thing I know I have receipts for is the plotting of our fake marriage.

That probably won't be helpful.

"I'm not sure what I have."

"Look into it and get back to me. I can talk to some colleagues and see what we can do."

You could knock me over with a feather with this show of support. "Why?"

"Why what? Isn't this what you wanted?"

"Well, duh. Yeah, but I thought you'd just blow me off as being flighty and frivolous again."

There's a pause on the line. "Ophelia, this could be huge. If what you're saying is true, we could gain a lot of publicity if we take you and Xavier on as clients."

I should have known. He's only helping me to further his career.

"Plus," my brother continues, "you're my sister and no one picks on you but Aiden and me. We're allowed and no one else."

I have to laugh. "That sounds more like it."

"So you need to do your homework. Call me tomorrow with an update."

We disconnect and I sit there, a surge of inspiration coursing through my veins.

It's not a plan—not yet—but it's a start.

Time to start finding receipts.

CHAPTER 44: XAVIER

No news is good news. Except for when no news is bad news.

It doesn't matter. I'm living in limbo, which is akin to hell in my book.

I should probably simply admit defeat and move back to England, tail between my legs. I've never been one to cower in the face of a challenge though.

It may be why I'm here, against my better judgment, doing a grueling circuit that includes burpees, dragon walks, jump squats, spiderman push-ups, broad jumps, and pistol squats. My quads hate me, but only as much as I hate myself.

I can't admit that I'm done, so I'm still here, training like a fool. Kenley, of course, is egging me on as if I'm going to be on the field for pre-season in two months. I finally hit my max, my legs buckling under the sheer fatigue, and I collapse down on the artificial turf of the Buzzards' training facility.

Three weeks have gone by and the only thing keeping me partially sane is pushing my body beyond the point of exhaustion. Kenley lets me in after the rest of the team is done for the day, but I'm fairly confident he's giving me the same sets they're doing.

I'm not sure why he let me crash in his flat in the first place. I'm quite certain he's punishing me in the gym for my overall crankiness and poor attitude. On the other hand, when I push my body to the point of breaking, it's the only time I don't feel like my heart has been ripped out of my chest and smashed beneath a boot.

Clearly, that's not a good feeling either, so I'll take muscles so worn out they simply cease to fire. It's better this way. Not sustainable in the least, but I don't know what else to do.

I close my eyes and clench my fists over my face, willing the burning to cease.

"Holy shit, Bird Man, you're a beast. You hit the highest reps of the team."

"Too bad I'm not on the team," I growl through clenched teeth.

"Yeah, I wish I could put your name on the leaderboard. It might spark a fire under these lightweights to know they've got serious competition."

"Who you callin' a lightweight?"

I don't recognize the voice immediately, so I sit up. It's Callaghan Entay, the keeper. He's been named co-captain for the upcoming season. But if he's in here, it probably means the rest of the team isn't far behind.

Bollocks.

I need to stand up and get out of here before I'm accused of trespassing. With my luck, it won't matter that Kenley let me in. I'll still be accused. Or Kenley will end up being sacked. I don't need that on my ledger. He's a right good mate, and I can't have him suffer for trying to help me.

Randomly, Ophelia's rant about birds being bad luck and harbingers of doom passes through my brain. Perhaps she was right about that.

"Fuck, Kenley, I'll go. I don't want you to get in trouble."

"Actually, I came to talk to you." Entay sits down. He glances around nervously. I'd be nervous to talk to me too. "I've got to make this quick though. Word on the street is that you're totally screwed right now."

"Good words travel fast."

"I got it from an inside source." Entay glances at Kenley. "Listen, those of us on this track know what it can be like. We get targeted for things all the time. Do you know how many paternity tests we've taken as a team?"

Kenley laughs. "Just you personally."

Entay shoots daggers at him with his eyes. "And the majority are unfounded. Kenley's working with you, helping you out. That leads me to believe that there's a chance you might not be as diabolical as the press is making you out to be. But you need to start speaking up for yourself."

"I'd like to hear this myself." Bjorn Janssen is there. Where'd he come from? Crap on a cracker. There's no way this is going to end well.

I sit up, running my fingers through my hair. It takes me a moment to get to my feet. If it weren't for the sudden jolt of adrenaline, I'm not sure I'd be able to stand at all.

"Let's go to the conference room and discuss this." It sounds like a suggestion, but when Coach uses that tone, we all know it's a directive.

My whole body is numb as I follow Kenley and Janssen into the office portion of the Buzzards' facility. Entay brings up the rear, probably to make sure I don't sprint off.

With the gelatinous mess my legs are from that killer workout, I wouldn't be able to run away if a bear was chasing me. I'd simply lie down and be bear food. That might be the more preferred option, as I feel as if I'm marching to the gallows. This is it. This is when they tell me to get out and never come back, and just like that my football career will be done.

"Can I shower first?" I'm stalling, I know, but I also smell. "I might be better prepared for a discussion not covered in sweat."

"No. Just sit down." Janssen opens the door to the conference room. This is so much worse than I anticipated. The room is full of suits. Most of them I don't recognize. One looks vaguely familiar, but I can't place him. I definitely recognize Robert Miller, owner of the Buzzards.

Bloody hell, this is going to be bad.

Coach Janssen points to a chair and I slide into it. There's a pitcher of water on the table in front of me. I pour a glass and promptly down it in one fell swoop. I refill my glass and drain that too.

It does nothing to quench the parchedness of my throat.

"Let's get this meeting started," the voice behind me says. I turn to look. *Camacho is here?* Shit. Absolute bloody shit.

Miller stands up. "We were just waiting on you, Vinny. Prompt as always, I see."

Camacho is so slick I'm surprised he doesn't slide off the seat when he sits down. "Xavier." He nods in my general direction.

I pour myself one more glass of water, this time if only for something to do.

"You've really stepped in it this time," Camacho continues. "I should have known you'd be a wild card with the reputation you came in with. Disgraceful. Who knows how many more people you'd leave in your wake of destruction? Do you know how hard you've been to pin down? Lucky for me, owners talk. I'm not sure what you thought you were doing here, training illegally." He opens his briefcase and pulls out a stack of papers.

Sliding them down the table, he continues, "That's a violation of your contract. Additionally, you violated your morality clause by engaging in fraudulent and illegal behavior with one Ophelia Finnegan."

I want to hiss at the mention of her name. How dare he even speak it?

"So if you'll please sign where the tabs are, you'll be officially terminated with the Baltimore Terrors."

Oh fuck. That water sits like lead in my stomach. I want to vomit it all back up. I look wildly around the table for a friend. An ally even. But all I see is stony faces.

"Do I have a choice?" I ask. I want to beg, to plead for someone to tell me there's another way.

Miller clears his throat. "I'm afraid not, Xavier. By working with Kenley here, you clearly violated your contract. You have no option but to sign the termination papers."

This is it. This is how it ends. With my hand shaking, I pick up the pen and begin to scrawl my name. Once, twice, three times, and then it's done.

Football is done.

My life is done.

I close my eyes as I place the pen down on the table. I hear the papers being pulled away. I sit back in the chair, eyes still closed, and elbows propped on the armrests. I knit my fingers together and try to focus on deep breathing. If I can't do something to still my mind, I'll absolutely lose it.

I've lost enough today. I'll keep what's left of my dignity, thank you very much. Though there's nothing wrong with a bloke crying, I won't give these suits the honor of seeing me do it.

I can hear low murmurs over the roaring inside my ears. Words swirl, but nothing clear enough for me to decipher. My brain struggles to process what they're saying. What I'm hearing.

"It's witnessed and notarized, Vinny. It's done, correct?" I think that's Miller, but I can't tell without looking.

"Done. Fair and square. Xavier Henry is no longer a Baltimore Terror. His career is finished, once and for all."

Slowly I open my eyes to see Camacho handing a stack of papers to the vaguely-familiar looking gentleman. Then I place him. Tanner Suarez. Commissioner of the USSL.

Bloody hell.

Not that there was much of a chance, but this seals the deal that no USSL team will ever even glance my way again.

Camacho stands. "Well, ladies, this has been fun, but now I'm off."

"Sit down, Vinny. I think you need to hear this." Miller's voice is commanding.

Camacho sinks down slowly, and I sit up straight. What's going on?

"Bjorn, whenever you're ready."

I don't know what else there is to say. I've been sacked. I'm banned from the USSL as well. They wouldn't have Suarez here if I wasn't. I don't need to hear them say it to know that it's true.

And the last thing I need to hear is my former coach telling me what a disappointment I am. I already know that. Every single cell in my body knows that.

"Thanks, Bob. Mr. Suarez, I'm glad you could join us today. We at the Boston Buzzards value integrity and honesty, as well as transparency in our business dealings."

Camacho smirks. "Yeah, then why did you want this guy?" He jerks a thumb toward me. "He's as shady and ruthless as they come. Need I remind you that he almost killed poor Phaedra Jones? Tanner, think about it. What if it was your daughter? Edmund Jones was right to ban him from the BFL."

"Yeah, about that," Bjorn says. He nods toward one of the suits, who begins clicking away on his computer. The projector screen at the opposite end of the room lights up as Zoom opens.

And there's Phaedra Jones.

CHAPTER 45: XAVIER

What the bloody hell?

"Hullo everyone, thank you for having me. Oh hullo, Xavier. Good to see you again," she says breezily, as if she didn't ruin my life.

I repeat, what the bloody hell?

"Who's that and what's she got to do with me? Can I go now? I've wasted enough of my time on this loser." Camacho stands up in a huff.

"That, Vinny, is the young woman you seemed to be so concerned about and protective of. Sit down, and hear her out," Robert Miller commands. No wonder he's taken the Boston Buzzards from the bottom of the barrel to second place in the league in two years. He understands leadership. "It's Phaedra Jones. Thanks for joining us, Phaedra."

"I'm chuffed to be here. This ... this has been a long time coming. Is Tanner there? I can't quite see everyone."

"I'm here," Tanner Suarez replies. "You asked for this meeting, Ms. Jones. Please go ahead."

"Right, okay then. So the thing is, I'm an addict. I'm an alcoholic and an addict, though I don't think that will come as a surprise to anyone who's met me in real life."

When she says this, practically everyone at the table gives Vinny the side-eye. It's obvious he had no clue about who Phaedra really was. Or is at all, actually.

"My father did a good job of keeping it out of the mainstream press for the most part, but it's not shocking or scandalous to anyone who knew me."

I think I may vomit. What is going on here? Why is she saying all this now? She threw me under the bus rather than admit she was an addict. What's changed? I want to get up and leave, but seeing as how Miller just put Camacho in his place, I'm afraid to move.

Phaedra continues, "I've only recently come to terms with the fact that I have a problem. I'm 236 days sober today, actually, so I'm still new to the journey if you consider the fact that I used for over ten years. And as part of my recovery, I'd like to set the record straight about the car accident."

This snaps me to attention, and I shift forward in my seat as if it will help me hear better.

"The night of the incident, I was drunk, high, and despondent. The only person who even noticed my distress that evening was Xavier Henry. I hit on him, but he would not accept my proposition because I was high, which says a lot about his character. When I left, he followed me out, concerned for my safety. He offered to call me a car or drive me home. I refused to listen. I was quite belligerent, in fact. I got in my car. At the very last second, Xavier jumped in, trying to convince me to stop. I wouldn't listen to him, but I quickly lost control of the car. When it crashed, all I knew is my father had told me if I messed up one more time because of the drugs, he'd cut me off forever. This was not the first of this kind of incident. My father was just skilled at covering it up. Let's say I learned from the best."

Christ almighty, is this really happening? Why is she coming forward now? It's too little, too late. My career is done. At least this will clear my name, but still, she ruined my life.

"I begged Xavier to say he was driving and that a bunny ran out in front of the car, causing him to lose control. It had worked for me in the past. Unfortunately, it didn't work for Xavier." Phaedra looks squarely at me. "Xavier, darling, I'm so sorry for asking you to lie. I'm even more sorry about Father's reaction. It's one of the many, many regrets I've amassed over the years due to my addiction. I let it go so long, rationalizing that you were still playing and that it didn't hurt you, but I know it must have. That was the justification of a selfish, struggling addict. It's taken me years to realize how my actions hurt others like you. Please accept my sincerest apologies. I'll understand if you don't forgive me, but I do want it publicly known that you are not a drunk driver and that you did not in any way injure or endanger me. Quite the opposite, really. Not only did you try to keep me safe that night, but even after everything that followed, you never went public with what happened. You never went to the press, even though they were crucifying you. You never told them I was high or a train wreck. Thank you for everything you did to defend me. You're a hero, Xavier Henry."

My mouth opens and then closes without producing any sound.

"And thank you, Ms. Jones, for clearing the air and Mr. Henry's reputation," Tanner Suarez says. "It's important for the USSL to be composed of players of integrity, and it seems as if Mr. Henry possesses such character."

I'm so confused.

"What are you saying, and Phaedra, why are you part of this meeting? How did you know about all this going on?" I ask.

"Tanner, if you don't mind, I'll go first so I can sign off," Phaedra says. "I've been out of the public for a while now since I went into rehab. I only downloaded ClikClak when I got out and was into my recovery. I particularly enjoyed the dating exploits of a certain American Clakker, who I found to be quite amusing. Then, a few weeks ago, the internet proved what a small world it is when I realized that Lovely Lia was married to the person I needed to apologize to. Well, when the ESPN story broke, I knew I had to step forward to make amends. I knew you'd never take my calls. Then I got a message from Lovely Lia—er, Ophelia— asking for help, and voilà! I'm here. But now I'll be signing off while you do your football business. Xavier, next time you're back in England, let's do lunch. I'd love to catch up."

And with that, the screen goes black.

I try to process all she just said. "Ophelia? Ophelia contacted Phaedra?" I don't even know I've said it out loud. "This doesn't make any sense. Why would Ophelia reach out to Phaedra?"

Bjorn stands up. "She's been quite busy, and quite persuasive too." He drops a stack of papers on the table in front of me.

"What are these?"

"The emails and documentation to refute nearly every single point in the ESPN article. I had several phone conversations with her, and at my request, she sent these over to me with alarming volume and speed. She can be charming, yet with dogged determination, as you well know. One would never expect that level of tenacity from her."

He should try spending nearly three days in a hotel room with her.

This is all happening at breakneck speed. The Buzzards obviously knew Phaedra and Ophelia had information to clear my name and reputation. Why didn't they say something before Camacho terminated my contract?

Miller nods to his lawyer who slides another folder down to me.

"What's this?"

"One-point-two for three years plus the standard bonuses."

Camacho's face turns as red as a tomato. "You can't be serious."

Miller looks at him, calm and cool. "You terminated him. In fact, you were happy to do it with an audience simply to humiliate him. You specifically asked Tanner Suarez to be here to verify the legitimacy of the contract termination. That was your request, not ours.

It was a bonus that Phaedra Jones asked for his witness as well. And since Xavier is unsigned and unattached to a team, we are free to sign him, as a non-citizen player, right now. I think that's all we need from you. Don't let the door hit you in the ass on the way out, Vin."

There is a moment of stunned silence before Camacho leaves in a huff. Miller turns back to me. "I understand if you want to have your representative look at these, but I also am under the impression that you are currently without representation."

I know I should have someone look at them, but I also don't want to miss this chance. I'm fairly confident I'm dreaming and that when I wake, this will all be gone. "Is this a dream?"

"Can I offer a solution?" Callaghan Entay steps up. "My agent, Justice Williams, would be more than happy to look at it and represent you. He's expecting your call."

I look around the room, still certain this isn't real. Kenley's there, grinning from ear to ear. "Ken, what's going on? I don't understand … how … why …"

The door opens at the far end of the room and Ophelia walks in with a tall brunette I've never seen before. Ophelia, dressed in an oversized ivory cable knit jumper and black leggings, is a sight for sore eyes. "Don't be mad at me for sticking my nose in. I … I had to fix this. And you know me. Before I could stop and think, I was messaging Phaedra and Hannah and emailing Bjorn when Mr. Miller wouldn't take my calls."

I don't know who Hannah is, and I really don't care. I'm on my feet and closing the distance between Ophelia and me in four long strides. I encircle her in my arms, picking her right up off the floor.

Her legs wrap around me, as they usually do, and it's enough to make me forget where I am. I bring her mouth to mine, hoping that my kiss can say what my brain cannot yet put into words.

Breathless, I pull back. "You did this for me?"

She looks deep into my eyes. "Of course I did. It was grand gesture time."

"You found Phaedra Jones."

"Technically, she found me first, but I did contact her and ask her to do this. I also found out lots of juicy info about Tony, none of which implicates you. Also, much to the chagrin of ClikClak, I'm not actually a sex worker. Not that there's anything wrong with that."

I kiss her again because I've missed this. I've missed her. And I love her.

"Ahem, are you two finished?" Miller asks. I hear him mutter, "So much for the marriage being just for show."

"One more thing," I say. "Thank you. I can't believe you did this for me. Why though?"

Ophelia smiles and the brightness of it nearly splits my heart in two. "That's easy. I broke rule number five."

"What's rule number five?" She'd mentioned rules before, but we never circled back to that.

"No falling in love. I broke it, because I love you, Xavier."

"Good, because I love you too."

CHAPTER 46: OPHELIA

W here to now?" Xavier asks.

It's been a long afternoon working out the details of Xavier's new contract. In the movies, they just cut to the next scene. In reality, it takes hours for the agent to get there, read it over, deliberate this point and then that one.

I tried to look attentive and not at all bored.

I don't think I was successful.

Lucky for me, and probably for Xavier too, Bjorn Janssen is definitely a Team Xavier person. I wasn't sure he'd remember me or respond to my emails, which is why I reached out to Hannah.

It was a Hail Mary pass, or whatever the soccer equivalent is. I should probably learn that. While waiting to see if Bjorn would respond, I searched and found Hannah LaRosa on ClikClak. She was the server at The Tower on our wedding night. I was desperate, and if Bjorn didn't come through, she was at least one more in I had with the team.

I don't think she was thrilled to have to reach out to Callaghan Entay, her former hookup, on my behalf, but she did it anyway. I'm so glad she did, because he's super helpful, getting his agent to agree to take on Xavier.

Team Xavier is pretty impressive if I do say so myself.

We should have shirts made.

I pull the car over into a Dunkin' parking lot. "Before we go any further, we need to talk. And I need you to let me go first, otherwise, I'm going to lose my nerve."

Xavier, sitting in my passenger's seat, unbuckles his seat belt and turns to face me. With a rolling wave of his arm, he says, "The floor is yours, m'lady."

"I understand that I'm impulsive. I always have been. That's not an excuse for what happened. I think my brain will always have a 'ready, fire, aim' tendency, but I need to make every effort to make sure that it doesn't hurt the people around me. The people I care about. The people I love. You."

My throat starts to get thick, making it hard to say the words. I push forward before I lose my nerve. "I didn't really know what love was until I met you. I know that sounds like some corny love song, but I don't have to tell you I'm not great at those either. But you—you were the first person to see me. The real Ophelia. And you liked me for me. I didn't have to try and be something I wasn't when I was around you. I didn't disappoint you. And you unlocked something in me that I thought I'd lost. My ability to write. From the time I was a small child, it's been my deepest desire. I tried a few years ago and … it didn't go well. So I threw myself into numbers, something I was good at. But it didn't fulfill me."

I take a breath and look at Xavier to make sure he's still paying attention. "So, yes, I was writing because of you. Inspired by you. That much is true. But I need you to take a look at this."

I hand him my phone, all queued up and ready to go.

"Ophelia, it's fine. I get it." Xavier holds up his hand. "I don't need to—"

"Just take it and read it. Please. For me."

Then I wait as his eyes scan my phone. His finger flicks the screen, scrolling. His eyes go wide. His mouth opens and closes. His head tilts to the side and his eyes squint a bit. Finally, after what feels like forever, Xavier looks at me. "What is this?"

"It's what I was writing. The story I published on Wattpad. The one the ESPN article claimed was about you."

Xavier looks at my phone again, scrolling up and down. "Unless I'm a vampire pirate with a thirteen-inch nob, then no. This does not resemble me in the least."

I start to laugh.

"Christ, Ophelia, the book is set at sea. There are literal vampires."

"I know. I wrote it."

He tilts his head as he continues reading. "Bloody hell, this is filthy. And is it even physically possible?"

I shrug. "Readers don't seem to care as long as it fulfills their fantasy."

He puts my phone down on the console. "This isn't about me at all."

I shrug. "I may have used some inspiration for the hero's backside. Yours is so fine, it should be commemorated in books. I'd take a photo and put it on the cover if I could. But otherwise, unless you're secretly undead and in search of your family's long-lost treasure, no."

"Why didn't you say something?"

I shrug again. "The other stuff, the Tony stuff, was big. And the social media stuff was true. I mean, I've gained over five hundred thousand followers just by being a hot mess. Hell, Phaedra was even following me."

That was a shock. And total coincidence that I saw her name on a post.

"Plus, you met my family."

"Yes, and at some point, we're going to have to unpack that bag," Xavier says.

Sighing I say, "I know. But in the meantime, I had to make this right for you."

"But I don't understand why."

"Why wouldn't I? Soccer is your dream. Your passion. You weren't ready to give that up yet, so I couldn't let some wanker take it from you."

He looks at me. "You really want nothing else from me, do you?" His voice is incredulous, like he can't believe what he's saying.

I don't want to lie to him. I don't want to keep anything from him ever again. "That's not totally true. There is something I want from you."

I see his chest rise and fall as he closes his eyes for a moment.

Quickly, I say, "I want you to marry me. For real. I want to be your wife, and all that goes with it. Soccer games, making smoothies, being a WAG. You tell me and I'll do it, as long as you'll marry me for real this time."

"Dammit, Ophelia."

Shit. No. He's going to jump out of this car and run far away. "I'm sorry. I know it's too much. But that's me. Always too much. We can get a divorce. Owen will figure out a way—"

My words are cut short when Xavier's mouth crashes on mine. He's holding my face in his hands, keeping me close to him. "No, dammit, Ophelia," he says, breathless. "I wanted to be the one to propose this time. Haven't you ever seen a romance movie? The man does it."

I laugh and he kisses me again, this time soft and sweet. A sigh escapes me. "So no divorce?"

"No divorce, but yes a proper wedding and proper marriage. But first, we need to celebrate properly, which may or may not include my fantasy of seeing you in nothing but my jersey with my name across your back. Now, where are we going to make all this happen?"

"Home."

EPILOGUE: OPHELIA

A proper wedding indeed. Well, as proper as we could put together on two months' notice.

It's on a Thursday still because that's the only day we could rent out The Tower, where the Buzzards had their cocktail reception. We're on the fourth floor, in the library, which is perfect for a bookworm like me.

Xavier starts practice next Tuesday with the Buzzards, so we'll be spending his last few days on a mini-honeymoon back at Avon Old Farms Hotel, complete with the four-poster bed.

I'm thinking of getting one for home. Our home. The apartment we picked out. We're in the back bedroom together, with the front bedroom as a guest room. Xavier's parents are staying there this week. Philip is up in the loft, sleeping on my ugly couch. He's quite the grump about it.

But for right now, I'm getting ready to walk down the small aisle toward the man I love. This time, I'm wearing a long white off-the-shoulder A-line dress made of the world's softest chiffon. Marley looks stunning as my maid of honor in her black dress.

There was no way I was getting married (again) without my ride-or-die.

"Here are your flowers," she says, handing me my bouquet. Naturally, I had the florist recreate the flowers Xavier gave me on our first wedding day. "I didn't threaten Xavier this time, but I can before we start. Should I?"

Of course, Marley gave Xavier the "talk" before our first wedding. I'd expect no less of her. "No, I think we're good there."

"Good. Are you ready?"

"Are the favors all set?"

Naturally, our guests will have full-size Oh, Henry! bars waiting for them.

"Good to go."

My mom is already sobbing. "I can't believe my little girl is getting married."

I have to laugh. I think she's been conveniently repressing the fact that this ceremony isn't legal at all, but rather a public declaration of our love and adoration.

Marley leans in. "Did you get *it* delivered?"

I nod. "Yes, Xavier's brother is taking care of it. And he promises that it won't kill me."

As an absolute show of my love, I'm having a white dove at our wedding. I was planning on releasing it, but then I looked into it and found that it's actually cruel to do this. I'm renting the dove, basically as a symbol, from a rescue facility, not dissimilar to Henry Hawkery. Philip's duties, in addition to being the best man, are to ensure the bird is well cared for tonight and that it doesn't peck anyone's—namely my—eyes out.

"Ready?" my dad asks.

"One second—" I hold up my left hand, which feels oddly bare without my rings. Xavier's going to give them back to me in a few minutes. I pull out my phone and press record.

This is it. We're having our wedding ceremony for friends and family to join us since we eloped last time. Thanks, ClikClak. In the most convoluted, most Ophelia way ever, you helped bring Xavier and me together. I can't wait to officially start our lives together. I swear, this really is something out of a movie. I couldn't make it up if I tried. Now I'm off to spend the rest of my life with the man I love. Kisses and hugs!

"A dove? Really?" Xavier leans over and whispers to me in the receiving line.

"It symbolizes honesty and integrity, as well as the pureness of our love. Even I can't find fault with that."

"Aren't you afraid it's going to kill you?"

I smile at him, then greet the next person in line. Another soccer player. I'm sure I'll learn all their names eventually. "Actually, no. Now that I realize my fear was not irrational and had a real reason behind it, I'm working on working through it. Having Daniel Dove here is a good step toward that. Plus, I wanted something to show you how much I value you. All of you. Even the feather-loving part of it."

"I have a surprise for you too." The last of the guests move through the receiving line, and Hannah is ushering us in to make the official entrance as announced by the DJ so we can have our first dance as husband and wife.

I don't count our dance to Billy Joel because that wasn't our song. This will be our first dance with the song Xavier picked out for us. I have no idea what he chose.

I'm guessing it won't be anything by Olivia Rodrigo.

"What's my surprise? Is it big? Is it small? Do you have it here on you? Is it in your pocket?" I begin patting him down like cops do in the movies.

Xavier pulls up his shirt cuff to reveal a small string of letters tattooed on the inside of his right wrist. I look closely, running my finger over it. "XOXO."

"Aww, you got a tattoo of my favorite hashtag. Kisses and hugs!"

Xavier shakes his head. "How about Xavier and Ophelia?"

XOXO

Tears threaten my eyes, but I'm saved by the DJ announcing, "And now please welcome Mr. and Mrs. Xavier and Ophelia Henry!"

Xavier leads me to the center of the floor, not letting go of me once. "What's the song?" I ask. For weeks, I've been asking him, and he's consistently refused to tell me.

As soon as the guitar starts, I know the song immediately. "'Home'? Phillip Phillips?"

Xavier nods. "I thought I'd lost my home. I thought since I couldn't be in England, I'd never be home again. Baltimore certainly wasn't. You showed me home is not a place. Home is a person. Home is you."

Choking back my tears, I say, "These are the five things you should know about me."

Xavier looks at me quizzically but allows me to continue as we dance.

"One. My name is Ophelia Henry. Like the Shakespearean character I was named after, I may do crazy things for love, but unlike the character, in the end, love is what grounded me. Two. I'm an accountant and an author. My debut novel is currently selling like hotcakes on Amazon. You should check it out. It's a super-steamy pirate vampire novel. Three. I don't like birds, but I'm learning to co-exist with them because my husband loves them. Four. I'm a reformed hopeless romantic. Right now, I'm quite hopeful because I'm in love with the most wonderful man in the world. And five. I used to do lots of dumb things in the name of love, but for once I did something smart, and that was falling in love with you."

Xavier kisses me. "See? Just like in the movies."

I have to laugh. "Are you kidding? Our story is just like me; anything but typical." But even as I say it, I can see the tagline for the movie poster, clear as if it were in front of me.

First comes marriage. Then comes love. Then comes forever.

THE END

ACKNOWLEDGMENTS

To Julianna Miner: Thank you for talking me down and through and over and around.

To Regina Dowling: Thank you for not only being such a loyal and vocal reader, but for sending me your favorite lines as well as my items to be addressed. Both of those are invaluable.

To my editors, Tami Lunch and Heather Balog: I can't thank you enough.

To my cat Sundance: Hazel was supposed to be the cat in this book, but I had to memorialize you someway. Your departure was too sudden and unexpected, and we all miss you dreadfully.

ABOUT THE AUTHOR

Telling stories of resilient women, *USA Today* Bestselling Author Kathryn R. Biel hails from Upstate New York where her most important role is being mom and wife to an incredibly understanding family who don't mind fetching coffee and living in a dusty house. In addition to being Chief Home Officer and Director of Child Development of the Biel household, she works as a school-based physical therapist. She attended Boston University and received her Doctorate in Physical Therapy from The Sage Colleges. After years of writing countless letters of medical necessity for wheelchairs, finding increasingly creative ways to encourage insurance companies to fund her client's needs, and writing entertaining annual Christmas letters, she decided to take a shot at writing the kind of novel that she likes to read. Kathryn is the author of many women's fiction, romantic comedy, contemporary romance, and chick lit works, including the award-winning books, *Live for This, Made for Me*, and *Underneath It All*.

Scan now to instantly receive FREE exclusive bonus content!

Stand Alone Books:
Good Intentions
Hold Her Down
I'm Still Here
Jump, Jive, and Wail
Killing Me Softly
Live for This
Once in a Lifetime
Paradise by the Dashboard Light

A New Beginnings Series:
Completions and Connections: A New Beginnings Novella
Made for Me
New Attitude
Queen of Hearts

The UnBRCAble Women Series:
Ready for Whatever
Seize the Day
Underneath It All

Center Stage Love Stories:
Act One: *Take a Chance on Me*
Act Two: *Vision of Love*
Act Three: Whatever It Takes

Boston Buzzards:
XOXO
You Belong with Me
Zero to Hero (2024)

www.ingramcontent.com/pod-product-compliance
Lightning Source LLC
Chambersburg PA
CBHW020933020726
47495CB00002B/474